Praise for Bingo Barge Murder

"Chandler launches her first Shay O'Hanlon caper with panache. Coffee, romance, murder, and a dog all make for Minnesota nice-nice."
—*Lavender*

"*Bingo Barge Murder* is a solid first entry in the Shay O'Hanlon mystery series. Chandler writes with a wonderful sense of place, plenty of humor, and a crisp pace. This is a great read from the very first page!" —Ellen Hart, author of the Jane Lawless series

"Chandler's debut is fast and funny ... crammed with memorably quirky Minnesota characters." —Brian Freeman, bestselling author of *Immoral*

"Jessie Chandler delivers a fresh murder motive in this engaging debut mystery." —Julie Kramer, author of *Stalking Susan*

"What do you get if you line up Shay O'Hanlon, owner of a café called the Rabbit Hole, a scrumptious police detective named JT Bordeaux, a computer genius drama queen, and a murder at the Pig's Eye Bingo Barge? If you said a rollicking, fast-paced black-out game of mystery and suspense, I'd have to yell—BINGO!"
—Mary Logue, Author of *Frozen Stiff*

"If anything happens to me, I want Shay O'Hanlon on my side! *Bingo Barge Murder* is a fun read with an emotional depth that sneaks up on you. The characters are interesting and quirky and the location is unique and well-developed. I hope this is just the first of many adventures for this 'Tenacious Protector' and her pals." —Neil Plakcy, author of the series of mysteries

Praise for *Hide and Snake Murder*

"Chandler follows up her *Bingo Barge Murder* with another tricky plot fully worthy of your suspension of disbelief."　　—*Lavender*

"Fast paced and witty. It is peppered with wonderfully colorful characters, making it a strong second novel in the Shay O'Hanlon Caper series."　　—*Lambda Literary*

"After reading her novels, I have come to believe Jessie Chandler is the illegitimate child of Raymond Chandler and Dorothy L. Sayers. She's funny—and she's good!"—Lori L. Lake, author of the Gun series and the Public Eye series

"Wild and wacky *Hide and Snake Murder* will keep readers guessing all the way to a slam bang finale."—Carolyn Hart, New York Times bestselling author of the Death on Demand series

"*Hide and Snake Murder* takes us to the beginning and end of the Mississippi, New Orleans and Minneapolis, capturing the quirky charm of both cities. It's a rollicking read with an entertaining cast of funny and fascinating characters. You won't be able to turn the pages fast enough."—J.M. Redmann, author of the Goldie award-winning novel *Water Mark: A Micky Knight Mystery*

"Jessie Chandler makes me laugh. A talented storyteller with a deft hand at pacing, she writes rollicking, raucous adventures that are sure to entertain."　　—Julie Hyzy, bestselling author of the Manor House Mysteries and White House Chef Mystery series

"*Hide and Snake Murder* is a unique story of zany friendship, tentative romance, and the deadly face of today's underworld."

　　　　—Elizabeth Sims, author of the Rita Farmer mysteries and the Lillian Byrd crime series

To the staff of Borders 531. We came, we saw,
we conquered, and we cried. Never fear,
Barney's Brain Train lives on,
for you are within the pages of this book.

JESSIE CHANDLER

A Shay O'Hanlon Caper

Pickle in the Middle Murder

MIDNIGHT INK
WOODBURY, MINNESOTA

FIRST EDITION
First Printing, 2013

Book format by Bob Gaul
Cover design by Lisa Novak
Cover illustration © Gary Hanna
Editing by Nicole Nugent

Midnight Ink, an imprint of Llewellyn Worldwide Ltd.

This is a work of fiction. Names, characters, places, and incidents are either the product of the author's imagination or are used fictitiously, and any resemblance to actual persons, living or dead, business establishments, events, or locales is entirely coincidental.

Library of Congress Cataloging-in-Publication Data
Chandler, Jessie.
  Pickle in the middle murder: a Shay O'Hanlon caper/Jessie Chandler.—First edition.
      pages cm.—(A Shay O'Hanlon Caper; #3)
   ISBN 978-0-7387-2598-7
1. Lesbians—Fiction. 2. Murder—Investigation—Fiction. 3. Minneapolis (Minn.)—Fiction. 4. Mystery fiction. I. Title.
   PS3603.H3568P53 2013
   813'.6—dc23
                                        2013001266

Midnight Ink
Llewellyn Worldwide Ltd.
2143 Wooddale Drive
Woodbury, MN 55125-2989
www.midnightinkbooks.com

Printed in the United States of America

ACKNOWLEDGMENTS

First and foremost I'd like to thank the staff of Midnight Ink and Llewellyn Worldwide. Terri Bischoff, Nicole Nugent, Courtney Colton, and the rest of the hardworking staff who make books happen—thank you from the bottom of my heart.

My apologies to the MPD and Scott County, for taking creative liberties with the titles and duties of their ranks.

Acknowledgements are hard. I know I'm going to leave out someone, or in this case, a number of someones, purely because my memory sucks. Please know how appreciated you are. Really.

Alyssa, thank you for telling me you wanted to see a dead body in an outhouse in my next book.

Huzzah, the Minnesota Renaissance Festival! Without the Fest, I wouldn't have found the privy, and without the privy, we'd be back to a boring old outhouse. Rose the Candlemaker, thank you for making beautiful wax roses and Smelly Bears, and for allowing me to drop you into my story.

Jill Glover, thanks for the rooster-in-the-city idea. I took it and ran!

DJ, it was an excellent roller coaster NaNoWriMoing with you at the Andover Caribou. Get that kick a** manuscript out there! And to the 'Bou Crew, thank you for keeping the Cinnamon Spice tea, turkey sandwiches, and dark chocolate hot chocolate with extra whipped cream flowing. You all do a darn good job, as do all of the Twin Cities Caribou and Starbucks in which I hunker down to write. Thank you for letting me take up space and bandwidth.

Pat and Gary of Once Upon a Crime Mystery Bookstore in Minneapolis, thank you so much for having such a great venue for mysteries and crime fiction, for sharing new favorites, and for anticipating the next release of our favorite authors. Remember, one more book won't hurt!

To my great team of readers and revisionists, including but not limited to Judy Kerr, Mary Beth Panichi, Patricia Lopez, Lori L. Lake, Sharon Carlson, Pat Cronin, Angel Hight, DJ Schuette, Liz Gibson, Brian Landon, my writing group (the Hartless Murderers), the BABAs, and many others who I know I am forgetting—thanks from the bottom of my heart.

Betty Ann, thank you for your continuing support, in so very many ways. I absolutely could not do this without you. And I forgive you for the dogs.

To all the booksellers out there who sell books because they love books: you are the ones who make things happen.

Last, but never, ever least, I send out a heartfelt thanks to my readers. If there were no readers, there would be no books, and that would be very depressing. Please keep reading, and don't forget to support your local, independent bookstores.

ONE

NOBODY EVER TOLD ME that a Renaissance faire would be a strange and surprisingly bawdy event. My girlfriend, JT, finally decided it was high time to introduce me to Elizabethan culture, twenty-first-century style. So on a glorious day in early October, she dragged me through a portal consisting of weathered, arched entry doors situated beneath a replica medieval castle gatehouse and keep.

It looked good from the outside, but inside, unfamiliar sights and sounds pummeled my senses. I heard Old English accents, smelled wood smoke, and saw that more than half the people in the courtyard were dressed like they'd just time-traveled from King Arthur's court. With roasted turkey legs.

But the strangest sight was a man squirming around on his back on the hard-packed dirt next to a giant pickle barrel. A ragged vest barely covered his naked chest, and dusty brown pants were tucked into knee-high leather boots.

He raised an enormous pickle in the air, looked me right in the eye, and shouted, "Come over here, miladies, and check out me huge, tasty tonsil tickler! It'll fill you right up!"

He waggled his brows and eyed me as through I were the last woman on earth. With a leer, he thrust his pelvis into the air.

I backed away in a hurry and turned to JT. "Tonsil tickler? I hope he's kidding. I had absolutely no idea the Renaissance Festival was so, so … " I frowned as I searched for the right word.

"Risqué?" JT cocked an eyebrow at me in amusement.

A man on stilts and dressed like a king's jester nearly knocked me down as he hurried toward the entrance.

"Not just risqué. I mean, it's strangely charming in its own sort of cheesy way."

As we listened to the pickle man's lewd patter, I wondered how long he planned to writhe around on the ground bragging about his huge pickle. Considering the number of briny cukes floating in the gigantic metal-banded wooden barrel, he was going to be in the dirt for a while.

Yet delighted fest-goers figuratively and literally ate up the pickle dude's antics, and I decided it was a good thing he had a helper taking dollars and doling out the cukes.

In all my thirty-two years, I had never had the time or inclination to attend the annual Renaissance Festival held in Shakopee, Minnesota. I was too busy with life in general and with the Rabbit Hole in particular—the coffee café I co-owned with my good friend Kate McKenzie—to take time out for Ren Fest, as the devotees call it. I thought it would be a goofy feudal fantasy world, perfect for Dungeons & Dragons types, but not for me.

JT gave me a nudge, affection radiating from her warm brown eyes. "Does this shock your proper Midwestern sensibilities?"

"Nope. But I swear I learn something new about my straight-laced, gun-toting cop girlfriend every day." My tone was teasing, but it was essentially the truth. Most of the time JT carefully toed the line. I truly had no idea she would be entertained by raunchy pickle peddlers, half-dressed wenches, jousting knights, and honeywine mead. Her enthusiasm was completely out of character, and although it surprised me, I loved it.

The sight of her happy, relaxed smile warmed my heart. She needed this. As a homicide detective with the Minneapolis Police Department, JT worked far too many hours, stressed too much, and didn't chill out enough. It was really hard for her to cut loose.

The sun glinted off JT's shoulder-length chestnut locks, which she'd worn loose instead of in her business-as-usual ponytail. She was easy on the eyes, but with her hair framing her high cheekbones and square, determined chin, she was breathtaking. She wore faded blue jeans and a soft, blue-and-black checked flannel shirt with rolled sleeves over a black T-shirt. Yup, definitely sizzling with a capital S. Sometimes I looked at her and couldn't believe someone like her would still be with someone like me after nearly a year. The length of our relationship was a record on my end. My MO was usually love 'em well and leave 'em fast, but there was something about JT that turned me upside down and inside out. I thanked my lucky stars for that every day.

At our feet, Dawg, my tank-sized boxer, leaned against my leg. His upper lip, as usual, was hung up on a lower tooth. He sat with his head cocked in curiosity as he watched the pickle man's shenanigans.

JT's recent canine addition, Bogey the bloodhound, energetically snuffled the ground nearby. He was a reddish-black police school dropout, a sweet dog with a nose addiction. After Bogey's previous owner, a rookie Immigration and Customs Enforcement agent, had been murdered last spring, JT'd volunteered to take him in. We hadn't realized the mutt's sniffing problems went beyond simple doggy ADD.

Bogey's nasal drug of choice wasn't cadavers, drugs, or criminals in hiding; it wasn't missing children or hikers lost in the woods; it wasn't cheeseburgers or even bacon. What made Bogey happier than anything else were crotches. Anyone's. Criminal or non-criminal. Man or woman. Child or baby. His only requirement was the more aromatic, the better. The hound was a work in progress, but he was learning to control himself.

The deep voice of the well-muscled pickle-hawker brought me back. "Come now, travelers. Eat me pickle. You know you want me pickle. It's juicy and very firm and only costs a dollar." The man tilted his head back and looked upside down at JT and me. "You know your mouth is watering to taste me big, hard, salty specimen."

"You want to taste his 'big, hard, salty specimen'?" JT asked me.

"No thanks. Maybe later. Why don't you go ahead and enjoy all that goodness?" I cut her a smirking, sideways glance as I shifted my backpack into a more comfortable position. After living with JT for the better part of four months, I knew she was not in the least tempted by anything soaked in vinegar.

"Ignore that rascal wallowing in the dirt like a beast! Come peruse the King's Nuts!" I turned to see a nearby woman bellowing under the shade of a large tattered umbrella that sported uneven yellow stitching reading KING'S NUTS. "They are shapely and crunchy. Much tastier than yon smelly gherkin." The umbrella was attached to a faded-to-gray wooden cart loaded with nut rolls of various kinds.

More bystanders stopped their window-shopping and gathered around to observe the slinging of food- and genitalia-inspired insults.

The purveyor of the King's Nuts wore layered skirts and a teal bodice that barely covered her chest. The constricting corset shoved her goods up so far she was close to having a wardrobe malfunction. I was afraid her boobs would explode out right into some potentially delighted but unsuspecting patron's face.

I tugged JT from the fray and we continued our ambling stroll through the sixteenth century. The sights and sounds were overwhelming already, and we'd hardly gotten past the front gate. It was odd seeing men and women playing dress-up and talking in the Shakespearean English. I wanted to find it juvenile, but deep down, I had to admit this whole medieval thing had an addictively ludicrous, over-the-top appeal.

Even the shop buildings that lined the rolling edges of the tree-filled grounds appeared authentic to the period. Huts with tall, gabled roofs stood proudly beside stumpy thatch cottages. The cement-like dirt ended where stones and rough wood planks had been laid as flooring within the shops. The sheer number of merchants and their varied goods sent my brain reeling. Even the store names were suggestive, like Cock 'n Dragon, which sold totally awesome rooster and fire-breathing reptilian artwork.

JT elbowed me as we wandered slowly along. "Come here," she said. She dragged me and the dogs up to a shop called Wax Werks by Rose the Candlemaker.

A crowd was gathered by the front entrance.

"Check it out, Shay," JT said.

I pulled my eyes from the doodads for purchase and moved over to where JT had entrenched herself in the throng. I craned my head to catch a peep of what everyone was looking at.

The shopkeeper, dressed in appropriate period regalia, slowly and methodically dipped a rose in wax, in water, and then in more wax of various colors. All the while, she chatted with her audience, answering questions and explaining how the whole process worked.

"Want one?" JT asked.

Before I could answer, the rose dipper glanced at us with a friendly smile. She looked from JT to me. "Oh, I think that is a grand idea, me dears. What is milady's favorite color?" She looked at JT, waiting for an answer.

It appeared as if I was about to have a hand-dipped rose whether I wanted one or not. "Purple," I answered before JT had a chance to run my colorful likes and dislikes through her brain.

The woman gave us a satisfied grin and went to town.

As was JT's style—and as was reinforced by her profession—she tossed casual questions at our flower creator as she worked. Before I knew it, JT had coughed up either "Master" Card or "Lady" Visa to pay for my stiff new flower. After an exchange of thanks, JT tucked the rose in the pack on my back. If you can't beat 'em, it was sometimes best to simply go along for the ride.

We followed the uneven, hilly pathway that wound through the Fest site. The sound of roaring cheers and laughter made it hard for me to hear JT attempting to explain the finer points of Renaissance fanaticism.

Finally I gave up and said, "What the hell is going on over there?"

"I don't know. Let's find out." JT led me toward the source of the chaos.

We rounded a two-story shoppe made of wooden shakes and smooth, worm-eaten logs and came upon a line of wagons ringing a baseball diamond–sized space. Between two of the wagons, a hand-painted sign tacked crookedly on a post proclaimed this area the GYPSY ROBIN HOOD STAGE. Beyond the caravans, a throng of people cheered at three energetic guys performing on an elevated platform.

My stomach rumbled loud enough to be heard over the crowd. "I guess I'm hungrier than I thought," I yelled in JT's ear.

She rolled her eyes at me, then surveyed the area for edible options. "Well," she hollered back, "there's a spinach pie place over there." She pointed to a shop in the distance.

I curled my lip.

She scowled at my expression. "Okay, then. I think you can get bangers and mash." I looked over at a shop where two bored vendors stood behind a counter with their chins propped on their fists. What did it mean when a crowd this size seemed to be avoiding the place?

A subliminal message was working itself out on my psyche. Maybe there was something to be said about the pickle guy's approach to slinging his wares. "I think I want a 'big, hard, salty specimen.'"

JT's brow furrowed in the cutest way when she tried to figure something out. It was furrowed now as she attempted to decipher my request, although I had no idea how she could forget something as bizarre as that pickle vendor.

With a laugh, I said, "A pickle, goofball. I want a pickle."

"If I didn't know better, I'd think you were pregnant."

"Not on your life, my love."

I grinned as I watched JT wrangle Bogey from a nosedive toward the zipper of the pudgy man standing next to us. He was cheering at the guys onstage and didn't seem to notice Bogey's rude manners.

Dawg woofed at Bogey, his forehead all crinkled up. Sometimes I thought he was actually embarrassed by Bogey's wayward nose. Dawg barked again and plunked his butt down on my foot, sitting so far back that his hind legs stuck up in the air. Very manly, my Dawg.

"Bogey!" JT shouted to be heard over the boisterous crowd. Bogey pulled up short, returned to JT's side, and heaved a frustrated sigh. Then he plopped on his stomach and slapped his chin on the ground with a disgruntled groan that I heard over the raucous crowd.

I looked at the pathetic expression on Bogey's face. "Maybe you could find me a nice big juicy pickle while I ply these two ravenous beasties with a treat."

JT laughed. "Okay. Stay and listen to the show. I think those nut jobs on stage are the Tortuga Twins. Coop would love them if he wasn't in Duluth with the Green Beans." Nicholas Cooper, better known simply as Coop, was my best pal. He loved this kind of stuff, including role-playing games and other such nonsense. He belonged to an environmental group called the Green Beans for Peace and Preservation that coordinated protests and gatherings to help promote awareness of environmental and social issues. Keeping Asian carp out of Lake Superior was their latest statement-making foray.

JT handed me Bogey's leash.

"Hurry up, fair wench. I'm not in the mood to wait for me vittles."

"I think vittles is more a cowboy-era term. How about victuals?"

"Whatever." I attempted a friendly cuff, but she ducked out of the way and danced backward a couple of steps. Then she blew me a jaunty kiss, pivoted, and disappeared into the crowd.

"Guess it's just you and me, boys." I tossed my beasties some Snausages, then turned my attention to the stage. Three men, all dressed in yellow shirts, black vests, and thigh-high leather boots stomped around a plank platform. I tuned in to their chatter and caught random rants about naughty Scottish girls, fuzzy Biebers, joystick humor, and grand-theft otter. When they started in on pickle hawkers, I realized JT hadn't yet returned with my hard, salty specimen. How long had it been? Ten minutes? Twenty? Where was my prompt cop?

I shifted from foot to foot. Those two bottles of water I'd guzzled on the way here had filtered through my system and were now looking for a way out. From the increasing screams of the crowd, I figured the show was about to wrap up. I searched the faces of the passersby, looking with increasing desperation for my babe.

Over the next five minutes, my need morphed from *gotta go* to *must go. Now.* I texted JT to ask where she was, then tried to concentrate on the show. My bladder grew more and more impatient as the seconds ticked by without a response. The excited throng ratcheted up yet again. I could hardly hear myself think.

Finally, I made an executive decision to bolt before it was too late.

"Come on, boys," I said as I turned in a circle looking for the Porta Potties I thought I'd seen not far away. They'd been dubiously renamed "privies" in an effort to give them a little more authenticity. I was pretty sure the only thing authentic to the period would be the smell.

Dawg bounced to attention beside me while Bogey lumbered to his feet, looking dazed. The howling behind us maxed out in volume. I was more than happy to skedaddle before the audience charged to the biffs themselves after standing immobile for the last forty-odd minutes. We passed beneath a white banner with a red hem tied to two tall posts that proclaimed the privies were dead ahead.

The outhouses were situated in an oblong circle surrounded by an eight-foot plank fence. Once inside, I scoped out somewhere to stow the mutts and was relieved to catch sight of a large handicapped biff. We would probably all fit.

I checked to see if there were any physically challenged people headed toward the smelly brown plastic house. Fest-goers popped in and out of the regular outhouses, but no one seemed to be in imminent need of the double extra-wide one. With one final glance about, we charged up to the door of the john and I yanked it open.

For one stunned second, I stood frozen, mouth agape, much like one of the mimes I'd seen working the crowd earlier.

Bogey bolted forward. He buried his face in the crotch of a man perched on the pot. Before I had a chance to back out and apologize, the man swayed and then started to tip forward. Bogey yelped and scrambled backward. One hundred pounds of freaked out dog tackled me ass-first, and I crashed onto my butt on the ground.

The man continued his slow somersault to the warped plastic floor. Strangely, a large, dark-green pickle protruded from his mouth. The sight mesmerized me until I lost sight of it when the top of his head gently thunked against the bottom of the john. Then the rest of his body flopped sideways onto the filthy surface, facing away from me. I scrambled to my feet and reached to shake his shoulder.

Oh my *god*.

The back half of his skull was missing. It was dripping down the back wall of the Porta Potty.

TWO

I keyed 911 into my phone with shaking hands and gave the dispatcher the particulars. Someone flagged down a Fest security guard as curious gawkers gathered.

I knelt a short distance from Half-Headless Dead Guy and scrubbed Bogey's face vigorously with wet wipes, all the while wondering where the hell JT was. She'd been gone forever, and that was entirely unlike her. Really, how the hell could this be happening? I'd seen more dead bodies in the past year than I wanted to, and they weren't even relatives at funerals. We were at the Renaissance Festival, for Pete's sake, not in some seedy part of town.

I finished rubbing every whisker on Bogey's just-touched-a-dead-guy face and remained crouched with an arm around each dog's neck. They watched the proceedings with wide eyes. I thought they somehow sensed this was bad. Very bad.

In short order, the Renaissance security platoon of maroon-caped men and women in yellow tunics crawled over the place like fire ants on a hill. Everyone but me was hustled out of the area. Two of the Ren Fest's Swiss Guard security people covered the entrance, and, just like that, this set of privies was closed.

One of the security people kept me company until the sheriff showed up and they could hand me over to detail the grisly facts of my find. My guard was a square-chinned young man with a neatly trimmed beard and big eyes. A stoic expression was frozen on his face, but he'd turned a little green around the gills when he first caught sight of the body. He held on for dear life to a staff topped by a yellow flag bearing a red cross, which apparently signified him as a Renaissance copper. When this was over, someone was going to have to pry his fingers off the wood.

"Hey," I asked when I glimpsed his pasty complexion. "You okay?"

Without tearing his eyes from the scene in front of the handicapped biff, he nodded stiffly. I hoped he wouldn't lose his lunch.

As suddenly as I'd forgotten about it, my bladder reminded me with a vengeance that it still needed attention. "Hey, I hate to ask, but I really have to go to the bathroom."

My pal lifted a hand and pointed to a biff five steps away. I handed him the dogs' leashes, which he absently accepted, and made a bee-line. I did my business with immense relief and returned to Green Face's side.

Where on earth was JT? Cripes, if I needed anything, it was her calm, reassuring self right about now.

The guards at the entry were busy waving people off. Maybe that was the problem. I said, "My girlfriend is Minneapolis PD, and she's looking for me. Can you tell those guards at the entrance to keep an eye out for her?"

"Nope. Sorry, ma'am. I can't leave. You'll have to wait until you speak with the sheriff's department."

I rolled my eyes. Wasn't I allowed a phone call or something? Then I remembered my cell. I pulled it out, expecting guard boy to grab it, unless he keeled over first. But his eyes remained locked on the dead dude. I glanced around surreptitiously and quickly hit JT's speed dial. It rang once and then kicked into voicemail. I ended the call without leaving a message. Good grief. Anger started to spread through my veins, mixing with the sick disbelief that was well entrenched in my gut.

After another five minutes, a door that I hadn't noticed creaked open in the fence between two of the Porta Potties. Beyond it a browning, grass-covered field extended as far as I could see. It was currently littered with the flashing red and blue lights of numerous squad cars and one ambulance.

"Sneaky," I said to my still-green friend.

Beads of perspiration rolled down his face. He pulled his gaze from the body and tuned into the action at the fence door. "Yeah, it's for emergencies."

Deputies funneled into the area and swarmed around the handicapped biff. A tall cop with ramrod-straight posture stalked over and spoke to one of the Fest guards, who pointed in our direction. The man turned on his heel and steamed our way.

He was at least six feet tall, with a shaved head. Lean and wiry, not an ounce of fat bulged where his gray button-down dress shirt was tucked into sharply pressed black pants. A gun and extra magazines were secured on the right side of his fashionable, rotten-banana-colored belt.

"So," he said to me as he closed in, "you found the body?"

I crossed my arms and really, really wished JT were here. "Yeah, I did."

He turned to my guard pal. "Beat it, kid." The sheriff or deputy or whatever he was tossed his chin in the direction of the gate entrance. The guard shot me a half-grateful, half-apologetic look and hustled off.

The cop's Neanderthal eyebrows were bushy and blond, overshadowing watery blue eyes. I'd bet anything those two facial caterpillars would grow wild, wiry hairs that stuck out at crazy angles when he got older.

The man introduced himself as Scott County Sheriff's Detective Clint Roberts. He pulled a palm-sized notebook from his breast pocket and rumbled gruffly, "Name?"

For the next few minutes I listed my vitals while watching for any sign of JT and at the same time struggling to keep Bogey from giving the man a snootful in the nads.

I was about to explain my foray into the handicapped biff when I noticed a dust-up at the entrance. I glimpsed a familiar chestnut head and realized the commotion was my wayward girlfriend. Thank God and about damn time. I opened my mouth to tell Detective Roberts that the party crasher was with me when JT managed to wiggle past the guards. She spotted me and charged toward us like a terrified bull zeroing in on an irritating picador.

She skidded to a stop next to me. As soon as she laid eyes on the detective, the panicked expression on her face immediately melted into either distaste or fury, I couldn't quite tell. Maybe both. I had just a moment to ponder that when she said, or rather, snarled, "Roberts. They have you on this?"

You could've cut the tension with a medieval broadsword.

The detective squinted at JT. "This is a crime scene, Bordeaux, and I'd advise—"

"Can it. Why are you questioning my girlfriend?"

I opened my mouth, but Roberts beat me to it. "It's *Detective* to you. She found the victim. Therefore she needs to answer my questions." He added sarcastically, "Minneapolis has no jurisdiction down here."

14

A muscle in JT's cheek bulged as she clenched her teeth, but she held her tongue. I'd never seen her act combative with anyone in her own profession.

Roberts waited a moment then nodded. "That's a good girl." He dismissed JT by turning his back to her. JT stiffened, and for a second I was afraid she was going to go after him.

Instead, she took a breath, then shifted around so she was again facing Roberts. From the way she crammed her hands deep in her pockets and pressed her lips in a straight line, I knew she was working really hard to rein her temper in. I casually slid a hand around her elbow in case she lost the fight.

"Okay, Ms. O'Hanlon," the detective said as he refocused his attention on me, "you were at the part where your dog attacked the deceased."

I said, "No, he never attacked—"

"Detective Roberts," a short, bald man dressed in a windbreaker called out, waving a brown wallet as he hurried toward us, "I have an ID on the victim."

JT pulled her hands from her pockets and propped her hands on her hips as she watched the exchange. I looked closely at her for the first time since she'd entered the crime scene. Her hair was in disarray, as if she'd flipped her head upside down and ruffled her fingers through it. Chunks of what appeared to be pickle bits were stuck to her shirt, and there were dark splotches on the material that looked wet. I wondered what happened to my salty specimen and why she might be wearing it. I leaned a little closer to her and sniffed. A sharp vinegary aroma wafted off her.

"Well, give it to me." Roberts snatched the wallet out of his tech's hand. He stared at it and blinked. Then he blinked again. "Well, I'll be goddamned."

15

His eyes rose from the wallet and met JT's fiery gaze. Without another moment's hesitation, he pivoted and stomped through the crowd of people surrounding the outhouse and the dead guy. He knelt, and called out, "Bordeaux, you might want to take a look at this."

JT met my eyes for a brief moment. The molten chocolate that usually stared back at me was hard as black diamonds. She walked over and bent down in the doorway of the biff beside Roberts.

They exchanged words and then both stood up. JT backed away as Roberts leaned toward her, grabbed her sleeve, and flicked something off. Probably a hunk of pickle. Then he pulled her closer, and took a big whiff of her T-shirt.

With a jerk of her shoulder, JT yanked the material out of his fingers. Roberts thrust himself right in her face. I was too far away to hear more than bits and pieces, but I did make out "pickle" and "this time" and "finally did it."

Before I could blink, the detective spun JT around. He whipped out his handcuffs, yanked her hands behind her back, and snapped them around her wrists.

The Tenacious Protector—the little thing inside me that came to life when anyone I cared about was threatened in any way—roared with a vengeance that startled even me. Without conscious thought, I bolted toward them. Dawg and Bogey were just a fraction of a step behind. The two dogs charged along as I howled out what could only be categorized as a war cry.

I'd almost reached my destination when two lean, mean deputies tackled me flat to the ground. Air slammed from my lungs. I did have the presence of mind not to let go of the leashes as I hit the hard-packed earth. One cop landed square on my backpack. The thought that there'd be no way my newly dipped rose was going to survive that squashing flashed through my mind.

I heard JT yelling, far away and muffled, but I couldn't make out what she was saying. Hands clamped tightly around my biceps and jerked me roughly to my feet. I swayed unsteadily between the two deputies.

Someone yanked the leashes from my hands.

As suddenly as it disappeared, clarity returned. Both dogs were barking and snarling. One of the deputies danced around trying to avoid their gnashing teeth and keep hold of the leashes. JT shouted at the dogs, and someone else was hollering at JT.

Detective Roberts had his meaty hands firmly on JT's upper arms, holding her back. "Jesus Christ," he shouted. "Get her the hell out of here. And those damn dogs too!"

I hissed in a breath, battling down the fury that continued to threaten to take my vision.

"Bogey! Dawg!" I yelled. Both dogs reluctantly stilled. The cop holding them looked like he might pee his pants.

Detective Roberts bellowed again, "Take her somewhere out of my sight and finish getting her statement before I haul her ass in!"

A thin, dark-haired, female deputy trotted over.

I shook myself loose of the two deputies. "I'm okay," I said hoarsely. "I'm not going to do anything. Jesus. JT, what the fuck is going on?"

JT said, "I didn't do this. Go find Tyrell, Shay. He'll know what to do."

I opened my mouth but nothing came out. My eyes flicked desperately between JT and Roberts.

Detective Roberts grinned as hateful a grin as I'd ever seen and addressed my woman. "JT Bordeaux, you're under arrest for the murder of Russell Krasski."

THREE

An hour later, after detailing my limited knowledge of prior events to the deputy, I was in the truck with both Dawg and Bogey, tooling toward Minneapolis's 3rd Precinct as fast as I could. I honestly had no idea what had just happened back there.

I tried, with no success, to get a hold of Coop. I knew he'd know what to do, and if he didn't, he'd help me figure things out. Damn dude. Maybe he was behind bars himself on disorderly conduct charges against the Green Beans. Wouldn't be the first time, and certainly wouldn't be the last. I left a message for him to give me a buzz.

There was no way JT killed anyone, even if she did pack a gun both on duty and off. But you better believe I was going to find out what was going on, and fast. JT's former partner-on-the-job, Tyrell Johnson, was a decent guy and a great cop who was now working Narcotics. I hoped JT was right when she said he'd know what to do.

I disconnected after dialing Tyrell's cell for the fourth time and swore some more.

For once the freeway wasn't clogged with a whole lot of traffic, probably since it was the weekend. As I headed into Minneapolis, I tried to organize the thoughts churning through my head. I saw Bogey's nose in a cadaver's crotch, the gargantuan pickle stuffed in the dead man's mouth, and then handcuffs being clicked onto JT's wrists—all these images appeared and disappeared from my vision like a slideshow. Why did JT smell pickley? None of this stuff was adding up.

By the time I pulled into the 3rd Precinct, twilight was turning into full-on dark. I prayed to the powers that be that Tyrell was within the dreary confines of the red-brick stationhouse.

I cracked the windows for the still-unsettled pooches and hustled between the cars in the lot. I barely missed mowing down an older couple leaving the station and nearly ripped the front door from the frame when I flung it open.

The lobby smelled of mold and fear-tinged sweat. A narrow bench occupied one side of a short hallway, and at the end of the hall were a couple of closed doors and an information window with thick, probably bulletproof glass. Behind the window, a cop with black curly hair shuffled through a sheaf of papers. Her nameplate read C. Chevalier, and she looked familiar. I'd probably run into her at one of JT's off-duty police functions.

The screech of the buzzer startled her. She looked up from her stack of paperwork and keyed a button. "Help you?" Her voice sounded tinny and bored through beat-up speakers nestled in the glass.

My heart banged within my chest. "Is Tyrell—Detective Johnson—here?"

Recognition dawned on her round face. Her dark eyes crinkled as she smiled. "You're with Bordeaux, right?"

Well, maybe this was going to be easier than I thought. "Yup, I am. But right now I'm looking for Tyrell. Do you know if he's in?"

"Hang on." She picked up a phone and punched in numbers. I watched her mouth move as she spoke to someone on the other end. After about twenty seconds, she hung up and keyed the mic. "He's in and will be down in just a couple minutes."

I expressed my gratitude and moved away from the window. A shiver shook me, and I wished I'd thought to grab the sweatshirt I'd left in the truck. With the adrenaline of the body discovery and JT's arrest, I was fricking freezing. I wrapped my arms around myself and wondered if word had yet gotten back to the station that one of their own was cooling her heels in a cage. Did agencies share info like that?

Despite her profession, terror over JT's well-being wasn't something I was used to, and the emotion welled up again unbidden. I'd fought panic's rising tide the entire way from Shakopee to Minneapolis, and every time I thought I had it under control, the force of it made me grind my teeth. I was going to have a jaw-ache before this was done. Typically I was pretty levelheaded. On the rare occasion when I lost it and the Tenacious Protector popped out to play, there was usually hell to pay on someone's part. If somebody somehow threatened my loved ones, I lost my mind—but there was no one to scream at or punch out about this. And right now it made me somewhat sick and impotently furious that I couldn't do a damned thing to help the woman I loved. Of course, I was pretty damn sure I was overreacting. *Come on, Shay,* I chided myself, *JT is a good cop with a good reputation. She won't be sitting in that cell for long.* But when I was in the midst of heart-pounding fear and supreme confusion, losing my mind was easy to do.

I toed a crack in the dirty linoleum floor and focused on regulating my breathing and slowing my heart. I was pretty sure I'd have a heart attack if I kept this up for too much longer.

After what seemed like twenty minutes but was probably only five, one of the doors swung open and Tyrell stepped into the lobby.

"Hey sugar. What're you doin' here?" A grin sliced his face and set his dimples dimpling. In two big steps he engulfed me in a bear hug. For a moment, Tyrell's cologne, Sean John's Unforgiveable, overtook the station stink, and I inhaled deeply. I knew what it was because JT and I had given it to him for his birthday a couple of weeks before. We'd spent twenty minutes at the Macy's men's fragrances counter, and I'd lost my ability to distinguish between scents before she settled on the Sean John stuff.

I dragged myself out of my cologne-induced reverie. As soon as I contemplated what I had to tell him, any calm I'd managed to gain during my wait evaporated. "Ty, we have to do something. I don't know what happened. They slapped handcuffs on her—"

"Cuffs on who? Eddy?"

"No! JT. He just—and she—" I was losing it again, hyperventilating. I gasped, "Half his head was gone—"

"Shay! Exactly who and what are you talking about?" Tyrell gripped my shoulders and pushed me to arm's length, alarm finally registering on his face. I wasn't usually quite so random when I spoke, but for the life of me I couldn't seem to put together a coherent sentence.

"The dead guy tipped over—with a pickle—I had to use the bathroom—"

"SHAY!" Tyrell gave me a good shake, making my teeth clack. "Calm down now and tell me what the hell happened."

I tried again. "They handcuffed her. Arrested her. They took her—"

"Arrested who? Took her where?"

Obviously Scott County and Minneapolis were not currently sharing information. Okay. I hauled in a shuddering breath. "JT. They arrested JT for murder."

———

With a foam cup of ghastly cop coffee in my hand, I sat on an old metal chair, its seat ripped from too many criminal butts. I faced Tyrell across the file-strewn mess he called his desk.

After he understood that it was JT who'd been cuffed and stuffed into a cruiser like a common criminal, he whisked me through a locked door and up a flight of warped, green-linoleum-covered stairs to a squad room. Desks, filing cabinets, and a long table at the back of the room filled the space. Only a couple other detectives were in residence, and both worked feverishly on computers sitting on top of their desks. They paid me no mind as we passed by.

Ty had led me to his desk and pushed me into the chair. "I'll be back in two shakes."

I'd tried to gather myself as I had stared at the dirty gray wall. I was on a rollercoaster that clacked its way up the track, rolled over the top, and finally dropped with sizzling speed into that breathtaking moment of free fall. Usually the cars would hit the bottom of the hill and head up the next incline. The problem was that I'd been in free fall since the moment JT disappeared through the fence toward the waiting squads in the field beyond. My heart had been in my throat ever since, and the end wasn't anywhere in sight.

I really needed to get a grip, but I had no idea how to regain my equilibrium. I tried to breathe slow and deep again, through my nose. That seemed to help a little.

Tyrell had returned with a cup of lukewarm joe and handed it to me. I took a sip and nearly choked on the bitter liquid that flowed over my tongue. It was nothing like the rich brew we served at the Hole.

He now settled in his own seat and said, "Okay, Shay, take it slow and start from the beginning."

I did, and for the next twenty minutes filled him in on everything that had happened. Maybe the horrible coffee had done its job after all.

"So," I concluded, "JT told me to come to you, and here I am."

Tyrell leaned back in his chair and crossed his heavily muscled arms over his heavily muscled chest. Tightly curled black ringlets framed his chiseled face. His hair was longer than I'd seen it before. That made sense; because of the position he was now working, he often went undercover. He pulled a big breath in and let it out slowly, his dark mocha complexion unusually pale. "Are you sure the name of the victim was Russell Krasski?"

"Yes, I'm positive." That name would forever be branded in my brain.

Tyrell ran a hand over his chin. "Shit."

"What's going on? Who's this Krasski guy?"

"JT never told you about him?"

"No."

Tyrell suddenly seemed very uncomfortable. He shifted and gave me a considering look, but I couldn't read his dark gaze. "If JT never told you about this, I'm not sure I should."

"Ty, come on." I barely restrained myself from jumping out of my chair and across the desk. "JT is sitting in a cell at the Scott

County jail right now. She needs our help. I can't help her if I don't know what the hell is going on."

Tyrell's jowls bunched as he clenched his teeth. "Let me call a couple people and see what's up. Then I'll explain."

I listened to two one-sided conversations and couldn't glean much from either except that JT was indeed in custody, and she was being held away from the rest of the inmate population because she was a cop—a well-known cop with a lot of busts. There were a number of cons she'd had a hand in putting away who'd be after whatever revenge they could get. My blood ran cold at the thought of JT in there, alone and possibly in danger. My heart revved and I fought the red haze that appeared whenever my Protector came knocking. *Deep, even breaths, Shay. In and out.*

Tyrell hung up and slid his right desk drawer open without meeting my eyes. He flipped through a number of files before shutting that drawer and opening one on the opposite side. After a moment, he pulled out a thick manila folder with the name *Krasski* scribbled in black Sharpie on the tab. He thumbed it open and shuffled through the contents. After a minute or two, he closed the file and threw it on his desktop. He then leaned back in his chair, threaded his fingers, and put his hands behind his head.

"Okay," he said. "Now, Shay, you sit calm while I tell you this. I can only give you the basics because the case is classified. So don't go all crazy on me, you hear?"

That didn't sound good. I felt like I was stuffed in the pouch of a cocked slingshot about to be flung to Kingdom Come. The slightest nudge would set me off, which is never a good idea when the person in front of you has a gun and badge. I breathed deep once, then again. *Oh God, just end this.* "Tell me."

Tyrell pulled in his generous bottom lip and chewed on it a moment. "Awhile back, JT and I were on a team that set up a sting on a ring that abducted kids, usually minority children whose parents had no resources and questionable status within the country. Girls were sold to the highest bidder, usually to someone overseas. The girls who couldn't be sold as marriage material, and all the boys, were bartered, traded, or sold as child slaves."

He paused. "For close to a year we worked the shit out of the case. We had the ringleader, Krasski"—he pointed at the file—"in our sights. He was a bastard of the highest caliber. He and his posse raped the girls and beat the boys to within an inch of their lives. Pretty soon those poor children were walking and talking robots. The kids that came from Krasski were in high demand. He used violence and the threat of violence against the kids' families, so none of them would rebel and attempt to escape."

Jesus. That was unspeakable. I closed my eyes a moment, then refocused on Tyrell, rampant emotion evident in his expression.

"The case was like JT's obsession. She researched Krasski, followed him, staked out his ass night after night. He was the worst kind of slimeball. The kind of weasel who was wrapped in Teflon—every charge we tried to slap on him somehow slid off. For the life of us we couldn't get a damn thing to stick."

"So what happened?"

"The night of the bust ... We had it all planned. Every stinking move. We finally managed to pull together all the evidence we needed to make an arrest, which would have shut down a huge Midwest operation." He inhaled sharply and held his breath for a moment before slowly letting it out through his nose.

I was riveted by Ty's tale, lost in the middle of some kind of horrifying psychological thriller—a horrifying thriller that involved the love of my life—instead of calmly looking at the hard facts of a real-life case.

"The operation went off without so much as a hiccup. We went in, busted a bunch of assholes, including Krasski. They were in the midst of—" Tyrell's face hardened. "God, it was awful. Anyway, we rounded up everyone. Not one person got away. JT and I had Krasski between us. We escorted him outside. And as we tried to stuff him in the car, he said something to JT. I missed it, and JT hasn't repeated it to this day." Tyrell closed his eyes. "She lost her freaking mind. With Krasski's hands cuffed, she beat the shit out of him. I needed help to pull her off him, and by then the damage was done. She put him in the hospital with a broken jaw and cracked ribs and I can't even remember what else. She nearly killed him. Goddamn it, the asshole deserved it."

Tyrell slumped back in his chair. His gaze was locked over my shoulder as he relived the memory. "JT was suspended. The case we worked so hard to make against Krasski fell apart."

Holy shit. "What about the others you arrested?"

"They were charged and most of them went down. But the number-one man was free. Once he healed up, the bastard could start up the whole thing all over again. JT was furious with herself. Talk about a boatload of trouble. She had to take anger management classes, do some other Internal Affairs crap."

"She's usually so in control. I can hardly imagine her on a rampage. If she snapped ... I can totally see where it'd be next to impossible to stop her." I stared at Tyrell. "She blamed herself, didn't she?" I knew JT well enough to understand that it would drive her beyond crazy that she was the reason a no-good criminal walked.

"Yeah. She ran herself through the wringer. When she came back to work, even I wasn't sure she was ready. While she was off, she decided it was her personal vendetta to nail the bastard somehow. Whatever it took, on the books or not. So she started following him on her days off, showing up at places he frequented. She wouldn't say anything to him. She'd just be there, make it obvious she was on his ass."

"Jesus."

"Soon things started to escalate. She became even more obvious. She'd pull him over with our unmarked car, harass the hell out of him. Started getting in his face."

"Oh my God," I whispered. This was a JT I didn't know. Why didn't she ever tell me any of this? I thought she loved her job, fully believed in what she was doing.

"Krasski wasn't stupid. He went to one of the watchdog groups that pull the police brutality card during trials. Got them all fired up. Wound up taking out a harassment restraining order on JT."

I could hardly believe my ears. A criminal had been allowed a restraining order? On my JT?

"Part of the order was if JT were to come within a hundred feet of Krasski, she'd be arrested. Basically, her career would be toast. I think the order's expired by now, though." Tyrell heaved a huge sigh. "So that's an abbreviated version of what's probably the worst thing JT has ever been through professionally."

I was still reeling over the fact that a badass hooligan had taken out a restraining order against JT. It was really hard to believe she'd never said a word about it to me. I could almost feel her pain, her shame, the incredible frustration she must have felt.

Tyrell said, "She tried to do what she could to prevent him from returning to the crap he'd been doing, but it was all just one huge cluster that spiraled into chaos."

"She had every reason to want to kill him. I get that. But, Ty, do you think she really could've done it? That she could completely lose her mind? I would never believe she'd be capable of doing that." Right?

Tyrell shrugged. "I don't know, Shay. I do know she's worked like hell to put this whole fucked-up nightmare behind her. I'll see what I can find out and let the guys who can help know what's going on. They'll have ideas on a lawyer. Try not to worry, hey?"

Yeah right. Not worrying wasn't an option.

FOUR

It was close to nine, fully dark, and maybe fifty degrees when I emerged from the station. After letting the dogs do their business, I drove off in a complete fog, despite both Bogey and Dawg periodically slurping me. They knew something was up. Dogs were like that.

I hit Redial for Coop's cell, tapping my thumb against the steering wheel impatiently as it rang in my ear, and hung up when voicemail kicked in. I didn't want to go through what I'd just learned with Judith, the name Coop gave the irritating robotic female voice that narrated most voicemail. I'd have started to worry about him if I wasn't already spending all my worry currency on JT.

Thoughts raged inside my head. One moment I was furious with JT for hiding all of this from me and the next I was terrified that she even theoretically may have hosed someone. Granted, it was someone who apparently deserved it, but the repercussions of her actions were unthinkable.

Waste. Whack. Pop a cap. Rub out. The words bounced through my brain like an echo from a megaphone blasting at full volume.

Instead of heading directly home, I decided I needed the cool, calm advice of Eddy Quartermaine, my ex-landlord and mom stand-in. She lived in Uptown in the back of a large Victorian she owned. The front half of the huge old house was occupied by my café, The Rabbit Hole, on the main floor. Above that was a dinky one-bedroom apartment I'd lived in for years until just a few months ago, when I'd moved in with JT.

I was an independent person, and it took some serious cajoling on JT's part to convince me to attempt to live in harmonious two-become-one-ness with her. We'd been cohabitating at her place now for a few months. In fact, I had surprised myself: I was actually pretty pleased with the whole situation.

Now the upstairs flat above the Hole was occupied by Rocky, a very endearing, somewhat challenged, multi-fact-spewing man of middling age who was mentally still in his teens. Almost a year earlier, Kate and I had hired him to help out at the Hole doing menial tasks and delivering rolls and coffee. The arrangement worked out nicely.

I parked in front of the detached garage just off the alley at the back of the house. My fingers were working about as well as my brain and I fumbled to open the gate to the fenced-in backyard. The motion light popped on, scaring shadows away. I filled Dawg and Bogey's water bucket from a spigot attached to the house and left them racing around after each other.

The screen creaked as I pulled it open. I keyed the lock, and the knob on the main door twisted easily in my hand. Eddy was a night owl, most likely watching reruns of *Cold Case* or another crime drama. It was her version of crack.

I stepped into a tidy, comfortably worn kitchen filled on this night with the familiar scents of vanilla and cinnamon. A deep sense of comfort and love settled over me. The light above the range was on, and the sound of the TV filtered through the doorway leading to the living room.

"Eddy," I called out, not wanting to be the cause of a heart attack.

"Shay!" she hollered. "Come on in, girl. Just let me pause this show. Don't know what I ever did without the wonders of a DVD player." She cackled with glee. The DVD player was a recent addition. Coop had tried numerous times to show her how to use the DVR that came with her DirecTV, but she promptly blocked him and the instructions out. I gave it another five years before we'd be able to cajole her into learning how to use it. Eddy didn't like change much.

Well-padded, almost-new carpet cushioned my footsteps. It was officially called Sand Swirl, but it looked to me more like the color of Dawg's belly hair. However, I doubted that Dawg's Fawn was the name of a color anyone would want to put on their floors.

I dropped onto the couch. Captain Frank Furillo's profile was frozen on the TV screen, his mouth open. I'd recently given Eddy the first two seasons of the early Eighties series *Hill Street Blues,* and she'd finally cracked the wrapper.

Eddy was kicked back in a recliner, Winnie the Pooh slipper-clad feet crossed. Her rich mahogany skin was a marked contrast to the white housecoat with frilly pink cuffs she was wrapped up in. She gave me a once-over. "Child, you look plum wore out. And sort of queasyish. Did you eat one too many Scotch eggs at the Renaissance Festival? Crazy people sell 'em, I know. Where's JT?"

I was attempting to formulate how to explain the events of the last half-day, but Eddy's comment about the Scotch eggs startled a laugh out of me. Something about the comment hit me as so inanely hilarious that I rolled from a gentle chuckle into a full-blown laughing fit in the space of a heartbeat. I gasped for breath.

With a sharp look, Eddy said, "You about done there? That wasn't funny."

I tried to compose myself and opened my mouth to speak, but the words that tumbled out weren't the ones I'd meant to say. "JT's been arrested."

Eddy cocked her head and frowned like Dawg often did. I thought for the briefest moment she was going to ask me what in the world I'd been smoking. Instead she said, "You best tell me what is going on."

I unloaded the whole mess on the poor woman, who sat through my recitation without so much as a question. She let me pour it all out.

When I finished, she said, "Well, that's one hell of a note."

My mind felt scrambled, bruised actually. My mouth ran off before my neurons had a chance to catch up. "Eddy, I can't believe JT held out on me from the moment we got together. Now she's a murderer. Well, a theoretical, could-be murderer," I amended. I leaned forward with my elbows on my knees and dropped my head in my hands. "What a mess."

"Shay, you stop right there." Eddy's voice dropped, low and deadly. "That girl no more killed someone than I suddenly became Olivia Benson from *SVU*. Or maybe Tina Turner would be a better comparison. JT had her reasons for not telling you. Anyway, the question is— what can we do to help her? We could bake her a cake with a file in it so she could saw her way out."

"Eddy." I said, and closed my eyes. At a base level I knew she was right about JT. My cop did everything by the book. Okay, maybe not *everything*, but most things. She sure as shit didn't kill anyone. No way. That would be beyond her. Wouldn't it? And even if she did kill this Krasski guy, so what? I thought the man deserved to die. But not by JT's hand, if only because of the repercussions she'd have to live with.

32

But then, what did that say about me? About her? The inside of my head was doing the swirlies again.

I was under the assumption that long-term lovers shared deep shit. I'd always shied away from divulging my true feelings and deep, dark skeletons with those I hooked up with. Come to think of it, hook-ups was exactly what they were *because* I refused to let anyone in. I never bothered to analyze my psyche deep enough to root out the cause of my recalcitrance. A mind and the depths of the soul can be scary things.

But amazingly, things were different with JT long before I laid eyes on the badge in her hand when she'd come to question me about Coop and the death of his employer eleven months ago. Trust was hard for me to come by, but for whatever reason, she made me feel safe. Like it was okay to have imperfections, self-doubt, and a complex, sometimes shameful past. That confiding those issues would make life easier to bear. I had coughed up most of my inner demons, and I thought I was getting the same in return. But JT had hidden her greatest pain from me, and damn, that stung like hell.

I stared grumpily at Eddy.

"Easy, child. Come on now. I'm kidding. We can get her one of those lawyers, like those Meshbesher and Spence people who are always on the TV, interrupting my shows."

With a great deal of effort, I managed to rein in my sparking emotions. "I think they're personal injury attorneys, not defense lawyers. Tyrell said he'd talk to some people."

"Well, whatever you want to call those shysters, make sure JT gets one—gets some, maybe more than one. What she needs is someone to figure out who did the deed. Killed Krasski the ass. That'll take care of the situation."

I shot her a look. She didn't usually take liberties with people's given names.

She said, "Dead man's name was Krasski, right?"

I nodded.

"See, he's got an *ass* in his name. K-R-A-S-S-K-I, get it?"

I rolled my eyes.

"So now we gotta find out who did the pickle stuffing and that'll get JT off the hook. Tyrell had a file, you said."

I could see where she was going with this, and I did not like it one bit. "Yes, he did, and it's locked up tight at the police station."

That troublemaking gleam appeared in Eddy's eyes.

"Oh no," I said. "No way. We are not going to steal Tyrell's file."

"It wouldn't be stealing. All you'd have to do is just a little peek. I'm sure there's a list of no-good scallywags in there who'd want to see Krasski swinging from the nearest flagpole. That'd be a start."

Prior to *Hill Street*, Eddy had been on a *Pirates of the Caribbean* kick.

"Besides, we need to piece together why the whole Krasski thing got to JT so bad. I'm sure she's seen lots of terrible stuff on the job, so why did this send her off the deep end? She's usually a steady, even-keeled little gal."

I wasn't happy with the *we* in her sentence, and that *little gal* had about eight inches of height on Eddy.

She continued, "It was certainly something more than the fact the man was evil. She deals with evil all the time." Eddy stretched and then recrossed her Winnie the Poohs. "You find out why that ass got to her and you'll understand the reason she couldn't tell you. And beyond that, why she became obsessed. Mark my words."

My brain was pretty much melted as I drove to the house I shared with JT. It was a little after ten, and I was wiped.

I pulled into the attached double garage and killed the engine. JT's two-story, redbrick colonial was originally owned by an aunt of hers. Somehow, JT managed to inherit the joint outright, which was fortunate since property taxes on a place overlooking Lake of the Isles were close to the same amount that a mortgage would run. Add utilities and upkeep to the equation, and JT wouldn't be quitting her day job anytime soon. Too bad that aunt hadn't left JT a nice trust fund to help out.

I shouldered open the truck door and exited. The two dogs clambered down onto the chipped concrete floor, and I slammed the door shut. It was past time for doggy din-din, and the mutts knew it. Dawg didn't think I was moving fast enough, so he gave me a healthy nudge in the butt and woofed. Bogey added his two cents by drooling a long, stringy trail of saliva onto my right shoe. I was still working on accepting his horrifyingly excessive salivation.

Together, we headed for the door that led from the garage into the house. It opened directly into a short hall that we used as a mudroom.

Dawg and Bogey scrambled past me and bolted into the kitchen, their nails scrabbling noisily on the linoleum.

A bench sat on one side of the tile floor of the mudroom with footwear neatly lined up beneath it. When I lived in my apartment, I was used to kicking off my tennis shoes and tossing them helter-skelter out of the way. But since I'd moved in, JT had been gently working on me to take the time to be less of a slob, and I was getting better about it. Most of the time.

Tonight, however, was not one of my more well-behaved moments. I toed my sneakers off, and with a flick of my foot, first one, and then the other shoe bounced against the wall and tumbled to the floor beside the bench.

Five coat hooks lined the opposite wall waiting for the heavy jackets that spelled winter in Minnesota. Soon enough they'd have more than windbreakers and sweatshirts hanging from them.

The hallway opened into a spacious dining room. It was filled with JT's aunt's ancient, heavy, hand-me-down furniture. They might be antiques, but they were so well used that I didn't think they'd be worth much more than family memories. The collection included an oblong table that probably weighed two tons and eight straight-back, walnut wood chairs. A matching gargantuan hutch filled with family glassware took up a big chunk of one wall, and a sliding patio door opened onto a nice porch that faced the backyard. I particularly liked the two-person rocking glider JT had tucked into the corner of the porch. We spent many evenings rocking and talking as the dogs exhausted themselves playing in the yard. I often wondered why JT's aunt had decided to leave all this to her, but I hadn't felt it necessary to be that nosy. Yet. Sometimes family politics worked in strange ways, and a grudge against one became the windfall of another.

The hall ended at the bottom of the stairway to the second floor. The rest of the main floor was taken up with a laundry room, the kitchen and living room, and JT's office.

I dumped my backpack next to the steps. The battered, broken rose JT bought me drooped from the zippered opening like an at-rest marionette. That's how I felt: bent and bruised, although not quite yet broken.

I scored the mutts their food, which they devoured in record time. I hadn't gotten anything to eat at the Renaissance Festival myself, and now, my stomach reminded me it was ready to rumble with a none-too-quiet grumble. I peeled a banana and smeared on Nutella, wolfing it down as I leaned against the sink.

Bogey wandered over and sat on his haunches facing me, one eye on the banana peel I'd tossed to the side of the sink. He'd eat just about anything—including plastic bags and tin foil—as long as it had any kind of food residue on it. He didn't much care for details, but he almost always managed to prove his guilt either by barfing up bits and pieces or leaving some interesting (and highly disgusting) doggie doo with remnants that pointed at exactly who the serial offender was. Luckily, he'd had no lasting negative effects. So far.

Dawg was Bogey's opposite. He never chowed on anything unless it was offered to him. I often wondered if his good behavior came from his horrible past life as a junkyard dog. Dawg had lived in daily fear of beatings at the hands of his jailer—I couldn't stoop to calling that man an actual dog owner—who starved the poor mutt on top of it. Now the jackass was lounging behind bars for murder. The best part was that he was cooling his heels in the brig because Coop and I stuck our noses where they didn't belong last fall while trying to prove Coop innocent of offing his bingo barge boss. The adventure was a success for the good guys all around. Well, except for Coop's dead employer, but he wasn't exactly a pillar of goodness anyway.

When I'd swallowed the last of the chocolate-hazelnut banana, I secured the banana peel in the garbage. Bogey huffed disgustedly at me, attempted to lick his chops (which just relegated more drool to the floor), and wandered off.

After wiping up after the mad salivator, I grabbed my backpack and stomped up the stairs. A hallway ran from one end of the house to the other and divided the space in two. Our amazingly spacious bedroom occupied one entire half of the floor, with two additional bedrooms situated on the other side of the hall. One room had become my office, and the other was used as a spare bedroom for overnight guests.

In my office, my mother's antique desk and wooden office chair took center stage. The set had been carefully hauled from my tiny apartment above the Rabbit Hole. Buttercream yellow paint covered three walls, and the fourth was taken up by mostly empty built-in bookshelves. A couple of filing cabinets and a new, buckskin-colored leather loveseat filled the rest of the room.

I set the backpack on the floor and dropped heavily into the desk chair. It squeaked as I leaned back and closed my eyes.

Everything that happened after five o'clock today was a surreal blur. I still could not wrap my mind around exhibit A: I'd found a dead body in an outhouse and that body had been iced. Smoked. Murdered.

Or exhibit B: a cop who apparently hated JT had arrested her, dragged her away, and locked her up like a common criminal. My JT, the maker and keeper of justice and the American way.

Then there was exhibit C: Russell Krasski. A man who did dastardly things, including trafficking *children*, had beaten the system and walked after JT'd wigged out and whomped him. I could feel the depth of self-hatred JT must have harbored against herself—and must still. I shuddered in my chair. It must have been absolutely awful knowing you were the one who was responsible for putting that spineless bastard back on the street. Would I have done the same thing had I been in her shoes? Probably. I suppose it depended on whatever Krasski had said that set JT off. I didn't lose my temper all that often, but when I did, it was a doozy. I really wondered what buttons he'd tweaked that pushed her into the deep end of the pool—wondered if she'd ever feel comfortable enough to tell me.

My day at the Ren Fest ran in Technicolor on the video screen of my mind. JT had been gone a lot longer than I'd expected fetching my pickle. I didn't know exactly where she was or what she'd been doing during that time, but I was sure there was no way she shot anyone. Wasn't I? Then I thought about the tangy wet spots on her shirt. The pickle chunks. Krasski had a pickle crammed down his throat… were the bits and pieces clinging to her shirt from that same pickle? I couldn't blame JT if she had indeed plugged him then stuffed him, though it still ate at me that she hadn't shared what had happened. She had to know by now that I would've completely understood.

Christ on a cracker, this was a lot for my poor gray matter to work through. I scrubbed a hand over my face and pressed on my temples. If JT had seen Krasski during her pickle quest, she theoretically could've followed him into the privies. The rowdy crowd watching the Tortuga Twins had been geared up, screaming at top decibel, and I wasn't sure if a gunshot would have been heard through the ruckus.

With a wheezing sigh, I sat up and watched the screensaver swirl its colorful patterns on the computer. Coop still hadn't returned my calls, momentarily distracting me from my morose thoughts. For the seventy-sixth time, I wondered what was going on at the protest up in Duluth. Open Rabbit Hole bills lay scattered off to one side of my desk, and my mind skipped from Coop to finances. Stress-induced ADD? I randomly picked up the electric bill and thought inanely that the total due seemed high. Costs just kept going up. And up. I tossed the bill on top of haphazardly stacked, color-coded Rabbit Hole file folders next to the computer.

My eyes caught a framed 5x7 photo of JT and me that I'd set close to my workspace, snapped a few months ago when we'd taken off for a long weekend in Duluth. We were on the pier at Canal Park, standing on the stairs leading to the lighthouse at the canal entrance, grinning like fools in love at the camera. JT was a step above me, her arms tightly wrapped around my shoulders. I loved that picture. It froze in time a moment of new love in carefree abandon. We needed to find that abandon again very soon.

I reached out a trembling finger and traced JT's face. Her long hair was pulled up in a ponytail, and wisps floated around her face in the breeze. Sunglasses rested on the top of her head. She was hot, she was beautiful, and somehow, she was all mine.

My throat constricted. I wished with every fiber of my being that she were home, safe and sound, in my arms instead of banging her head against the bars of a jail cell. Alone. Ugh.

I pulled the backpack onto my lap and gently slid the waxed flower from the bag. The colorful head was somehow still mostly intact, barely attached to the stem. I chucked the stem, hauled myself out of the chair, and gingerly set the head on an empty shelf. Better some than none.

The house was unnaturally quiet and depressing without JT. My jaws popped in a huge yawn. I desperately needed to sleep. Whether or not it would come was another question.

I descended the staircase to turn out the lights on the main floor.

Dawg was curled up on one corner of the couch, his head propped on the arm. At the sound of my footsteps, he hopped off and followed me as I extinguished the lights in the dining room and entered the kitchen to do the same. He licked his lips and gazed longingly from me to his bowl and back again. His entire upper lip was snagged on his lower teeth, giving him the most pathetic, irresistible face ever. However, tonight even that wasn't working.

"Sorry buddy, that's it. You don't want to be up all night with indigestion, do you?"

He whined and put an even more woeful look on his squashed face. I gave him a vigorous cheek rub that flapped his lips up and down.

Then I turned my attention to Bogey, who was sprawled out on the kitchen floor. I stroked the soft fur between his eyes and he gave me a slow, deep sigh. He peered up at me with big brown eyes, and the loose skin on his forehead crinkled up. I patted the frown down, and he sighed again.

Life was sure easier when you only required some decent food, a nice yard to play and poop in, and lots of unconditional love.

———

Sleep, unsurprisingly, was hard to find. Time and again I jerked awake after groping for JT's solid warmth and finding nothing but cool sheets.

I rolled over yet again and stared at the glowing red numbers on the clock radio. 7:15. Not the way I liked to start my Sunday mornings. With a frustrated sigh, I sat up and snapped the bedside light on, illuminating the room. When I moved in, we'd redecorated the bedroom to make it feel a little more like mine as well as JT's. The walls sported a light orange color that at first I thought would be disconcerting, but now I actually kind of liked it.

A couple pictures of Coop, Eddy, and the rest of the café gang graced the walls, along with a few shots of JT's folks. Above our bed was a headboard-sized painting done by Alex Rodriguez, a local artist pal of mine. She'd given it to JT and me when we'd finally decided to live in sin together. It was an abstract desert scene, done in both muted and vibrant desert colors. I had to admit it went well with the orange walls.

I threw off the covers and stood, the beige-speckled loop and pile carpet soft under my bare feet. I padded into the large bathroom and flicked the light. Three bulbs at the top of the medicine cabinet popped on, making me squint. I was headed toward the shower when I caught sight of myself in the mirror. What a case of bed head! My dark hair was flattened on one side and shoved up in tufts elsewhere. A line ran down the left side of my cheek where I'd laid too long on a fold in the pillowcase. Haunted, bloodshot eyes stared back at me. I turned quickly for the comfort of a hot shower, which did little to clear the fog in my head.

I rolled through the motions of dressing myself, pulling on black jeans and a semi-clean purple First Avenue T-shirt I'd tossed across the back of a chair earlier in the week. Fortunately, I didn't have to work at the Hole on this dreary, misty morning. I was so distracted I'd probably give hot chocolate for coffee orders and serve up whipped cream instead of tapioca pudding.

Both Bogey and Dawg were still conked out at the foot of the bed when I was dressed for the day. They didn't stir as I passed by.

I descended the stairs slowly, feeling the effects of being tackled by two lawmen. I sure wasn't getting any younger. I stopped in front of the patio door and hollered, "Who wants to go out?"

For a count of three, silence greeted my words.

Then there were a couple of thumps overhead. The sound of nails scrabbled against the hardwood floor in the upstairs hall. Then the dogs banged down the stairs, bounded around the corner, and raced toward me. If I didn't know them better, I'd have been afraid that two nearly hundred-pound canines would send me head over keister and crashing right through the sliding glass door.

But even though Bogey had a hard time controlling his snoot and Dawg enjoyed bouncing on anyone he loved, they both managed to screech to a halt just before plowing me over. Their muscles quivered in anticipation of the great outdoors, misty or not.

I slid the patio door open and they nearly tripped over each other as they burst outside. I followed them to the edge of the covered porch and leaned against one of the two carved pillars that framed the short set of stairs leading to ground level.

It was damp and chilly. I hugged myself and watched the pooches chase each other around the yard. They charged around the corner and out of sight down the run beside the house and then zoomed back again. After some vigorous snuffling and taking care of biz, they returned to careening around the now mostly brown lawn, carefree and exuberant.

Carefree and exuberant I was not. I was a study in contrasts, on edge and raw. Panic bubbled within me, in turns manageable, and then unbearable. The thought of JT locked away, probably terrified, conflicted with my darker contemplation of her tangled web of secrets. The crappy night of sleep wasn't helping any.

I squeezed the back of my neck and blew out a long breath. I had to do something. Eddy often liked to tell me when I was younger that action was always better than contemplation. As usual, she was right.

With the dogs romping contentedly, I headed back inside to fill their dishes and pour myself a bowl of Lucky Charms. Maybe some of that little leprechaun's luck would rub off.

I slumped into a dining room chair and chowed my breakfast. Once I washed down the last bite with a glass of orange juice, I dialed Tyrell's cell. Hopefully he'd have good news for me.

On the fourth ring, he picked up. "Johnson." His voice was hoarse and thick.

Oops. "Ty, it's Shay. I didn't mean to wake you."

I heard rustling and a couple of soft grunts as, in my mind's eye, he probably struggled to sit up. "No problem. You okay?"

"Hanging in there. Mostly. Did you hear anything more last night?"

"No. I tried. The Scott County Sheriff's Department is pretty much locked down when it comes to anything related to JT's arrest. Not sure why they're being such dickheads."

"It's got to have something to do with that Clint Roberts, the detective who arrested JT. I've never seen her so hostile with another cop before."

"Dunno, maybe he is the stumbling block. I'll try again and see if he'll play. Why the hell would JT have a beef with the guy, though, is what I don't get. She gets along with everyone." He sounded almost envious.

Did Tyrell let himself entertain the damning yet impossible notion that JT might actually have pulled the trigger? I had to admit that the circumstances did look terrible—considering the pickle chunks and juice splattered on her shirt, combined with the amount of time she'd been MIA. But I just couldn't see her doing the deed. However, I knew better than most that even good people can be pushed into doing things they typically would never consider. I prayed this wasn't one of those cases.

Eddy's file peeping suggestion nagged at the back of my mind, and no matter how I tried to tune the thought out, it kept popping up and waving at me. She was right again. If Krasski was really as reprehensible as it appeared, the man would have enemies galore. Knowing how thorough both JT and Tyrell were, there was sure to be a list of potential killers in that file.

"Shay, you still there?"

I pulled myself back to the conversation I was supposed to be having. Might as well ask. "So, in that file you have on Krasski..."

"Yeah?"

"Are there others who might want this piece of horse hooey dead?"

Tyrell was silent so long I could practically see his wheels turning as he tried to figure out where I was going with this.

Finally, he said, "Oh, hell yes. The man doesn't have many friends, especially after a bunch of his pals wound up in prison after the botched bust and he didn't. I'll do everything I can to get a hold of the detective on the case and make sure he has the full picture."

"You know I appreciate it. Do you think they'll let me see her?"

"Don't know. I'll see if there's any strings I can pull. I'll let you know when I hear something."

"You going into the station today?"

"Nope, I've got to head back under for the next couple. Have a rash of homeless beatings I'm working. But I promise I'll call and let you know as soon as I hear anything. And Shay?"

"Yeah?"

"Stay out of trouble, okay?"

FIVE

I PACED AROUND THE house like a lion stalking the fence around his enclosure. The next logical step was to follow Eddy's advice: figure out who offed Russell Krasski and get my girlfriend back home where she belonged.

Tyrell wasn't going to be at the station today, so this was the perfect time to take a crack at having an unauthorized look-see in Krasski's file. I hoped it was still on the desk where Tyrell left it. The big question was how was I going to manage to weasel my way into the heart of the cop shop. No police officer was about to allow me access and then hand over confidential files so I could figure out where to start my search for vigilante justice. If I really was going to attempt this insane scheme, that was the sticking point.

Maybe I could claim I forgot something at Tyrell's desk when I talked to him last night? He wouldn't be there to contradict my story, and it was Sunday, so maybe the place would be empty. Now *that* would be dreaming.

A plan started to congeal in my thick head, and, as harebrained as this course of action was, it made me feel better to have some kind of goal.

Action is better than contemplation. Remember that, Shay. However, before I ran off on this wild pheasant hunt, I needed to do one more thing.

I looked up and dialed the number to Scott County jail.

After a fifteen-minute runaround, the person in charge of visitation finally came on the line. I launched into my spiel one more time.

"I want to find out if I could visit someone being held at your facility. JT Bordeaux."

"One minute." The dude sounded as if I'd woken him from a Rip Van Winkle nap. Or he was busy smoking Marlboro's instead of working a jail. He put me on hold and one minute turned into five. Hold music would've actually been nice. I leaned against the arm of the recliner in the living room with my feet crossed at the ankles. My top foot was shaking back and forth so hard I nearly lost my balance. Nervous energy at work. I stood up, putting my foot to work instead, and paced some more. At the eight-minute mark a loud beep sounded in my ear, and he was back.

"Yuh, Bordeaux's here."

No shit, Sherlock. "Can I see her?"

"No, ma'am. No visitors."

"Why not?"

"Security risk, ma'am."

This guy was a man of few words and those few words were pissing me off.

"How is she a security risk? She's a cop, for Pete's sake."

"Orders, ma'am."

"From who?"

47

Papers rustled. "Detective Roberts, ma'am."

I was right. "Can I at least talk to her?"

"No, ma'am."

I swore to god if he called me ma'am one more time I was going to reach through the receiver and pull his tongue out.

"Can you tell me *when* I might be able to either speak with her or physically see her?" It was a monumental task not to sound too sarcastic.

"Court's open tomorrow. Maybe then. Maybe not."

"Okay. Thanks ever so much." This time the sarcasm came through loud and clear.

I hung up and moaned in frustration. I'd run out of options; it was time for action.

———

I procured a parking space close to the café on 24th just off Hennepin. The dogs and I piled out of the truck and they trotted ahead of me on their retractable leashes. Bogey's tail whipped the air, and Dawg's butt wiggled in thrilled excitement. There was never a lack of petting hands and treats inside, and they knew it.

The bells above the front door jingled merrily as I swung it open. The rumble of caffeinated chatter filled the space with a comfortable "you're home now" buzz, and the scent of cinnamon mixed with the pungent smell of brewed coffee made my mouth water.

It was a typical Sunday morning at the Hole.

I unleashed the hounds and Dawg headed toward the counter, stopping along the way to greet customers who'd become friends and try to make new ones. I was still waiting to be busted by the city for allowing four-legged critters in my establishment. Our standing story was that Bogey and Dawg were service dogs, although we weren't exactly sure what service they might provide. No one had turned us in yet, so we hadn't had a chance to try out our story. Thank goodness; Dawg loved people, and I'd hate to keep him away from his fans. He was all about, "Hey, I'm a good pal. Can I be your pal, huh, huh? Can I? Please? Huh? Huh?" *Wag, wag.* "You look lonely. Just pet me and you'll be happy. You'll feel even happier if you rub my tummy!" *Wag wag.*

Attention hog.

Bogey was Dawg's opposite. He would wait with a sour, put-upon expression for someone to reach out to him. He was happiest either crotch-sniffing on his own terms or snoozing in front of the fireplace. That pooch was just plain strange. I had to say, though, that he did remarkably well not inhaling our customer's nether regions while he was in the Rabbit Hole. Maybe he was afraid we'd toss him out on his delicate schnoz. He was actually worse when he was on the leash, out of his comfort zone. I guess snorting crotches was his form of Valium. Maybe he needed a canine psychiatrist.

The Rabbit Hole wasn't too big, and it wasn't too small. The walls were painted in a swirling vortex of cozy colors. The shades fit the fall season nicely and reflected the warmth Kate and I wanted to extend to our customers.

Most of the three-foot-round French café tables were occupied with the pre-church or just-waking-up crowd. Even the two groups of overstuffed chairs that flanked a gigantic stone fireplace were filled with lounging caffeine and tea junkies.

Doyle Malloy, my first—and last—high school boytoy, sat at one of the tables with his girlfriend, Amanda.

Even before high school, I knew I was different from most girls. They wanted to play dress up, and I wanted to play war. They loved frilly things, and I loved my mud-encrusted adventure clothes. By the time I hit high school, I realized I didn't mind the frilly things on someone else. That *someone else* just didn't happen to be Doyle, although for all I knew, maybe he liked to wear frilly things too.

Regardless, I'd wanted to make sure I gave the male species every opportunity to prove my same-sex instincts wrong. Doyle and I had only been seeing each other for a few short weeks when he—unfortunately—walked into the school's band storage room during the annual Queen of Hearts dance at a very inopportune moment. I'd fallen off the testosterone wagon and was busy defrilling—although not yet defiling—a sizzling-hot cheerleader. Oops.

Now Doyle was an ex-Minneapolis PD Homicide detective. The ding dong had resorted to hiring a private dick to help him solve his cases. When the MPD realized this, they canned his ass. Turned out the private eye he employed was an ex–Scotland Yard inspector, and now he and Doyle were running their own show out of an old dentist's office in Minneapolis.

"Hey, Big D!" I stopped at their table and slapped his arm. I added, "Hey, Amanda."

Amanda raised her coffee cup at me in greeting.

Doyle said with a big fat smirk, "If it isn't the turncoat in the flesh." He claimed to still resent the fact I'd swapped teams during our doomed romance, and he brought it up at least once in each conversation. Deep down I thought he was kind of proud of himself for thinking he was the reason I "became" a lesbian. He had trouble grasping the whole "it's biological" concept, but only because he was a numbskull, not because he was at the anti-gay end of the spectrum.

The one great thing Doyle was always reliable for was cop gossip, even if he wasn't a cop anymore, and I was pretty sure Amanda was now working for the St. Paul police department. Maybe one of them had heard something about JT. The trick was in getting Doyle to share his (usually ill-gotten) information without giving him too much in return. His penchant for gossip ran both ways.

I ruffled his hair affectionately and smiled at Amanda. "So what're you two doing slumming it in Uptown? I thought you were St. Paulie folk now."

Doyle took a noisy slurp of his coffee and waved the cup at me, sloshing tan liquid down the front of his light-blue shirt. Somehow he managed to wear a bit of everything he consumed. He brushed ineffectively at his front and said, "It's the battery acid you make. It goes down slicker than a hooker in the shower."

I cast an all-too-knowing glance Amanda's way at the disgusting yet complimentary comment. She shrugged, her expression of semi-horror mirroring my own. God only knew where Doyle came up with his array of inappropriate editorials.

"So," I said, pointedly refraining from commenting on hookers and showers, "you two heard anything through the grapevine lately?"

Doyle leaned toward me.

I leaned toward him.

He whispered loudly, "I got laid this morning."

This time it wasn't me who whacked him.

Amanda cut her eyes at the man. "I think when he woke up this morning, his brain remained deeply embedded in dreamland." Then she focused on me. "Other than a couple of gang-related incidents in the last few days, everything's been quiet."

I asked, "No rumblings from the burbs?"

Doyle said, "The burbs? You're kidding, right?" For him, if it didn't happen in Minneapolis or St. Paul, it may as well have happened in the North Pole.

Amanda said, "Nothing more than the usual stuff. Why?"

Bite your lip, Shay. "Oh, no reason. I—"

"Shay!" Kate's sister Anna called across the café.

Oh, thank you, lord of the crappy liars. I slammed my jaw shut, looked up, and called out, "Be right there."

I bid the duo a friendly adieu and skedaddled over to where Anna stood behind the pastry case. She said, "Thought you might want the last cinnamon roll." We'd recently hired the kid on as extra help, and she was rocking it, as evidenced by quickly learning my favorite edibles and drinkables.

"Hot damn, you bet I do," I said with extra enthusiasm. Saved by my sweet tooth.

"I'll whip you up a coffee, too." Anna went to work prepping my little bits of heaven. Unlike her sister—who was petite and willowy, with an ethereal build and spiked, multi-colored hair—Anna was almost as tall as Coop's six-four. Plus she was ripped, not scarecrow thin like Kate. She could probably do a chin-up with one hand. The young woman had broad shoulders, curly blond hair that hung to the middle of her back when not tied back, and twelve-pack abs. She would've been right at home with Xena and the Amazons. Anna was a third-year mechanical engineering student at the U of M, and one of the highly unusual brainiacs who also possessed a healthy dose of common sense. She was similar to Kate in her ability to anticipate the wants and needs of her customers, me included. I adored her.

Kate was behind the cash register finishing up with a customer. She was a dear friend and fantastic business partner. We'd done college together and, after parting ways for a few years, we reconnected and opened the Rabbit Hole. Neither one of us was particularly good at following established, expected paths. The café suited us both.

Today, green hair sprouted from Kate's head like spring grass on a misshapen bowling ball.

"Nice hair," I said.

"Thanks. I was going to do Rock Star Red, but I want to hold onto summer a little longer." Kate's short locks sported varying shades of every color under the sun. I wasn't sure what her true hair color actually was anymore.

"Nice."

"What brings you in this early?"

I wasn't typically a morning person, although being in this line of business meant I saw plenty of sunrises. However, on my off days, it was rare to see me in before noon, if I showed up at all.

"I'm dropping Mopey and Dopey off for visitation."

Kate's gaze settled on Dawg as he wandered from one customer to another. "Okay. Dopey's working the crowd. Where's Mopey?"

We both glanced around, and then Kate pointed. I followed the direction her finger indicated. Bogey was flopped upside down on the rug in front of the fireplace, eyes shut, huge lips splayed out on either side of his head. A toddler was snuggled up beside him.

I leaned a hip against the counter and grumbled, "He's doing what I only wish I could be doing."

"Aren't you Little Miss Freaking Sunshine." She tilted her head and studied my face. "You look stressed. How'd you like the Renaissance? Late night?"

I wished it were a crazy fun night with JT that had me dragging.

"It was … " I squinted, trying to think of a succinct way of giving her the rundown. "Interesting."

"Oh?"

"Well, it was kind of cool, actually, until we got to the part where I found a dead man in one of the privies."

Kate eyes widened and she gasped. Literally. "Oh no. You're kidding."

"Dead serious—no pun intended. And it gets worse."

"Anna!" Kate barked.

Anna popped over to the register. "What's up?"

Kate fumbled to untie her apron. "I have to talk to Shay a minute. Can you—"

"Get outta here," Anna told Kate and passed me a large hazelnut latte and a plate bearing my sweet roll fix. A fork protruded from the sticky mess.

I trailed Kate into the kitchen.

She whirled on me as soon as I crossed the threshold. "What on earth happened?"

I stabbed a hunk of roll and popped it in my mouth. My taste buds did a happy dance despite the circumstances. "They arrested JT for murder," I said as I chewed.

"No fucking way." Kate's eyebrows rose so quickly they almost flew off her forehead.

"Fucking way." I picked up my cup and slurped the foam from the top of my latte. "She's down at the Scott County Jail."

"Oh my god. Oh. My. God." At one time, Kate had designs on JT, before JT and I got together. She'd been a good sport, though, and now she and JT had become pretty good friends.

"It was so strange. Horrible. The cop that arrested her…" I trailed off and stuffed my face some more.

Kate widened her eyes at me.

"Sorry," I said after I swallowed. "He and JT were oil and water. I've never seen her like that. With another cop, no less."

"Well, how would you react if you were getting arrested for murder? Why did they think she did it?"

I related the rest of the story, ending just as I drained the last of my cooled latte into my mouth.

"How is it that you always manage to attract the strangest shit ever?"

That was the question of the decade.

I said, "I haven't been able to get a hold of Coop. I wonder if he's in the pokey again."

"No, not this time. He's back, without any jail time, you'll be happy to hear. He came in last night and was back in really early this morning to help Rocky out with his phone books."

"Phone books?"

"You really haven't been paying attention lately, have you, Shay?"

I shrugged, feeling more than a little lost. It wasn't that I wasn't paying attention so much as I was just absorbed in . . . what? Okay. Evidently, I wasn't paying as much attention as I should have to what was going on around me.

"Coop hatched a plan to help Rocky earn more money for his Tulip trip."

"Does Rocky need a raise?"

"No, I don't think a raise is necessary. He just wants extra money to add to his savings for his Tulip trip. Delivering the phone books was Coop's bright idea, so I had no qualms about calling him bright and early to get over here and help."

Tulip was Rocky in girl form. She was a street vendor who hawked balloons she twisted into animal shapes near Jackson Square in New Orleans, entertaining kids and their parents for five bucks a pop. Rocky met Tulip the previous spring when Eddy and family friend Agnes took him to Louisiana on his very first vacation. And was it a doozy! Between a stolen toy snake, drug money, and hit men, the Big Easy wasn't for the queasy. Once we'd made it back to Minnesota in one piece—well, except for the toy snake—we had to deal with a ruthless Mexican cartel. I was happy to report we all made it through the fireworks okay.

Thanks to Kate, Rocky and Tulip had begun "dating" through Facebook. Rocky was beside himself, dying to return to the land of zydeco and beignets to visit his Tulip. To that end, Eddy had established a Travel To Tulip fund, and we all pitched in a few bucks here and there for the cause. At last count I think he was up to almost three hundred bucks.

Kate said, "You should go into the backyard and check it out."

"Check out what?"

"The phone books, knucklehead."

———

I eyeballed the mountain of undelivered phone books stacked haphazardly against the house within the fenced-in backyard. I was sure they hadn't been there last night. Of course, it was dark, and I was wound up, so was it possible I hadn't noticed? I looked again at the bulk of plastic-encased paper. I doubted it.

Eddy was in her kitchen when I went back inside. She looked up from a cookbook that was open on the counter as the screen slammed shut behind me. "Hey girl. I was just looking up the recipe for Kitty Litter Cake. How are you doing this morning?"

"I'd be a lot better if I was still asleep, and did you really just say Kitty Litter Cake?"

"Sure did. It's almost Halloween. Gotta make something that fits the holiday." Eddy patted me on the cheek and then pulled me down into a hug. I loved this woman with every fiber of my being, Kitty Litter Cake or not.

She said in my ear, "It's going to all work out. Have you heard anything from JT?"

I squeezed Eddy hard, then released her and stepped back. "No. Tyrell's working on it. I called the jail, but they won't let me see her or even talk to her."

Eddy rolled her eyes. "Figures. You decide to follow my advice yet?"

"You give a lot of advice. Which advice?" I knew exactly what she meant, but it was fun to stir the pot every so often.

"When are you gonna start listening to this old lady, child? I told you last night you needed to find out who else might be in the market for a dead Krasski. Tyrell had a file that I just know is plum ripe for picking names that would fit—"

"I'm way ahead of you. Want to come with?"

Eddy slammed the cookbook shut. "You bet your bottom twenty dollars, sweet cheeks. Now where'd I put my breaking-the-law shoes?"

———

Five minutes later we were cruising up Hennepin Avenue.

Eddy said, "Maybe we should invite Coop along for this escapade. It's always good to have a little extra backup."

"Good idea. Do you know where Coop and Rocky are delivering those phone books?"

"Of course. When are you going to learn I know all? They're over in Lyn-Lake, by that teeny weeny little bookstore on 26th and Lyndale near the French Meadow Bakery." The teeny weeny little place was a mystery bookstore called Once Upon a Crime. Gary and Pat, the husband and wife proprietors, along with their wonder dog Shamus, were cool—often helping me find CSI-type forensic mysteries that Eddy chewed up and spit out faster than I could keep up. Too bad one of them couldn't help us solve this whodunit.

I cruised slowly down Bryant, cut over on 26th, and headed up Colfax. Plenty of cars lined both sides of the street, but I didn't see Coop, Rocky, or Eddy's rusty yellow truck that she said was serving as phone book home base. We circled a couple more blocks before finding it. The truck was parked between a red Honda Civic and of all things, an old rusty 1960-something Ford Galaxie that was dwarfed by a huge, expensive boat on the shiny silver trailer hitched to its rear end. It was hard to believe the car was still running in this day and age, much less pulling that behemoth. It was a strange world.

The back end of Eddy's pickup hovered inches above the asphalt under the weight of the books, and the front was practically lifting off the ground.

I parallel parked a few cars away and we scanned the area for the phone book boys. It was still overcast. A downright chilly breeze prickled my skin as we exited my truck. What a difference from yesterday. But then, that was weather in Minnesota. You might be wearing short sleeves in January and shoveling snow in May.

Curled brown and orange leaves crunched underfoot as we strolled toward the phone book pile. A few of the trees that lined the street stubbornly hung onto the last of their leaves, refusing to give in to the inevitable pull of the season.

Eddy said, "They'll be along shortly, I'm sure."

"I hope so." I shivered and jammed my hands in my pockets.

"Hey, Shay! Eddy!" Coop's voice echoed behind us.

"Hurry your butt over here," Eddy hollered at him.

Coop closed in, dragging a noisy Radio Flyer wagon behind him. Time for another load. A cigarette dangled from the corner of his mouth. He kept trying to quit but hadn't yet managed to conquer his addiction. He was wearing a Green Beans for Peace and Preservation hoodie with blue hockey-skate laces at the neck and faded jeans honestly worn at the knees. He had to stoop to reach the wagon's handle. I didn't envy him the backache he was going to have after this.

He said, "I knew you'd hear my psychic plea for help. I'm going to kill whoever gave Rocky the idea to deliver phone books for cash." Coop tossed shaggy, ash-blond hair out of his bloodshot eyes. He looked exhausted. "Oh, wait," he grumbled. "That was me. Go ahead and shoot me now."

I propped my hands on my hips and scanned the uneven mound of various-sized telephone books that nearly spilled over the sides of the truck onto the street. "Where did you come up with this looney idea?"

"Back in the day, I did this to make my rent payment when it was phone book delivery season." For a long time—years in fact—Coop had struggled to keep a job and pay his bills. He didn't starve to death because both Eddy (through cooking) and I (through a donation of lunch money) helped supply him with grub when he needed it. Between his fight for peace, preservation, and environmental activism as a member of the Green Beans—and an equal if not even more powerful craving to spend his days in computer game oblivion—holding down a steady source of income was something of a challenge. Things changed in a big way about a year and a half ago.

Coop had been a supervisor on an old bingo boat on the Mississippi River between Minneapolis and St. Paul. The giant rust bucket, better known as Pig's Eye Bingo, had recently been sold down the river for scrap. Its rather piggish owner, Stanley "Kinky" Anderson—Coop's former boss—had been murdered onboard, and there wasn't a soul around who wanted to deal with a poltergeist of that magnitude.

One good thing came of the fiasco. During his time as a bingo slave, Coop had honed his computer systems programming techniques, both legal and illegal. Since then, he'd moved on to designing customer rewards programs for gaming establishments, and he frequently worked with Eddy's Mad Knitters and their friends on their computer skills. They were generous with their pocketbooks when they finally grasped what he was trying to teach them.

The Mad Knitters, a group of between three and fifteen or so gals, regularly met at the Rabbit Hole to work on their latest knitting projects. However, they usually wound up in Eddy's apartment playing Texas Hold 'Em, Mexican Train dominos, or lately, Mahjongg. I'd tried a couple of times to learn how to play myself but gave up. I had no idea how the ladies did it. The strangest terms came out of their mouths, and they'd do fancy moves and other things with the tiles as they shuffled them out and played them. Too much brainpower for me.

Now Coop was making enough moolah off his reward programs and the crazy knitting crew that he no longer had to worry about where his next buck was coming from. It was a nice but still-unreal change.

Coop rubbed his hand over the stubble on his chin and frowned as he considered my words. "I don't think back in my phone-book-jockeying days that there were four different books for each address. Kind of puts a kink in my fast and easy money-making plan." He shrugged. "Oh well. If it helps out Rocky, I guess it's worth the pain in the back. He told me he feels bad that we're all giving him dollars when he thinks he should be earning it. Although if I ever try a stunt like this again, do whatever you need to do to put me out of my misery immediately. Please."

Eddy said, "We'll have to shoot you later. Shay needs to borrow you for a little while before I pull the trigger."

Ten minutes and an abbreviated regurgitation of my tale of trauma later, Coop shook his head. "How on earth do you do it?" He stared at me incredulously. "You're a badass magnet for trouble. Poor JT." He stubbed his cigarette out and carefully tucked the filter back in the box. I had to hand it to him; if he had to do the deed, at least he was a responsible puffer who refused to litter the ground with his butts.

Eddy and I then outlined the task at hand. "So," I finished, "are you up for the job?"

"Hell yeah—"

"SHAY O'HANLON!" Two arms flung themselves around my midsection from behind and squeezed hard. "Shay O'Hanlon! I am so happy to see you! I have missed you!"

The pure delight in Rocky's voice never failed to warm the cockles of my heart.

He let go of me and latched onto Eddy. "Eddy! Oh Eddy! Did you know I am bringing great volumes of information to every household? There are two thousand fourteen pages of knowledge in that yellow book," he pulled one arm free and pointed at a four-inch-thick tome on the tailgate of the truck, "One thousand four hundred thirty-five pages in the white pages," he paused to take a breath, "One thousand thirty-three pages in the Dex, and then a miniscule four hundred thirty-five pages in the Century Link book."

Rocky finally relinquished his grip on Eddy and tottered around to face us. He was round and stocky, with a smile just waiting to burst across his face. A rarely removed teal aviator cap sat at a jaunty angle on top of his head, and he was encased in an oversized Twins parka that would keep him warm at twenty below.

He said, "Nick Coop agreed to help me make one hundred sixty-three dollars and seventy-two cents to add to the three hundred twenty-four dollars and forty-seven cents I have already saved up so I can go to New Orleans, Louisiana, in the United States of America, to see my Tulip." At the mention of Tulip's name, Rocky's face brightened even more. "That is exactly one thousand two hundred twenty-five point three three miles from here."

SIX

Rocky decided he wanted to come with us. I didn't think we'd be gone too long, so we locked up Eddy's jalopy and hopped in my truck. I know Coop was praying for someone to come along and steal all the phone books, but I was sure most people would stay as far away from them as they could get.

The city streets were quiet; folks were probably inside getting ready to watch the Vikings lose another one. With luck the cop shop would be empty, too.

Only half a dozen cars were parked in the precinct lot when we pulled in. Eddy decided to wait in the pickup. If she couldn't be in the thick of things, getaway driver was her next favorite option. Rocky, Coop, and I trundled through the imposing iron and glass doors.

Inside, a teen of indeterminate age sprawled on one of the benches in the lobby. The hood of a frayed black sweat jacket covered the top of his head, and his hands were stuffed in his armpits. He tried to appear insolent, but the constant bouncing of his knee told the real tale. I wondered what his story was.

I hoped the same officer I'd talked to yesterday would be on duty again. No one was behind the window, so Coop leaned on the buzzer.

About three minutes later, to my relief, C. Chevalier appeared at the window. I stared at her nameplate as she sat down, and something clicked in my brain. Chandra. Her first name was Chandra.

She keyed the mic with a friendly smile. "Shay, right?"

I nodded and crossed imaginary fingers. "Yeah, right. Hey, Chandra, when I was here last night I think I left my wallet on Tyrell's desk."

Her smile faded. "He's not in—"

"I know," I said quickly. "He told me to come on down and check." A small lie for the greater good, right? Hopefully this wouldn't get back to Tyrell.

Chandra's gaze slid to Coop and Rocky, who were crowded in right behind me. "Well, I can see who's in to escort you up, but your two friends will have to wait here."

"I don't need an escort, I'll just dash in and right back out."

Her lips pursed a moment. "No one's supposed to come into any secured area without an escort."

Before I could say anything else, Chandra scooped up the phone and dialed a number. And waited. After what had to be a full minute of ringing, she said, "No one's picking up in the squad room. I—"

"Hey," Coop interjected, "You can guard Rocky and me here while Shay just runs up quick to see if her wallet's there or not. If she doesn't come back, you can arrest us." He gave her a dazzling, irresistible grin.

"Well, I really shouldn't . . ."

She was weakening. I added, "I know the way, and it'd be just a second. I won't get lost, promise." I flashed her my own pandering smile and leaned conspiratorially toward her until my forehead touched the glass. I lowered my voice. "Chandra, I really need my wallet. Without it it's hard to buy, you know, items for my monthly . . .

feminine needs. No cash. I'm in a bit of a pinch here, and I don't really want to explain that to these goof balls." I jerked my thumb toward Coop and Rocky.

A knowing look crossed Chandra's face. Items for monthly feminine needs were something she could relate to. There was definitely something to be said for the sisterhood of the travelling pads. Or tampons.

She gave me an exaggerated nod of understanding, bit her bottom lip. Then she said, "All right. But be quick, okay?"

"Like a gazelle," I assured her and headed for the door Tyrell had propelled me through the night before. A muffled buzz sounded, and I pulled the handle. The door popped open, so I squirted through it. I caught a fragment of Rocky saying, "Chandra Chevalier, did you know that the Minneapolis phone book has exactly two thousand fourteen—" before his words were cut off as the door clicked shut.

Between Coop and Rocky, Officer C. Chevalier would be well entertained until I returned. With luck, the distraction would make it much less likely that she'd call anyone else to let them know I was on the way up.

I took the stairs two at a time and burst into the squad room. Praise be, the place was devoid of life. I scuttled over to Tyrell's desk, and sure enough, still laying on top of his mess was Krasski's file. With a quick inhale, stale coffee, old building, and fear of getting caught played over my senses. My hand hovered over the manila folder, and I again darted glances all around. The room was still as empty as it had been a moment before.

I was tempted to grab the entire file and run but quickly reconsidered. My lungs froze as I flipped the cover open. Paper-clipped to the inside was a mug shot of the same man I found in the privy—minus the pickle protruding from his mouth and with his entire skull intact, of course. I tore my eyes away from the photo and focused on the rest of the papers that were stacked none-too-neatly within.

The first pages were police reports. I rapidly scanned through them but didn't see what I was looking for. I really wanted to find a note titled KRASSKI ENEMIES. Or, to make it even clearer, something with a nice, neat rundown of who wanted Krasski dead. Fat chance of that.

The next few pages were newspaper clippings starring the bad boy himself. He'd been hairline deep in a number of nefarious criminal activities. Started his criminal career when he was in elementary school and got nailed hotwiring the principal's car. Damn. He must have had terrible influences growing up.

My heart hammered so hard I had to stop every couple of seconds and make sure I didn't miss the sound of someone coming through one of the numerous doors that led into the room. I hauled in a frazzled breath and again refocused on the file. I quickly flipped through a copy of the restraining order Krasski had taken out against JT. I still couldn't believe that he'd managed to secure a restraining order, or that she'd never told me. When I got mad enough, it was an out-of-body experience. Like watching a movie that starred me through the red haze of anger and panic. JT should have known I'd be on her side against this monster, that I would understand.

Frustration made me want to growl or cry. Maybe both. That line of thought wasn't going to do a damn bit of good, so I shoved it away and kept sorting through the file.

My ears were pricked for the slightest sound of returning cop, and the muscles in my legs and back were so tense they trembled. There were only a few more items in the folder, and I was pretty damn certain this dumbass plan was hatched for nothing. I scanned yet another report that meant nothing to me. As I flipped the page, I spied a tattered sheet of paper torn from a spiral-bound notebook.

I again scanned the room, then refocused on the creased page. I recognized JT's handwriting. In neat, precise block letters she'd printed KNOWN KRASSKI ASSOCIATES. Below it she'd made a list of names in a column. After a few of the names, she'd made notes about where they lived and their status. Three of them had lines drawn through them, and I wondered if that meant they were locked up or dead.

Then a terrible, yet sickly amusing thought hit me. What if the people who'd been crossed out had been murdered? Maybe JT was pulling a Dexter and killing off the baddies in a misguided attempt at justice. Maybe she was a serial killer killer. I almost snorted in demented laughter. I considered cramming the sheet in my pocket and hightailing my ass right out of there.

The sound of two voices filtered in from the door that led to the kitchen, where Tyrell had gotten me coffee last night. I froze, one arm outstretched as I reached for a pen to use to jot down the names.

Holy shit.

The voices were closer now, right on the other side of one of the thresholds. I didn't recognize either of the gruff tones.

One guy said, "If I drink one more cup of this shitty sludge, I'll have to go to HCMC and have my stomach pumped."

A man with a deep, growly voice said, "It'd help if the last one out at night would shut off the coffee maker." The whirring sound of a microwave revved up. "That's why I stick with tea. Can't go wrong. Have you tried Flowery Orange Pekoe? It's fruity, delicate to the palate. You can try mine in forty-five seconds." Interesting words coming from a guy who sounded like James Earl Jones.

"Fruity? Palate? What the fuck. Are you kidding me? You know I don't drink tea, Gibbs. Jesus."

"You should try it. Calms the nerves."

"Some goddamned decent coffee would do the same thing."

Forty-five seconds. By now, probably thirty. I needed to get my ass out of there and not become mesmerized by crazy cop convo. But damn, I really wanted that list.

Then the light bulb burst over my head as bright as fireworks after a show at the State Fair. My phone. I prayed that they'd hang out in the kitchen while Gibbs's tea finished brewing.

I whipped my phone from my pocket, clicked the home button, slid a shaking thumb across the bottom of the screen. Waited forever for the fricking thing to load. That'd teach me to upgrade when I had the chance. The camera on the newest version of the iPhone was supposed to open in no time flat. Guess that's what I got for being thrifty.

"Come on, come on, come on," I chanted under my breath. I was so tense I thought I might shatter into thousands of guilty little pieces.

Finally the list of names came into focus. I tried to keep an eye on the door to the kitchen and blindly snapped two pictures of the names. The two cops were still yapping at each other. In a separate space in my mind, I wondered if they were street partners. If they were, it sounded like there'd be plenty of daily verbal fisticuffs.

I slapped the file closed and dumped it back on the desk. I'd taken two steps toward the stairs and freedom when Gibbs said, "Hey there, little lady. Something we can help you with?"

Uh oh. I froze, then pivoted on the balls of my feet to face them. My knees were literally shaking. I tried out a sickly smile. "I forgot my wallet on Tyrell's desk last night." I fished it from my pants and held it up. "Got it."

A thin, broad-shouldered man said, "Yeah, I remember you. I was here for-fucking-ever typing up that goddamn report."

Gibbs, who looked about ten-foot-seven, rumbled, "Too bad you lost the coin toss, Zappo. So it *was* you who left the coffee on all night."

That set them off again. I gave them a wave and hustled for the stairs.

"Admit it, Zap. It's better to come clean."

"Hey, Johnson was up here last night. He drinks coffee too—" his voice was cut off as the door shut with a snick behind me.

I rattled down the dingy green stairwell as fast as my legs could go and burst into the lobby with enough force that the door slammed against the wall. The racket startled Hoodie Boy, and he jolted from his insolent slouch and sat up straight.

Coop and Rocky, who were still at the window talking to Chandra, spun around at the clatter.

My wallet was still in my hand. I held it up to show Chandra. "Got it."

Her voice sounded even tinnier at this distance. "Oh good. That's a relief. Hope you make it in time." This was accompanied with an exaggerated, knowing wink. "Coop and Rocky, it was so nice to meet you."

Rocky turned back to face her. "Officer Chandra Chevalier, it was very nice making your acquaintance as well. Don't forget that the FBI says that in 2010, fifty-six law enforcement officers were killed in the line of duty, and thirteen of those killed were part of a city with at least two hundred fifty thousand residents." He turned on his heel and bounced toward me.

Officer Chevalier was still smiling, so that was a good sign. She gave us a wave and walked away from the window.

Coop brushed past me. "Come on, Shay, what you waiting for?"

Rocky zoomed along after him, and I fell in step with the little man. I said, "You did a great job, Rocky. Thank you."

"It was no problem, Shay O'Hanlon. Officer Chandra Chevalier is a very nice lady."

"Yes, Rocky. Yes, she is."

As soon as we cleared the doorway, we hoofed back to the truck. Eddy had the engine running, and we dove in.

Before we'd slammed the doors, Eddy shifted into gear and pulled out of the lot at a surprisingly sedate pace. That was rather impressive since she wasn't known for driving anywhere close to what could be considered sedate. The farther away from the cop show we got, the more her natural driving habits returned.

Once I managed to get buckled in and righted myself from a sharp left Eddy made onto Lake Street, I tossed my phone at Coop.

He caught it. "Find anything?"

Eddy slammed on the brakes and squealed to a stop at a light that switched from yellow to red. The shoulder strap of the seat belt locked down as my upper body jerked against it, and I put both hands on the dash for balance.

"Uh," I grunted.

"Sorry," Eddy said.

Over my shoulder I told Coop, "I took a picture. Just in the nick of freaking time, too. Two cops fighting about the coffee almost busted me knee deep in Krasski's file."

The cab was silent as Coop scoped out my photo.

After a minute he said, "I can read all the names on it if I zoom in."

"Nick Coop," Rocky said, "What are you looking at?"

Coop said, "Shay took a picture of the names of some bad people."

I prayed we weren't going to enter the "why?" conversation maze.

In the visor mirror I watched Rocky settle back against the seat. He said, "You should use Google to do your search. It gives you results in one-third to one-half a second. That's faster than I can blink. Faster than even you can blink, Shay O'Hanlon."

I laughed. "I see you've moved on from Facebook, Rocky."

"Oh," he said. "No. Never. I can never, ever leave Facebook. I love Facebook. I love Tulip on Facebook. Soon," he rubbed his hands together gleefully, "I will have enough money to go and visit my Tulip."

Rocky's round face beamed in the reflection of the mirror. Oh man.

Coop said, "As soon as I get home, which with any luck will be in just a couple of hours, I'll start checking on these guys. I'll just send this…" he poked the buttons on my phone, "to my email." Technology was an amazing thing. The things Coop did with that technology was scary. His skills probably put him on a covert government watch list.

"Thanks." I cut a glance back at Coop. He caught my eyes, and in their depths I could see compassion and affection. We'd been friends almost as long as I could remember. If I'd liked boys, I'd have hauled his butt to the justice of the peace and made an honest man out of him long ago. Coop was one of the kindest people I'd ever known. He was usually honest, gentle, and stood up for what he believed in. With the newfound confidence born of not one but two dangerous situations in the last year, he could kick some serious ass. In my heart of hearts, I knew he'd do anything for me, and the feeling was mutual.

Eddy signaled and made a squealing right onto Lyndale. "Nicholas, I'll drop you and Rocky off to continue your deliveries. Shay, we'll hash things out over a nice hot chocolate."

Soon enough we'd dropped off the two phone book delivery boys and were zooming toward the Hole. Eddy pulled around to the alley and parked in front of the garage. As usual, I was ready to spring from whatever vehicle Eddy piloted and drop to my knees in thanks that we made it to our destination alive. She was a demon who usually went from zero to sixty and back to zero in the space of a block. Just because Eddy was driving *my* truck didn't mean this ride was any different, and my legs trembled in a mix of adrenaline and fear as I stumbled from the cab.

I propped my hands on the side panel of the pickup bed and dropped my head between my arms.

Eddy jumped to the ground and slammed the driver's door shut. "You all right there, child?"

"Yeah. I just need to think for a minute. Go on in."

"There'll be a cup of something good for what ails you waiting. Take your time."

Eddy knew me well enough to know when I simply needed space or when I needed something more, like a swift boot in the seat of my pants. As usual, she'd read me right on.

I stood quietly as Eddy strolled toward the back door of her place, letting my body acclimate to solid ground. The insanity of the last day roared through my head.

This craziness belonged on a half-assed television show, a sit-com, maybe. Not in my *life*.

Again.

I closed my eyes and breathed deep. Eddy was right. Since I couldn't get the dirt straight from JT's mouth, I was going to have to do it the hard way. Talk to those who knew JT best and see if I might be able to unravel why this part of her life had been so deeply hidden. I knew what shame could do to a person. It was an emotion I knew JT would wear deep under her skin, where no one would see it. She could be a damn stubborn, mule-headed woman. Maybe that's why we got along so well; her stubbornness gave my orneri-ness a run for its money.

So who exactly could I talk to? JT had a brother, but he was last known to be living in the mangroves of Key West. I had no idea how to go about getting a hold of him. After retiring, her parents had travelled the US and abroad and had finally settled in Seattle. I'd never met them, and to my knowledge, they hadn't come to the Cities since JT and I'd been together. The few aunts and uncles she had still above ground were scattered across the states.

There was one living grandparent in the metro, and he was cool-ing his jets at the Shady Grove Nursing Home in St. Paul. He'd been a Minneapolis cop, and JT idolized him. She had followed in his footsteps, much to the chagrin of her parents, who wanted her to go into something a little less dangerous and a lot more profitable. They'd always expected her to take up a career that would line her pockets in the shortest possible time. They wanted her to be a per-sonal injury attorney, insurance broker, or maybe a financial advisor who could place their well-hoarded finances in long-term growth stocks and mutual funds. Instead, JT flipped them the figurative bird, went the blue-collar route, and played rough with the rabble.

JT said her grandfather was the only one—aside from her dead aunt—who seemed to be delighted with her career path. Sadly, his mental capacities had declined at an alarming rate in the last few years. Now, from what I could glean from JT, he was in a moder-ately severe stage of memory loss. JT didn't talk much about it. I'd dropped her off at the nursing home before, but she never wanted me to go in with her. I respected that and found myself a joint close by called Izzy's Ice Cream to hang at while they visited.

Maybe now was the time to introduce myself to JT's grandfather. There was a chance the old man could give me some insight into the damaged, painful parts of JT's psyche. What were the odds he knew what really happened? That he might know truths that were never put into the police reports or in the restraining order? It was worth a shot, and at this point I didn't have many other options. Better than sitting around doing nothing.

That decided, I stood up straight and did a neck roll. My entire body felt stiff, most likely the result of the cops who'd piled on top of me yesterday at the Renaissance Fair. I was going to send them the bill for the chiropractor visit I was pretty sure was in my near future.

I headed into the house, passing by the still-gargantuan stack of phone books waiting to be delivered to disinterested homeowners. Who used phone books anymore anyway? Those boys better hope it didn't rain, or that was going to be one huge pile of soggy newsprint.

The screen door squealed as I pulled it open and stepped inside, then banged against the door frame behind me. The kitchen was empty, but a steaming NYPD mug sat on the tabletop. I picked the mug up and brought it to my nose. The heavy, mouthwatering aroma of chocolate and booze tickled my nose. I took a careful sip and sighed as warmth spread down my sternum and fanned out into my chest. It was good stuff.

Another scent registered in my nose: cigar smoke. I followed the odiferous trail into the living room. Three Mad Knitters sat at a rickety card table in the middle of the room. I recognized two of them.

Noxious smoke curled from stogies clenched between two of the Knitters' dentures. Somewhere along the line Eddy had moved the group from playing their various games at the kitchen table to the card table in front of the TV so she could watch her crime shows. Crazy woman.

Eddy was just coming through one of the French doors that separated the Hole from her living room, and she kicked the door shut with her foot. She was carrying a to-go container with three hot beverages in one hand and a platter of coffee cake in another. She saw me and said, "There you are, child."

"Here I am," I faintly echoed as my nose wrinkled involuntarily at the pungent cigar smoke. Eddy liked teasing me that one day maybe the Knitters would score some pot and haul out the bong. I could just see them toking up like Dolly Parton and crew in *9 to 5*. Hilarious.

"Hey ladies." I gave them a wave that was more about clearing the air than saying hello. I nodded to Agnes, a string-bean-thin gal with bluish-white hair. She was the family friend involved in the New Orleans stuffed-snake incident.

"Hello, Shay," Agnes said in a gravelly voice. "Have you met the newest member of our troupe?"

"Nope, I don't think so." I carefully took a sip of my hot chocolate.

Willie, one of the longest-standing members, said, "Whee! It's wonderful to have fresh blood. Isn't it, girls?" Willie was about two-foot-three and was as round as she was tall. Her enthusiasm for life was expressed by uttering "whee" at least once during each conversation. She should've been the one to do the voiceover for Maxwell the Geico pig in the insurance ads on TV. It wasn't surprising she and Rocky got along really well.

Agnes pointed at the only person in the room I didn't know, a petite woman with short, brown hair who was sitting quietly, observing. "Molly Panzer. Get it?" Agnes elbowed Molly, who grunted once.

"Do you get it, Shay? Panzer," Agnes repeated. "As in those big guns used in World War Two, I think. KA-BLAM!" She slammed her fist on the top of the card table, making the Mahjongg tiles bounce.

I raised my eyebrows and glanced at Eddy. She said, "Oh, Aggie. You shut your yap about that. There's much more to Molly than big guns. Take her fabulous cookies, for example." Eddy beamed at Molly, who gave her a weak smile in return. I bet anything she was wondering what the hell she signed up for in joining this group.

Molly said, "It's nice to meet you, Shay. I've heard all kinds of things about you."

I'll just bet she had. I said, "Nice to meet you too. Eddy, can I talk to you for a minute?"

"Of course, child. Just let me pass these goodies out." Eddy handed off the coffees and placed the platter of coffee cake at the edge of the card table, clear of the Mahjongg tiles.

I headed back into the kitchen. After a minute, Eddy came though the door and said, "What's up?"

I leaned against the kitchen table. "I'm going to go talk to JT's grandfather."

Eddy's expression brightened. "Now that's a darned good idea, if I do say so myself. I'll come with."

"But—" I jerked a thumb toward the living room.

Eddy waved a hand at me. "Don't you worry about them old ladies. They were here before I got home and they'll probably be here when we get back. Mahjongg takes awhile to play anyway."

If she wanted to leave cheroot-puffing gals playing a crazy tile game in her living room, that was fine by me. The mug was now lukewarm. I drained it and rinsed it out in the sink.

"You're doing the right thing, Shay," Eddy said as she watched me. "You mark my words."

Eddy always had a way of reassuring me. If words didn't work, she got the switch out so I was quickly reassured about whatever point she was trying to make. She said, "Good thing I think I feel my second wind coming. I'd love to meet Dimples."

I shot her a sideways look. "Dimples?"

"Yes, silly girl. Haven't you ever talked to JT about her grandpop?"

76

"Well, yeah. She says he's losing his mind and that it's nothing I want to see. She always shut me down after the first question."

"That's because you don't know what the right questions are yet, child. Just you remember, with age comes wisdom and lots of hot gas."

Truer words were never spoken.

SEVEN

FOLLOWING EDDY'S OBSERVATION ON the value of sucking up to old folks through canine companionship, we rounded up Dawg and Bogey and loaded them in the truck.

The Shady Grove Retirement and Assisted Living Facility was a newer complex with beautiful grounds. For the last few years, Dimples had been happily ensconced at Shady Grove in a one-bedroom apartment in the memory care wing.

Bogey's chin rested on Eddy's shoulder, and a string of drool had worked its way out of the corner of his mouth and was nearing the corded knit of her forest-green sweater. Her fingers were busy scratching his ear. Dawg leaned against the backrest, letting Bogey hog the space between the seats.

When Dawg first came to live with us, it took Eddy awhile to warm up to his canine charm. Once she did, that dog had her wrapped around his not-so-little paw. I'd been worried how she'd react when she found out JT was going to take Bogey in, but Dawg had done his job; she hardly blinked. Drool, dog poo, and shedding hair everywhere hardly made a blip on her radar anymore.

Once we'd cleared ramp traffic and merged onto I-94 east, I asked, "Are you sure they'll let dogs in?"

"Almost all the geezer places nowadays let animals come visit. If they don't, the dogs can just wait in the truck for us."

"True. So I'll go to the front desk and ask for JT's grandfather. Do you have any idea if he has a name other than Dimples?" How could anyone stand to be called a facial dent? That's what I really wanted to know.

Eddy shrugged. "Nope. But I'm sure they'll know who he is."

A few minutes later we pulled into the parking lot. The complex was located south of 94, not far from its namesake, Shady Grove Park. It was brick and majestic, with a covered front entrance that tried to imitate a hotel instead of a place for the geriatric set to land.

I took Dawg while Eddy wrangled Bogey, and we hoofed it for the main doors. A little old lady wrapped in a yellow housecoat with a blanket tucked around her sat in an electric wheelchair to one side of the entrance. She was so stooped over her face almost met her lap. I wasn't sure if she was awake or asleep, but when we passed by her, she said without looking up, "Careful, or they'll keep you here. They're wily, they are."

Eddy stopped.

I kept a wary eye on Bogey in case he attempted to go crotch diving. He'd probably accidentally break her nose.

Eddy bent over and attempted to make eye contact. "Elva, that you? I thought they had you boxed up somewhere in Golden Valley."

The woman's head remained facing her lap, but she said, "Was. Too much traffic. My son decided to corral me here where I can tour the parking lot. Less chance of getting flattened."

Eddy stood and squinted at the lot. "There's lots of nice trees I guess. If you can see 'em. Gotta run, Elva. Catch you on the backswing if they haven't locked you down by then."

We trooped through glass doors that automatically slid open as we approached. The lobby was large, and the vaulted ceiling allowed natural light to fill the space. A dark, granite-topped reception desk sat off to the left, and three hallways branched off, probably leading to resident rooms. A convenience store/gift shop faced the front doors, and two or three elderly shoppers browsed within.

A bespectacled older gentleman with neatly trimmed iron-gray hair bustled around behind the reception desk. He wore a brown and yellow plaid button-down shirt under a mocha-colored leisure suit jacket that sported white stitching. Thirty-five years ago, he'd have been at the peak of style.

"Help ya?" the man asked, a friendly smile on his craggy face. I was distracted by his eyebrows. They grew huge and bushy, more impressive than Andy Rooney's. His still-sharp blue-gray eyes lit up when he saw Dawg and Bogey. "Nice dogs!" he said as he circled the counter and approached us. The polyester pants he wore were smartly creased high risers. There wasn't a wobble in his stride.

I said, "This is Dawg. D-A-W-G, Dawg. And Eddy there has Bogey."

The man reached a gnarled hand out and gave Dawg a chin rub. "If I had a treat, I'd give you one, young fella," he told Dawg. Dawg slurped his fingers.

Then he turned and took two steps toward Bogey, who was straining at the end of his leash. Before I could make a move to give Eddy a hand, Bogey embedded his nose right in Leisure Suit's family jewels like a homing missile, his tail wagging wildly. After an alarmed

"Bogey!" from Eddy and a wrestling match between me, Eddy, and the mad sniffer, we were back under control.

Through it all, Dawg watched from the sidelines with a look of utter mortification. If he'd been human, I think he would've shook his head and said, "Bogey, you're an embarrassment to the canine race."

"Sir," I said, "I'm so sorry. We're working on it, but ..."

"Not to worry," Leisure Suit said, his grin still firmly in place. "That's the most action I've gotten in a long time."

Eddy said, "You need another jolt, just say the word and we'll be happy to accommodate you. Say, you don't know Dimples Bordeaux, do you?"

Oh God. Eddy had such a way with words. Good thing was, it often produced the results we wanted.

Leisure Suit rubbed his chin and peered at the ceiling. "Yes, I surely do. He's in the C wing, has a bit of a time recalling things, if I, myself, am recalling correctly. The tectonic plates are starting to slip, in more ways than one." He rapped his forehead with his knuckles. "Nice chap. Let me just look up his room number." With that, he practically skipped to the other side of the desk and shuffled through some sheets of paper. "Here he is. Unit C room 21. Though you might find him at the pool. Likes to watch the ladies"—he pursed his lips and seemed to search for a word—"swim."

Apparently JT's grandfather still had an eye for the gals. I could just see an elderly JT hanging out poolside and ogling wrinkly chicks as they attempted to follow an overly enthusiastic water aerobics teacher through a reduced-impact shallow-end-of-the-pool routine. Is that what was waiting for us when we hit retirement age? I started to panic, then realized Eddy wasn't anything like that, and we wouldn't have to be either. Sheesh.

"Well, thanks, handsome." Eddy stuck out her hand. "What did you say your name was?"

The man took Eddy's and tugged her a bit closer. "I didn't, you little vixen, you. It's Olaf Madsen, at your service."

"I'm Edwina Quartermaine, and this here," she jerked her thumb at me, "is Shay O'Hanlon, my long-lost daughter. Our colors might not match, but our hearts do. You've already met the drooling duo. You let four-legged friends into this joint?" Eddy leaned forward over the counter and beamed at Olaf. "You're a real rascal, aren't you?"

"You stop by again, and we'll see just what kind of a rascal I am, Edwina. Oh, yes, we do allow most all four-legged friends. Well, except rats and mice, of course."

We thanked him and headed off across the lobby toward the C wing. I leaned in toward Eddy and whispered, "Edwina? Really? What's up with that? No one calls you Edwina."

She elbowed me. "Shush, child. My, but he was a looker, wasn't he?"

"Yes, he was." For a gentleman of a certain age, Olaf was indeed quite handsome.

She wagged her head slowly, the expression on her face one of pleasant surprise. We hit the wide hall and started counting brass numbers attached to the wall beside each door. The place was bigger than it looked. We were looking for C21 and we'd just passed C2.

A few of the heavy oak doors were open, and in the short glimpses I could steal, I saw what looked like typical apartments.

The sounds of televisions at substantial volume floated through the air. Dawg and Bogey sniffed their way down the hall. There were plenty of new smells for them to puzzle over here.

Two staff members passed us and paused to greet the dogs, then continued on their way. Finally, I saw C21 on the wall next to a closed door. "There it is."

Eddy knocked, and there was no answer. She rapped again, to no avail. "Should I see if it's open?"

"Yeah, maybe Dimples can't hear too well anymore." I tried to remember if JT mentioned anything about her grandfather's hearing but drew a blank. Maybe I needed my own memory addressed.

I tried the knob. The door silently swung open on well-oiled hinges. Eddy and I looked at each other. Eddy said, "Whatcha waiting for? Go see if he's in there. I'll wait here with the gruesome twosome."

"Chicken."

"Hey, he might be all keeled over in there. You're the one who keeps finding dead bodies. You got practice with that. I'm good at the after-the-fact business. Once the body is gone stuff."

I handed over Dawg's leash and stepped through the threshold. "Mr. Bordeaux? Sir? Are you in here?"

Silence greeted me. The apartment felt empty.

A tidy galley kitchen was on my left, sporting a refrigerator and microwave but no stove. Folding closet doors were to my right. The short entry ended in a T. Down the tiny hall to the right was an austere, neatly kept bedroom. Above the bed was a picture of a smiling, dark-haired young man in a policeman's uniform with an attractive woman in a wedding dress on his arm. Most likely JT's grandparents. It was obvious where she scored her good looks.

I stuck my head into a dinky bathroom. It was unremarkable save for metal handrails that were mounted on the walls along with a red emergency call cord situated near the toilet.

The living room was another story altogether. An old, twenty-inch TV sat against one wall. A recliner faced it, along with a couple of side chairs. It was a spare room, not in size but in the fact it missed the usual clutter of a life well lived—with one glaring exception.

Pictures.

There were photographs everywhere.

One wall was dedicated to photos of JT from infancy to adulthood. I had taken one shot of JT not two months ago when we'd gone running around Lake of the Isles. The expression on her face pulled no punches regarding how she felt about the person on the other end of the camera.

I sucked in a half-breath as phantom pain sliced through my soul. *Now is not the time to fall apart, Shay*, I chastised myself. There would be time for that later.

There was also a series of portraits of JT as she progressed through her police career, through promotions and honors. For all the good JT had done as a cop, it was a damned shame that she had to hold so tightly onto the one incident that should've, by now, been dealt with and tucked far away. Then again, maybe tucking away trauma was something cops had a hard time doing. No, that was definitely not true; JT could compartmentalize with the best of them.

I sighed and turned my attention to the rest of the living room. There were photos of Dimples and his wife, along with shots of JT's mom and dad. There were a couple pictures of her brother as a kid. There was no doubt this man was proud of his family.

"Shay!" Eddy called from the front door. "Is he dead in there or what?"

I tore myself away from the Bordeaux family memories. "No one's here," I said and booked it out of the apartment.

We struck out to find the pool. After asking three residents, two staff members, and accidentally getting lost in the caverns of the basement, we succeeded. A set of glass doors accessed the pool, and they were thoroughly steamed over. When I pulled one of them open, a hot chlorinated fog slithered out, wrapping its tendrils around us. The thumping bass of pounding music vibrated my frame.

I waved my arm. "Holy cow, it's a bit warm in there."

Eddy squinted. "It's so the old farts don't freeze to death. Come on." She and Bogey marched into the warm, humid space.

Dawg and I followed, and the door retracted behind us. Once the temperature equalized, the air cleared. Dawg whined, straining on the end of his leash toward the pool. Over the summer JT and I found out he *loved* water. I gripped the leather tighter in my hand lest Dawg decided to try and take a dip.

The pool was huge, Olympic sized. A school team could come here for practice and there'd still be plenty of room for senior water polo.

An energetic gal of advanced years led eight women, seven of whom wore brightly colored swim caps, in a sloshing pool-side rendition of the Village People's "YMCA." The music blared loud enough for even the hardest of hearing to pick up the beat.

Not far from the splashing, three men bobbed in the aerobic backwash, face-up atop bright blue foam mattresses, watching the geriatric bouncing with intense interest.

On one side of the pool, round white plastic tables with yellow umbrellas—to keep the fluorescent light off aged skin?—were lined up, and lounge chairs occupied the opposite side. Two women reclined atop towels on the loungers, reading.

Since our quarry was most likely one of the guys floating in the pool, we headed toward them. As we drew closer, I realized all three gents weren't merely watching the action, but were staring intently at the water dancing divas and periodically elbowing each other. Apparently one was never too old to ogle.

We stopped at the edge of the pool.

"Excuse me. Mr. Bordeaux?" I called out to the three mostly hairless pates. I received nary a twitch.

Eddy elbowed me aside. "Dimples!" she hollered at the top of her lungs.

One of the men craned his neck to take a gander at us but couldn't turn quite far enough around.

"Over here," Eddy shouted, adding a little wave.

The man in question, floating between the other two gents, tried paddling first one way, then the other in an attempt to turn his floating mattress around. I could hear him swearing a blue streak as he bashed into his companions. Finally he managed to paddle our way, steaming slowly along feet-first.

When the rubber mat eventually ran into the side of the pool and stopped his forward motion, he hooked gnarled fingers under the edge of the cement deck to keep himself from drifting away and squinted up at us. Whitish stubble covered his chin, and orange swim trunks came to just below his man-boobs. "Can't see shit without my glasses. Whaddya want?"

I knew it was going to sound ridiculous, but it had to be done. "Are you Dimples Bordeaux?"

"What's it to ya?" he growled.

The tone of his voice startled Dawg, who squeaked and pressed himself hard against my leg. He was still skittish in certain situations. I put a calming hand on his head.

Eddy said, "We want to ask you some questions about your grand-daughter."

"What's that? Speak up, for Chrissake."

Bogey crept closer to Dimples, who now floated parallel to the cement side of the pool. Blue veins showed through the thin skin on the back of the hand that gripped the edge of the pool. Eddy held Bogey back and planted her feet wide in order to maintain control.

I yelled, "JT. We want to talk to you about JT."

86

At the sound of his granddaughter's name, the man broke into a wide smile. It was then I realized exactly why people called him Dimples. He had more divots in his cheeks than a golf course for beginners. JT's chin was an exact replica of his—square and well-defined with an adorable dent in the center.

"Where's that JT? She here?" He peered around.

"No, she's not," Eddy said loudly and took a step toward Dimples. That was all it took to get Bogey in sniffing range of the pool's edge. He pulled Eddy another step forward, stretched his neck out over the floatie, and tried to plant his schnoz in the middle of Mr. Bordeaux's swim trunks.

"BOGEY!" Eddy yelled as she tried to hold him back.

The application of a large dog nose to the groin startled Dimples, and he shoved away from the pool edge with a howl.

Bogey did his best to stay with his quarry. He leaped into the air like an obese gazelle, leash stretching taut as he reached its limit. He hit the water with a resounding splat, barely missing landing square atop Dimples. His weight pulled Eddy off balance, literally dragging her to the pool's edge. I dropped Dawg's leash and made a frantic grab for Eddy, missing her by a fraction of an inch. She toppled, slow motion, arms windmilling, into the pool.

Something in me snapped. The giggles started even before Eddy'd spluttered back to the surface.

Bogey paddled desperately around trying to get a fix on his target.

Dawg quivered, just waiting for me to give him the high sign that he could join the rest of his pack in the water. What an irresistible game it must have looked to him.

My giggle grew into a howl of hysterical laughter.

Eddy shot me a dirty look as she splashed around searching for Bogey's leash. "Shay! Don't just stand there," she spluttered. "Do something!"

She finally got a grip on the leash and gained a foothold. She grumbled under her breath and struggled toward the cement steps at the end of the pool. Bogey paddled along behind her.

By now the aerobics class had ground to a halt, and all of the colorful swim caps were pointed in our direction. Eight pairs of rheumy eyes stared at us with intense interest, plus those of the two gentlemen on the blue floaties.

Dimples's own eyes were wide as silver dollars, and a look of amused delight was firmly planted on his face. He said, "Damn, that was worth a nudge in the nuts."

With effort, I finally got a tentative hold on myself and hustled over to give Eddy a hand from the water. I grabbed Bogey's leash as Eddy sloshed up the stairs like a diminutive sea monster rising from the ocean depths. The hem and sleeves of her sweater were stretched far below where they belonged. She looked like a little kid trying on her dad's clothes! That thought sent me into another paroxysm of hilarity as Dawg and I stepped aside to let Eddy and Bogey onto the deck.

Bogey scrambled from the water and decided it was time to excise the pool from his body. He shook and sprayed everything within a fifteen-foot radius, including me.

Streaming rivulets of water spread in a growing puddle at Eddy's feet. "Well," she said, trying to look as dignified as she could under the circumstances, "we better do what we came here to do."

Dimples skirted Eddy and wrestled his floatie to the deck.

"You need some goddamn towels," he told Eddy.

Eddy grumbled something under her breath.

I said, "Oh, Eddy, I'm so—" I lost it again as hysterical giggles bubbled up from my core like lava.

Dimples returned with an armful of blindingly white towels and held two out to Eddy and one to me. "Here ya go, little ladies." Then he turned on me and said, "She gonna kill you for laughing?"

I swallowed another guffaw that threatened to burst forth. "She just might."

He said, "Well, come on then. Let's get things figured out while you're still breathing and you tell me why my JT isn't here."

———

Ten minutes later, we were seated in wobbly plastic chairs at one of the round tables next to the pool, the umbrella doing its job to protect us from those harsh, dangerous rays from above.

Eddy was bundled up in a fluffy white robe while her clothes tumbled in a huge dryer just off the pool deck.

Dimples had pulled on a robe of his own, and black horn-rimmed glasses now perched on his nose, making his cloudy eyes appear larger than they were.

Dawg sat by my leg, still not sure he liked what was going on. Bogey stretched out on his side, exhausted from his escapade.

Dimples leaned forward and propped his elbows on his bony knees. "So whaddya want?"

Eddy said, "Mr. Bordeaux, can I call you Dimples?"

"Sure you can. Everyone else does," Dimples said as he continued to stare at me. Then he snapped his fingers. "Why, that's it! You're Taffy, aren't you?"

I frowned. "No sir, I'm not Taffy. My name is Shay—"

"Ah yes, Taffy Abernathy. I remember now."

Just let it go and cut to the chase, Shay. I said, "I'm hoping you can tell us a little about JT."

"Taffy, you went to school with JT. Got homesick at bible camp with her. Spent all your damn time together. What's wrong with your memory?" He did the squinty thing again. "Oh no, you aren't going senile already, are you?"

Who the hell was Taffy? I exchanged a confused look with Eddy.

"No, sir, I met JT a year or two—"

"You damn kids," Dimples said, "You forget everything."

"Sir," I said, "I'm not Taffy. My name is Shay O'Han—"

He waved me off. "Pshaw, don't you go trying to fool an old geezer. The kids used to tease you," his voice pitched up into singsong range. "Taffy, Taffy, Abernathy. Taffy, Taffy, Abernathy."

Oh dear God, that poor girl. "No, I didn't know JT—"

Dimples continued right on. "You two used to get in some mighty hot water. I remember the time JT got a hold of my hundred-proof hooch and shared it with you." He hee-hawed. "That was bad news. So, Taffy, what are you up to these days, hey?" He reached out and thwacked my leg. "You got any little Tootsie Rolls underfoot?"

I opened my mouth, but nothing came out.

Eddy came to my rescue. "You wouldn't know where Taffy lives, do you?"

Dimples shot Eddy a cantankerous look. "Ask her yourself. She's sitting right here." He stabbed a crooked finger at me.

Eddy said, "Dimples, we're needing to find out what happened between JT and one of the criminals she's had troubles with."

I said, "Do you remember the Krasski incident, Mr. Bordeaux?"

A definitive flash of recognition lit up his face. "Krasski? What's that a-hole done to my JT now?"

Before either Eddy or I could say anything else, he said, "Taffy, you're the one who showed me that album you put together about Krasski. Why are you asking me about it? And it was all over the news. I suppose you kids don't watch the news anymore. Do you even know how to read?"

I stiffened. Taffy had an album on Krasski? Why? And how on earth could I have missed the papers and apparently the television blaring JT's fall from grace? I knew I tended to ignore current events, but this was a little beyond that.

Eddy's eyes met mine, and she widened them at me. Taffy was going to get a visit, very soon. And I was going to start keeping tabs on the evening news.

"So tell me, Taffy, do you still keep track of everything like you used to? You were the class historian, if I remember rightly. Waste of time in my opinion."

"About Krasski," I said, hoping to right this perilously tipping Q&A, "did JT—"

"JT did nothing wrong." He stuck a finger in a nostril, wiggled it around, pulled it out and flicked something off his fingertip. Luckily not in my direction. I tried to keep my face from scrunching up in horror, and I saw that Eddy's expression mirrored my own. This interview needed to end soon.

Before I could think of something to say that didn't include boogers, Dimples said, "So Peaches, did you find a cop job yet?"

I blinked and had to process for a second before I realized he was now on an entirely different track. "My name isn't Peaches, either, Mr. Bordeaux."

"Oh. That's right, you're Taffy. The old memory banks are sometimes a little slow." He thunked his forehead with a knuckle.

"No, I'm—never mind. Who's Peaches?" What was with these edible names?

"Peaches Reker. JT went to the academy with you, er, her. Thick as thieves, they were." Dimples scanned the area. "Where is that girl, my JT?"

Holy cow, the memory banks weren't *slow*, they'd completely shut down. I said gently, "She's not here."

"Well then, I guess it's just you and me, and," he glanced at Eddy, "that cute little thing over there. She's looking a little soggy." He gave Eddy an exaggerated wink. "You know, for years we had Crown Vic squad cars. Then the a-holes downtown got Chevys. Crappiest cars ever. We want the Crown Vics back."

I peered at Dimples in confusion. Eddy had that pinched, semi-constipated look on her face that usually meant she was dealing with a nut job. Or a stubborn dog.

One more time. I would try one more time. "Mr. Bordeaux, can we talk about JT?"

"Sure. Where is she? Can you make that good pineapple upside-down cake now?"

Oh boy. This little heart-to-heart was over.

Eddy realized we were done too. She stood. "Thank you for all your help, Dimples. I'll just go gather my clothes." She traipsed off to the laundry room, leaving me alone with daft, delirious Dimples.

I smiled at him. "Thanks for talking with us, Mr. Bordeaux."

"Hell, Taffy, this was the most fun I've had in ages. Did I tell ya about what those damn pencil pushers downtown did? Bastards got rid of our Crown Victoria squad cars…"

EIGHT

WE REGROUPED AT THE truck. Eddy's clothes were mostly dry, but her sweater had shrunk so much the sleeves now ended well above her wrists. If she had a belly button piercing, it would've been exposed.

For the dogs, I poured water in two ingenious collapsible bowls I'd found at Petco. They happily lapped the liquid up and then scrambled to the truck. Eddy bundled Bogey into the extended back of the cab behind her seat and climbed in. I tucked the bowls away and dispatched Dawg to his spot behind me.

"Well," Eddy said, "That was enlightening." She sat with her legs out, wiggling bare toes as she held her soggy red Converse high-tops to the vents in a futile effort to help them dry.

"No shit. I'm going to call you Splash from now on."

"Watch your mouth, child," Eddy grumbled, then she threw a still damp sock at me.

"You have to admit that was classic. I so wish I could've gotten it on camera. Or video. That would've been even better."

"Yeah, yeah. Go ahead. Rub it in. This old lady could have died, and you'd have just laughed your fool butt off." Eddy's voice sounded stern, but I could see by the way the corners of her mouth curled up that she found the entire incident amusing as well.

"So," I said. "What do you think about Taffy Abernathy?"

"I think we should give her a nice little Sunday afternoon visit. Don't you?"

"Yeah. But we need to find out where she lives first." I pulled out my phone and wagged it at her. "Don't you just wish you had a smart-phone, Eddy?"

"I'll take the dumb one that's hooked into my telephone line back home, thank you very much."

Smartphones and dumb phones were a running joke between us. Eddy hated cell phones and refused to own one. Sometimes that made life more than a little complicated.

I hit Rocky's favorite site to search for Taffy Abernathy, since that was surely a nickname. Curiously, two Taffy Abernathy's appeared in my search. One was in Alabama, and the other had a Minneapolis network listed, as well as a phone number. I keyed in the numbers and waited for the connection to do its thing.

Three rings later, a high-pitched voice answered. "Abernathy residence."

I wasn't sure if I had a squeaky adult or a young kid on the other end. "Hi," I said. "I'm looking for Taffy Abernathy." I wondered if she hadn't married since she was still using her original last name.

"She's not here right now."

From the inflection, I figured I was talking to a kid. "Do you know when she'll be home?"

There was a long pause, and I could hear Dawg's soft snuffing be-hind me. "Are you there?" I asked.

"She's at the suppository."

I pulled the phone from my ear and stared at it for just a second. Did I have a mini Dimples on the line? "She's where?"

"DADDY!" the voice shrieked in my ear. I jerked the phone away from my head again.

Bogey woofed at the vocal echo that banged through the cab. The kid had a set of lungs on him. Or her. I cautiously put the phone back to my ear. Through the ringing in my head I heard scraping sounds followed by a sharp thud. Then a man's voice came on the line. "Hello?"

"Hi," I said and shifted in my seat. I needed to regain my brain, fast. "I'm organizing the class reunion from—" Where the hell did JT go to school? St. Joseph Academy! "From St. Joseph's, and I'm trying to get a hold of Taffy."

"She's working now, but she'll be home later." The man sounded distracted. I could hear the TV in the background and the sharp blast of a whistle. Football, probably. Then at almost the same time, something came across the line that sounded like a goat bleating. The kid was probably doing his kid thing and making irritating noises. Another reason not to have any.

I said, "I keep losing track of Taffy. Where is she working these days?"

"She's at the Central Minnesota Cryogenic Depository."

"Cryogenics? Is that a—"

"Yup. Sperm bank."

Oh my. "They're open on a Sunday?"

The man laughed. It was a big, booming, friendly sound. "Oh yeah. Donation and ovulation don't stop for the weekend."

"No, I don't suppose. Thanks for the info. I'll catch her later."

We disconnected.

"Well," Eddy said. "Where is she? Let's go."

"She's at the suppository."

Eddy did a double take. "What?"

I chortled. "The suppository."

"What are you talkin' 'bout, child?"

Keeping a straight face was a losing battle. I choked out, "She works at," I struggled for control, "the sperm depository."

"Oh, really." After a couple of beats she said, "Well, what are we waiting for? It's off to the suppository."

I fell apart again.

———

The Central Minnesota Cryogenic Depository was located in Friendly Fridley, just south of Interstate 694 in a 1970s-era three-story office building that had seen better days. I pulled into the parking lot, which was in dire need of a coat of tar.

The air temp was cool enough to comfortably leave the dogs in the car, so we bid them adieu and strolled inside. A directory listed the cryogenics office on the third floor.

We rode the elevator up and entered a cozy, whimsically decorated waiting room. Giraffes, lions, and gazelles chased each other over a savannah painted on the walls. Brown carpet covered the floor, muffling the footsteps of the clientele. Chairs ringed the room. Two women appeared to be reading magazines. I wondered if the chicks were there for implantation or whatever it was that happened when one patronized a place like this.

The receptionist looked up when we'd opened the door. A curious, bemused smile played on her lips as she took in Eddy's shrunken sweater and generally damp appearance. The woman screamed hippie. Long, straight blond hair parted down the middle was braided on either side of her head. A leather cord was tied headband-style around her forehead, keeping wisps of loose hair out of her eyes. Her face was heart-shaped, and she had pouty lips. She wore a kelly green, poofy-sleeved peasant shirt with multicolored flowers embroidered on the chest.

I sniffed the air, half expecting to smell incense and pot.

She asked, "What can I do for you?"

Eddy said, "We're looking for Taffy Abernathy."

The woman's forehead crinkled. "I'm Kathy Abernathy. Still known to friends and family as Taffy."

Bingo! I barely restrained myself from breaking into a jig.

I said, "Kathy—or Taffy?"

She laughed pleasantly. "Oh, if you know me already as Taffy, just call me that."

I smiled. "Well, Taffy, do you know JT Bordeaux?"

She laced her fingers together, rested them on the desk, and leaned forward. "I do." Then a look of alarm hit her, and her eyes got big. "Nothing's hap—"

"She's okay," I hastened to assure her. "Well, not exactly okay, but ..." I trailed off. "Anyway, do you remember JT being involved with Russell Krasski?"

Taffy stared at us for a good three breaths. Then she said in a far more businesslike tone of voice, "Why are you asking?"

Eddy said, "JT's in a bit of hot water, and we're"—Eddy scrunched her face as she searched for the right descriptor—"trying to pluck her out of it."

Taffy frowned. "Are you cops?"

"No," I said. "Nope, we definitely are not the police."

She had to know JT was gay. Didn't she? Well, she was going to now if she didn't already. A quick breath in and I said, "I'm JT's partner, the name's Shay O'Hanlon." I jabbed a thumb at Eddy. "This is a close friend of ours, Eddy Quartermaine."

Taffy's eyes widened and she brightened. "Oh. Hey. I wondered if JT settled down. I haven't heard from her in, oh—maybe a year or more." She stood and looked me up and down. That's when I realized Taffy was not only fine-boned, but she was short. Like, shorter-than-Eddy short.

With a gleam in her eye, she said, "You devil, you. You finally took the good detective off the market."

"She sure did," Eddy said and poked me in the shoulder. "Now they're like two little old ladies, spending their evenings in, no more bar-hopping and carousing."

Like I was ever a carouser. Well, okay, maybe that wasn't exactly true. JT's arrival in my life had brought about a number of positive changes that I hadn't anticipated, and quiet evenings in were one of them. I said, "Can we get back to Krasski?"

"Sure." Taffy stared expectantly at us.

Might as well ask flat out. "Did you put together some kind of album about what happened between Krasski and JT?"

Now her brow wrinkled again, the crease between her nose deepening. "I did, but how in the world do you know about that?"

"Dimples," Eddy said.

"Ah." Taffy nodded once. "JT's grandpa."

Someone in the depths of the office yelled, "Kathy, we need you for a minute."

"Be right there," she called back, and then faced us again. "How about you meet me at my house in"—she glanced at her watch, which was secured to her wrist with a two-inch-wide purple leather band—"an hour? I'm off about one, and that'll give me time to get home and sort things out."

She wrote her address on the back of one of the cryogenic doc's business cards and handed it to me. I reached for it, but she yanked it from my grasp just as my fingers closed around it. "By the way, how did you find me here?"

I grinned. "I talked to someone at your house who told me you worked at a suppository. Then your hubby filled in the rest."

Taffy rolled her eyes and handed the card over.

————

"Shay," Eddy said after we once again settled ourselves in the truck. "I suppose I should get back and check on the old ladies. Drop me at home before you catch up with Taffy, will you?"

"No problem." I shifted into Reverse and glanced at the two pooches as I backed out of the parking spot. Dawg was sprawled across the narrow bench seat and Bogey had somehow wedged himself on the floor between the front and back seats. "Maybe Coop's done, and he can come. Especially if Ms. Taffy is a true-to-life hippie and is growing some Maui Wowie in her house."

Eddy cut me a look. "Maui Wowie?"

"Pot, Eddy. Marijuana."

Eddy raised her lip in distaste and refocused her eyes on the windshield. "You kids."

It was an uneventful twenty-minute ride home. I pulled up to the curb half a block from the Hole, and we scrambled from the cramped confines of the pickup.

Dawg and Bogey did their business, and then we descended on the Hole. I headed for the counter, which was surprisingly quiet for the number of customers seated in the café. Eddy scooted off to check on her Mahjongg-playing flock.

Kate had a rag wrapped around the milk steamer and was working off the residue. "Welcome back, stranger," she said.

"Where's Anna?"

"This is the first breather we've had all morning. I sent her in back with some lunch."

I cocked a brow. "This is the third Sunday it's been this way. You think we need more help?"

Kate lifted a shoulder. "I'm not sure if it's busy because it's cooling off and people want to cozy up or what." Her eyes scanned the place. "Feels good, though, even if it's temporary. Here." She handed me a plate with a crumbled slice of chocolate chip banana bread that had been sitting on the back counter. I accepted it with glee.

It sure did feel good that the economy was at least moving in the right direction. The last couple of years were rough on everyone, particularly on small businesses. If we hadn't had Eddy's support and willingness to forgo our monthly rent once in awhile, we would have been in real trouble. It felt damn good to be in a financial upswing, no matter how tentative it may be.

"Shay O'Hanlon!" Rocky zoomed through the doorway leading to the back room. "Did you know Anna is going to make virtual reality worlds for burn victims to escape to when they are being treated for their injuries? They have to go through terrible treatments. Daily wound cleaning to remove dead tissue. Do you know how bad that hurts, Shay O'Hanlon?"

Before I had a chance to answer with a resounding no, Rocky foraged full steam ahead. "I do not know either. But it has to be very, very bad. More than four hundred fifty thousand people are burned every year, usually at home." His eyes got real big. "Almost four thousand of those people die. Die dead, Shay O'Hanlon. Deceased. Expired. Croaked."

Ouch.

Before Rocky had a chance to wind himself into a burn facts statistical frenzy, I asked, "Where's Coop, Rocky?"

He pointed over to one of the groupings of easy chairs. Now that I looked closer, I caught sight of the top of Coop's head peeking over the back of a chair that faced away from the counter. After exchanging a few more morbid comments with Kate and Rocky, I headed toward Coop.

The four chairs that circled a large, low coffee table were all occupied. I gingerly set my items on the round tabletop and studied my best friend. He was out like a light. The Duluth gig, playing phone book delivery boy, and helping me sneak into the cop shop must've really done a number on him. One hand rested on the edge of an open notebook computer that was balanced precariously on his lap. His other arm hung over the side of the chair, fingertips dangling a breath away from a to-go cup of coffee that rested on the floor.

I stepped over his sizable feet and perched on the table's edge.

He didn't stir.

I picked up my bread and took a couple bites. The blissful burst made my taste buds do backflips. I chomped happily and considered my snoozing pal. Coop would never win awards for fashion sense. He wore a holey, button-down sweater over a faded Pink Floyd T-shirt. Blue jeans with fraying cuffs covered the top of well-worn, brown work boots.

I crumbled off another piece of bread and leaned forward, holding it under Coop's nose. His nostrils twitched. Then he inhaled deeply. I waved the chunk a little. This time he cracked an eye and peered blearily at me.

"You better be sharing," he said, his voice hoarse.

The grin that'd been playing at the corners of my mouth blossomed into a full-fledged smile. "Sure. Open wide, little boy."

He complied and I delivered. His eye drifted shut again as he chewed slowly. Once he swallowed, he said, "I'm on the case of Krasski's friends and enemies. Just taking a fiver."

I nudged his calf with my tennis shoe. "I need you to do something else first."

"What?"

"Come with me to visit the hippie queen of Minneapolis."

This time both eyes popped open and he blinked, his eyelids not quite in sync with each other. "Come again?"

"We're going to visit a friend of JT's. Her name is Taffy Abernathy."

"Give me another bite. And you're a liar."

I handed him the rest of the crumbly mess. "Nope. She and JT are pals from way back."

Coop shoved the rest of the bread in his maw and chewed. He managed to say around the food, "Never heard of her."

"Me either. But she knows a crap load about Krasski. Maybe why JT's been so…" I trailed off with a grimace. "Why she never told me, never told any of us, about Krasski or the restraining order. Wait till you hear about Dimples."

Coop swallowed and licked his lips. "Who the hell is Dimples?"

"JT's grandfather."

"Really." He looked skeptically at me as he shut down the computer and slid it in his backpack. "Dimples? Seriously?"

"Yeah. It's not his real name, but it's what he goes by. When he smiles, you can see the name is perfect. He's looney as a drunken pigeon. Come on," I said and proceeded to fill Coop in on Eddy and Bogey's deep-sea dive and the rambling dirt we'd mined from

Dimples. Once we were buckled in the truck and headed toward Taffy's, I finished the story.

Coop took a sip from his now lukewarm caffeine-infused beverage. He said, "If she's a hippie, maybe she has a little wacky tobaccy." He waggled his eyebrows.

"I told Eddy the same thing."

One of the many things I loved about Coop was that he could make me laugh no matter what.

———

I pulled to the curb in front of a cream-colored bungalow that sat on a corner lot in Minneapolis's St. Anthony neighborhood. A cedar plank fence enclosed the backyard. Reddish-colored ivy covered a good portion of the fence. The yard was full of orange and brown leaves, and it could use at least one more good raking before the snow flew.

We mounted a set of on-the-brink-of-crumbling cement stairs and I rung the doorbell. After a few seconds, Taffy swung the door opened. Now that I could see her from head to toe, she was even tinier than I thought. The peasant shirt hung loosely around her hips. Faded jeans and Birkenstocks completed the ensemble.

"Come on in," Taffy said with a welcoming smile. "My husband took the kids out for ice cream so we could have a little peace and quiet." She turned her attention to Coop. "And this is?"

"Nick Cooper," I said. "A good friend of mine." I added as an afterthought, "Of JT's too. Eddy had things to take care of, so I hauled him along for the ride."

"Well, come on in, then. Nice to make your acquaintance, Nick."

They shook hands. "It's just Coop," he told her. Eddy and Coop's on-again off-again girlfriend, Luz, were the only two people who dared call Coop by his given name.

"Coop it is then." Taffy backed up to allow us entrance.

That's when I noticed a puffy, snow-white something on the floor near her feet. It scrabbled backward as we stepped inside, nails making a scraping sound on the hard surface.

I did a double take. The thing had bright white feathers and a little red doodad on the top of its head. "Is that a . . ."

Taffy followed my gaze. "A chicken? Yup. We raise a lot of our own food. It's Shay, right?"

I nodded, my eyes glued to the chicken.

She said, "Shay and Coop, meet Chelsea 'I Really Am a Big Scaredy-Chicken' Chicken."

Chelsea had moved away from us and stood on two thin legs in the hall, bobbing her bright-red combed head and keeping a beady eye on Coop and me.

I wondered when Taffy said they raised a lot of their own stuff if she meant they snacked on Chelsea Chicken's drumsticks when the time came or if they simply ate eggs she might produce. I hoped it was the latter.

Coop read my mind. With a look of fear, he asked, "Do you, um, you know, fry her up?"

At that, Taffy looked horrified. "Oh no. The kids would never go for that. Chelsea and a few other chickens that we keep out back live pretty happy lives here. If they stop laying eggs or don't take to the city, we bring them to my sister's farm in Wisconsin. There they can live in peace and quiet until they go to the big poultry coop in the sky." Taffy laughed. "As long as I don't wear Chelsea on my head when we cross into Wisconsin, we're good. That's a crazy, little-known Minnesota law that's still on the books."

Coop sighed. "That's the kind of life I want, minus the poultry coop in the sky."

We followed Taffy into the living room. While it was evident that kids lived here by the scattering of toys across the floor, the place was actually pretty neat. It didn't smell like a chicken coop, either. The room held a bright blue couch, two contrasting yellow recliners, a coffee table made out of weathered wood, and a large hutch displaying family pictures filled the room. The walls were covered with framed—and what looked to be original—movie posters of the four Herbie the Love Bug films.

Coop and I settled on the couch. Taffy sat across from us on the edge of one of the recliners.

Chelsea bobbed over and, with a couple of soft clucks, perched smack-dab on top of Taffy's right shoe. Taffy looked at the blob on her foot with affection. "She likes my feet for some reason. Even takes a ride around once in awhile."

I glanced past the arm of the couch. Lying in a polished log-frame pet hammock was the strangest-looking dog I'd ever laid eyes on.

Taffy said, "That's Hemingway. He's our pet pygmy goat. We make our own goat cheese, yogurt, butter, that kind of thing. Even lotion. We do things a little differently in this house. We try to turn established rituals upside down. Take married names, for one."

"Ah," I said, "I was right. Abernathy is your maiden name, but your kid answered the phone Abernathy residence. Did your husband..."

Taffy grinned. "He took my name instead of me taking his. We thought it would be a good lesson for the kids that nothing has to be set in stone."

Coop said, "That's actually a good idea. I'm all for shaking up the establishment."

At that moment, Hemingway swung his head toward Taffy and gave a little bleat. I figured this was going to be a doozy of a story, regardless what we found out about JT and Krasski. That thought brought me back to the reality of why we were there. A fist of distress gave my heart a fast squeeze as I wondered what JT was going through right now. Scared and lonely, for sure. Those emotions mirrored themselves inside me. I hoped to hell they were keeping her safe in the clink.

"So," Taffy's voice brought me back, "You wanted to see my Krasski souvenir book." Her tone took on a sarcastic edge. She hefted a dog-eared, wire-bound notebook that had newspaper clippings hanging out from three sides off the coffee table and plopped it on her lap. "What exactly are you looking for?"

How much to tell her? She'd been through quite a bit with JT. I decided to let it fly. "JT's in jail, Taffy."

"In jail? As in, inside a jail cell in jail?" Any vestiges of humor melted off her now-pale face.

I nodded. "We were at the Renaissance Festival yesterday, and, well, one thing led to another. I kind of stumbled on a dead body in one of the privies. Then they arrested JT."

"Whoa, hold on," Taffy said, leaning forward, elbows on her knees, hands on her cheeks. "A dead body in one of the Porta Potties?"

I nodded.

She asked, "What did they arrest her for?"

I closed my eyes. "The murder of Russell Krasski."

The next few moments were filled with dead silence. Not even Hemingway or Chelsea made a peep. The ticking of a clock on top of the hutch sounded unnaturally loud.

Finally Taffy cleared her throat and said hoarsely, her voice filled with a mix of disbelief and relief, "The bastard's dead." After a few seconds, she refocused on me with narrowed eyes. "What exactly happened?"

I explained, ending with the chat that Eddy and I had with Dimples that led us to her.

"Wow. What a mess." Taffy cupped a hand over her mouth and stared off in the distance.

Coop said, "Yeah, it's a cluster. But," he patted my leg, "don't you worry. We'll spring JT." I wasn't sure if he was comforting Taffy or me.

I said, "What we'd like to do is take a look in your scrapbook and see if we can figure out who else would've liked to see Krasski hung out to dry."

Taffy patted the book and choked on a derisive laugh. "There's plenty of suspects in here, I'm sure. But before you start your hunt, I have a question."

"Okay," I said.

"Did JT ever mention communion wine to you?" Taffy peered first at Coop and then at me.

Communion wine? I shot Coop a puzzled glance. What could that have to do with what was going on?

"No, she didn't," I said. To my knowledge, JT wasn't the least bit religious. Other than comparing notes on our feelings regarding organized religion when we first hooked up, and learning that we both loved the Christmas season anyway, church and all that went with it wasn't part of our lives.

I steeled myself for more new revelations in the continued shakeup of my world.

Before Taffy had a chance to launch into it, Hemingway the Pygmy goat chose that particular moment to rouse himself. He let out a cross between a *bleat* and a *baa*, somehow bounced out of the hammock, and landed on his cloven hooves with a thud. He rocketed himself straight up in the air and then launched his stumpy body toward Taffy. Chelsea Chicken let out a startled squawk and tumbled off Taffy's foot. She righted herself, and the chase was on. Chelsea charged out of the room, wings flapping, with Hemingway on her three-toed heels, white feathers swirling in their wake.

In a matter of seconds, they came roaring back, this time with Hemingway in the lead bleating bloody murder. Chelsea *bawk, bawk, bawked* sharply, flapping her stumpy wings hard and leaping up and pecking Hemingway's butt every few steps. They raced through the room and out the opposite door, the racket fading and then disappearing altogether.

"Sorry about that," Taffy said as she tried to stifle a strained laugh. "That's their after-wake-up exercise routine. They're outside now."

Coop clapped a hand to his chest. "Holy macaroni. How'd they get out?"

"My highly intelligent, yet highly procrastination-prone husband installed a one-way pet gate in the back door. It allows the menagerie to go outside but not come back in unless we're here to supervise."

I thought we had it bad with the dogs.

Taffy settled back in the chair. "So where was I?" Then she leaned forward again. "Jeez. I'm a terrible hostess. The story is kind of involved. Can I get either of you something to drink? Or snack on? Iced tea? Water? Trail mix?"

I said, "Water, if you don't mind."

Taffy looked expectantly at Coop.

"Iced tea would be great. Thanks, Taffy."

"Groovy gravy. Should've thought to ask sooner." She stood up and headed out the same doorway that Chelsea and Hemingway had fled through.

After she'd cleared the room, Coop leaned toward me. "What the hell's up with communion wine?"

"No idea," I whispered. "How about living with a chicken and a goat in your house? Gives a whole new meaning to fighting like dogs and cats."

"No shit."

Taffy returned, cutting off our brief conversation. In one hand she held two sturdy, blue-gray clay mugs by the handles. They looked familiar. In her other hand she had a glass of clear liquid. She handed me the glass, set one of the mugs on an end table by her chair, and gave the other to Coop.

Coop held up the mug and studied it. There was a raised seal on one side, and it looked like it'd been thrown on a potter's wheel. The vessels were hourglass shaped. He said, "These are great, Taffy. Are they from this year's Renaissance?"

"We go every year."

I snapped mental fingers. That's where I'd seen the mugs. As JT and I threaded our way through what little we managed to see of the Festival before all hell broke loose, I'd seen a number of free-standing carts selling Ren Fest shirts and medieval-looking mugs in various shapes.

Taffy settled back into her chair with a sigh. "Okay. I'm not going to go into too much detail, because half of this is JT's story to tell. But maybe I can share enough to give you a sense of what drives her where Krasski is concerned."

I was pretty sure I was in the midst of having an out-of-body experience. The revelations about JT just kept rolling in, whether I wanted

109

them to or not. I didn't realize I'd begun to bounce my knee more and more frantically until Coop clamped a large hand on my leg to still it.

Taffy said, "As kids, JT and I were close. Best friends, almost blood sisters if you count the bloody scrapes we pressed together. We lived two houses apart and went to the same school and St. Joe's Catholic church." The word *church* came out in a semi-snarl. "We were ornery little monsters. Got into plenty of dumb trouble. We pulled pranks, got ourselves into places and situations we shouldn't have been in. Swiped dime-store stuff from Woolworth's. That kind of thing."

Whoa. JT hardly ever talked about her past, and even more rarely about her childhood. The JT I knew was straight-laced. She tried to follow most of the rules most of the time. When she did let go, it was a real leap of faith on her part, and it didn't happen often. It didn't mean that JT was cold or distant, but she tended to carefully calculate the things she said and did. Doing something on a whim without a plan was a real challenge. It was hard to imagine my girlfriend being a normal, pain-in-the-ass kid.

Taffy said, "One summer morning we were bored, hanging out up in our favorite climbing tree in JT's backyard." Taffy stared at the ceiling as she lost herself in memory. "I dared JT to sneak into the church vestry where the communion wine was stored and drink some. She refused unless I went along with her." Taffy rolled her eyes. "As if I wouldn't have. Anyway, the church was just a few blocks away. Evening mass wasn't for hours. We hopped on our bikes and ditched them in the schoolyard next to the church. We made it in without anyone seeing. Man, to this day I still remember the stink of frankincense that filled that old building." She shuddered.

"So we made it into the vestry. JT had just pulled out an unopened bottle of wine from the wine rack when we realized we had no idea how to get the cork out. Before she could put it back, we heard Father

Frank's voice. We dove into a closet. If only we'd closed the door all the way." Taffy shut her eyes, took a breath, and opened them again.

"One of the choir boys was with Father Frank. We couldn't hear exactly what he was saying, but he was scolding the poor kid. I remember JT grabbing the back of my shirt and pulling me away from the door so she could see better. I managed to press my face against the rough wood framing the door, right below hers. I wanted to see what was going on too.

"So Father Frank was railing on the kid, and, well, one thing led to another, and this guy was just like the hordes of other priests who are finally being outed as sexual predators. JT burst out of that closet like a bee stung her in the ass. She had the bottle of wine in her hand and started bashing Father Frank with it. The kid took off. I remember her shouting at me to run." Taffy put her hand on her chest. "I just stood there for a second and then bolted. I still feel guilty about that to this day."

I asked, my voice tinged with trepidation, "What happened to JT?"

"Maybe five minutes later, she came streaking through the back-yards and scampered up our tree."

Taffy paused and was silent so long I wondered if she were going to say any more. She heaved a heavy breath and continued. "JT swore me to secrecy about what we'd done and what we'd seen. She was absolutely terrified. She said Father Frank told her that if she breathed a word of any of it to anyone, hellfire and brimstone would be rained upon anyone and everyone she loved." She scrubbed her face with her hands. "Who the hell tells a little kid something like that? I still get worked up when I think about it."

Coop asked, "Did he hurt JT?"

Holy shit, I wanted to know that too. The Tenacious Protector stirred, and I bit the inside of my lip hard enough that I tasted blood.

It was like waking up a sleeping beast. I managed to force the beast back in the bottle and concentrated on Taffy's voice.

"She never spoke about what exactly was said or what happened after I left. I'm pretty sure Father Frank threatened her, beyond the whole fire and brimstone thing. She never told me specifically what the bastard said except that he told her everyone that both she and I loved would go straight to hell if we so much as uttered a peep about what we saw that day.

"At that age, after having the power of the church crammed down your throat for so long, you believe what they tell you. The incident changed us both. After that she became much more cautious. She refused to go back to church, no matter the punishment her parents inflicted. Believe me, they tried."

I said, "That sounds a whole lot more like the JT I know. The one who likes to plan everything, who has a tough time being spontaneous. I think it's a control thing. She doesn't want to break the rules, but she will if she thinks it's for a greater good."

"Exactly." Taffy slumped back. Retelling that story couldn't have been easy. "She rallied for the underdog. For anyone she felt was being taken advantage of. I think that may be why she followed her grandfather into police work."

Coop slid me a sidelong glance. "Sounds a little like someone I know, minus the cop part."

Huh. I hadn't ever thought in those terms about JT and me, but it was true.

Taffy raised an eyebrow and then looked at Coop. "Another fighter for the good?"

One corner of his mouth curled. "You could say that. So how did you handle what happened? Like JT?"

"Heavens no. Pretty much the opposite. I acted out, rebelled. Flounced around in tube tops and mini skirts, even when my parents managed to drag me back to church. The term 'wild child' didn't even begin to cover it. I started smoking pot, dropping acid, embraced my inner hippiness and took it to all new levels." Her brow quirked. "But I guess the one good thing, if you can call it that, is that I wound up volunteering at CornerHouse. I've been there for the last fifteen years."

I asked, "What's that?"

"It's a nonprofit started back in 1989 here in Minneapolis. Since then they've partnered with," Taffy squinted her eyes in thought, "I'm pretty sure it's four or five law enforcement agencies and a couple hospitals. Their vision is for all children to grow up in a world free from abuse. We're pretty darn far away from that goal, but you can never, ever stop trying. In fact that's where I met Sam, my main squeeze."

I smiled wryly. "At least something good came from the whole affair."

"Absolutely true."

Coop shifted and crossed his ankle over his knee. "So why did you wind up keeping this?" He pointed at the scrapbook.

"JT and I kept in touch after high school. Our paths led different ways, but we'd meet for coffee or a movie every few months. When the Krasski thing went down, it brought so much back for me—for the both of us. I started keeping track of the newspaper coverage. Not sure why, exactly. JT was absolutely inconsolable after she lost it and ruined the case. But something struck me about that slimeball."

I said, "Must've been the class historian in you coming out."

Taffy glanced sharply at me. "How did you—"

"Dimples remembers *some* stuff," I said.

"So," Taffy said, "how about we all take a peek at this thing and see who might be a killing candidate?"

For the next half-hour, we scanned clipped newsprint articles, website printouts, and notes that Taffy had made. I didn't realize just how much press the fiasco and fallout had garnered. My stomach constricted as I read headlines like MINNEAPOLIS COP BUSTS UP OWN BUST. Poor JT.

In the end I typed into my iPhone the names of four men who were linked to Krasski in various capacities. I wasn't sure if any of the names had been on the list I'd photographed at the precinct, and I didn't want to take time to check.

We thanked Taffy for her time. As we climbed into the truck, Taffy's husband, Sam, pulled up in the driveway in an ancient VW van. The rattletrap coughed up three kids, one of whom had a respectable Mohawk dyed bright orange. It reminded me of the red thing on top of Chelsea Chicken's head. I wouldn't put it past the Abernathys to encourage such individuality in their offspring. They were good people.

NINE

COOP AND I HEADED to JT's place. Home. Damn, I really wanted to think of the place as ours, but it was hard. Maybe my issue was because I was such an independent person. Eddy and JT both would probably modify *independent* to *stubborn* or *willful*.

Coop stayed outside on the porch for a smoke while I went in to grab chips, Top the Tater, and a couple of Cokes. Then I scooted up the stairs to my office to boot up my computer. Kate, Anna, and I had dubbed Coop "Blitz Man" one night not too long ago because of his uncanny ability to find information over the Internet, through both legit and questionable channels. If anyone outside the cop shop could find dirt on bad dudes, it would be Coop.

As I neatened up the office space by removing paperwork and straightening file folders, I thought about what we learned from Taffy. If nothing else, that chat reinforced my gut feelings about JT. As unhappy as I might be with the fact that JT hadn't confided in me about the Krasski thing or told me the asshole had taken a restraining order out on her, I got it. JT was a proud person. She didn't want to show weakness. In her position, I understood that too. But the whole thing still stung.

"Hey," Coop called from downstairs, pulling me from my meandering musings. "You bring some grub?"

"Chips and dip," I yelled.

A herd of elephants thundered up the steps, and Coop appeared in my doorway, slightly out of breath.

"Dude, you really need to try and kick that habit again. Look at you, puffing from just a few stairs."

"Yeah, yeah. Out of my way, beyotch." Coop snagged the bag of potato chips and stuffed his hand inside. He hip-checked me out of the way and dropped into my chair.

"Wipe your fingers before you goo up my keyboard." Sometimes Coop's common sense switch needed a flip.

"Hey," Coop mumbled as he crunched a mouthful of chips. He swallowed and said more clearly, "Who's the one who scored you this fab setup?"

"Who's the one who cost me three arms, two legs, and my right eye?"

He grinned. "Why, that would be your best pal ever. Look at this sweet all-in-one computer with a bitchin' twenty-two-inch screen. It's a thing of beauty."

"Indeed." I gave him a whack. "Get to work. With non-greasy fingers, please. We need to get my woman's butt out of the clink. The sooner the better."

For the next hour and a half, Coop ran the names from the known associate's list I had snapped at the cop shop as well as the ones we got from Taffy.

Only a few names came back as still in circulation. Krasski definitely hung out with the wrong crowd. Of the eighteen or so miscreants, two were dead, twelve were currently hanging out in jail or prison, and four were still on the streets.

I hoped the logic that Eddy had come up with was solid—that it had to be someone who knew Krasski and harbored a grudge. For all we really knew, this search could be a wild goose chase that wouldn't do one bit of good. But in the long run, what else could we do, aside from planning a jailbreak?

"Okay," Coop finally said, one bag of chips, three-quarters of a container of Top the Tater, and two Cokes later. "Here's what we got." He hit the print button.

The printer creaked and groaned its way to life. While it warmed up, I asked, "So how's Luz?"

Coop lit up like a Christmas tree with LEDs. "She's okay. I talked to her while I was in Duluth."

Luz Ortez had been the formidable ex-leader of what was probably the largest drug cartel in Mexico. We'd met her a few months back during the Baz the Spaz Incident. At the time, we were pretty sure she wanted us dead, and at one point I'd felt the cold steel of her gun pressed against my forehead.

However, one thing led to another, and not only did she keep us much alive and kicking, she helped shut down one of the most notorious drug cartels in the world. She'd been involved in a long-running covert "black ops" operation that we were clueless about until everything was pretty much wrapped up. Which was probably a good thing, because if we'd had any idea what we were getting ourselves into, we'd have run home crying for mama.

There'd been an instant attraction between Coop and Luz, and they'd managed to date, if you could call it that, in a long-distance sort of way. She'd flown Coop to Cabo for a weekend and to Puerto Vallarta for a few days too. I had no idea how it was going to work out for them, but Coop seemed happy enough at this point. Not that I wanted him to crash and burn, but the whole romance seemed way too far out of the realm of possibility. That kind of thing just didn't happen. But then, a lot of odd things were happening around me lately that I couldn't account for.

"This is a bunch of scary-ass people. Here." Coop handed me a sheaf of still-warm copy paper. He'd neatly synthesized and compiled a mug shot and the pertinent information for each potential suspect in plot points down the page. It couldn't be argued, greasy fingers or not, that the man wasn't efficient when he put his mind to it. If he weren't so antiestablishment, he'd be in high demand by more than one law enforcement agency.

I scanned the sheet on the top of the pile. "Hey, Coop, this bad boy looks like he eats skinny vegetarians for lunch." Coop was a vegetarian, and he was plenty bony. Poor guy. One of these days he was going to kill me.

"I'm happily ignoring you," he said as he held up the now empty bag of chips. "This vegetarian is still hungry."

"Let's take these downstairs. You can spread everything out on the dining room table and I'll whip you up something."

"Yeah, another one of your fabulous peanut butter and Nutella sandwiches?" He smiled and batted his eyelashes.

"Stop smirking, veggie boy. You know what they say about beggars."

We assembled in the dining room, and I laid out the papers across the oak surface.

"Going out for a minute," Coop called as he headed toward the patio door.

The sliding door swooshed open and banged shut a second later.

I turned my attention to the sheets on the tabletop and picked up the paper on top. The name in the header was Shawn Geller, and according to Coop's research, he'd been incarcerated in the St. Cloud prison and then been transferred to Stillwater before he was released. He'd been convicted of varying drug-related charges, attempted human trafficking, and other equally sleazy infractions. His picture reflected a hulking man with thinning hair who looked like he was constipated or about to throw up. I assumed getting booked might do that to a person. Geller had been sprung not long ago, and the sheet listed his last known address as a motel in St. Paul.

Possible suspect number two was a mean-looking guy named Mike Handler. He smiled at the camera in such a way that it looked like he wanted to burst off the paper and strangle someone. He'd been busted and incarcerated for sexual battery, and that was just the tip of the iceberg. What a disgusting piece of work. He'd been a known associate of both Geller and Krasski. He'd been out of the big house for the last six months and was reported to be living in a halfway house in Minneapolis.

Carlos Montega was known as a cat burglar as well as a minor soldier in a lesser-known drug cartel based near Monterrey, Mexico. That was interesting. Maybe Luz would know something about that. He was tall and thin, with a wiry build similar to Coop's. He was suspected of helping move Mexican kids across the border into the US for the purpose of human trafficking. However, no case strong enough to do any good had been made against him thus far. His last known location was an address in the suburb of Shoreview.

The last possibility we had was a bald-headed Asian man of epic proportions staring at the camera so intently it felt like he was looking directly into my soul. With effort I pulled my eyes away and focused on the description of his bad deeds. His name was Jin Pho, and he was one mean SOB. From the age of sixteen he'd been in and out of the slammer on charges that started tame enough—grand theft auto—and had moved into more serious, harder core crimes. Drugs, assault both with and without weapons, attempted rape, and numerous other charges filled the page. The address Coop found for him was somewhere in Anoka.

I dropped the sheet back on the table and headed into the kitchen to whip up some sandwiches. I'd just dipped the knife in the Skippy jar when my cell rang. The number was blocked. I didn't usually bother answering those kinds of calls, but these were no ordinary circumstances. I pinned the phone between my ear and shoulder and continued my slathering. "Hello?"

"Shay, glad I caught you. You free?"

Tyrell. My heart rate sped up. Good thing I answered. "Yeah. What's up?"

"I pulled some strings. If you can hustle your butt down to the Scott County jail by six thirty, you can see JT. Can't guarantee for how long, but you can at least verify that she's in one piece."

My legs went weak. "Did you see her? Talk to her?"

"No and no. I'm still working, but doing what I can from this end. You need to go in the main entrance and ask for Jake Rasmussen."

"Ty, thank you so much—"

"Don't thank me till you've seen her with your own eyes. Get going. Leave a message on my cell after you're done. I want to know how she is too."

"You got it."

We disconnected, and I hurriedly finished smearing the peanut butter and slapped the tops of the bread on the two sandwiches. No Nutella this time.

I wrapped the sandwiches in a paper towel and stuffed Coop's reports in his backpack. I slung the pack over my shoulder as I made a beeline for the porch, hollering his name at the top of my lungs.

———

The clock on the dash read 6:19 as we pulled into the Scott County jail parking lot in downtown Shakopee. Thanks to Coop's fast use of the mobile map on his phone, we made it in record time.

We bailed out of the truck and hustled to the front entrance. I still wasn't used to it growing dark before eight or nine, and it was plain depressing.

The jail was a newer, two-plus-story, beige stone and metal-paneled building. It housed almost three hundred inmates and was connected to the courthouse via an underground tunnel. Coop had recited these facts to me through sticky bites of his PB but not J sandwich.

The doors opened to a rotunda. I approached the buzz-cut, blond-haired deputy on duty.

"Hi," I said.

The deputy's name badge read THURSTON. My mind flashed back to Thurston Howell III from *Gilligan's Island*, but the beefy cop in front of me didn't look at all like the stranded millionaire.

He said, "What can I help you with?"

I chanted the name over and over again on the way here. Now I let it rip. "Can we please see Jake Rasmussen?"

"I can let him know you're here. Who are you?"

Coop and I handed over our identification, and he picked up a phone and dialed a number.

"Rasmussen, hey. I have a"—he paused to peer at our licenses—"Shay O'Hanlon and Nicholas Cooper here for you."

He listened a moment, frowned at whatever was said and responded with a reluctant, "Okay." Then he hung up.

"You," Thurston said to Coop as he handed his license back, "need to wait here. Benches are over there." He pointed to a couple of unadorned wood benches against a wall.

Then he addressed me. "Wait over there by that door." He indicated one of a number of doors leading only God knew where. Nowhere, I was sure, that I really wanted to find out about.

Coop met my eyes and gave an encouraging nod. My stomach quivered and I regretted eating the peanut butter sandwich that was now a big lump in my innards.

I refocused on Thurston. Everything in my periphery felt a bit out of whack. "Do I get my license back?" I asked.

"When you come back, I'll return it. Regulations," he said with a shrug.

Coop headed for a bench while I crossed the polished floor and waited by the door the deputy indicated. It wasn't more than two or three minutes before it swung open, and a tall, slender man with short, walnut-colored hair stepped out. He was wearing a short-sleeved, button-down plaid shirt and blue jeans with polished-to-a-sheen black boots. His entire bearing screamed military.

"You Shay?" His voice was deep, his speech measured.

"Yes."

He stuck a hand out. "Detective Rasmussen. You must have some pull with Tyrell. He's been saving this marker for a long time."

I wondered what Tyrell had to work with to make this happen. "He's a good friend."

"That he is. Well, come on back. I'm sure you understand this visit needs to be kept quiet."

"Yeah, I got that."

I followed Rasmussen into the depths of the jail. I was usually pretty good at directions, but if he ditched me, I wasn't sure I could find my way back out of this maze of identical hallways.

We finally stopped at an unmarked door. He produced a key, unlocked it, and waved me inside. There, sitting at a metal table in the tiny room, arms crossed, eyes granite and glaring, was JT. She was dressed in an orange shirt. I couldn't tell for sure what she was wearing on the bottom half. Her hair was up in a messy ponytail, and her normally dusky skin appeared pale. There were dark smudges under her eyes. She was exhausted.

The moment she saw me, she stood.

"You've got ten minutes, Bordeaux." Rasmussen stepped from the room and pulled the door shut behind him.

I stood frozen. Seeing JT in county lockup duds would've been laughable before this moment.

JT broke the spell first, moving around the table toward me. I met her halfway and wrapped my arms around her, holding on tight. I buried my face in her neck.

"Jesus, JT, what the fuck is going on?" I whispered.

"Oh god, baby." She pulled slightly away, sliding her hands up and framing my face, her thumbs caressing my skin. "Hey, look at me."

I turned my head and kissed her palm, then met her eyes. They had dissolved from hardass granite into the pools of rich mocha that I loved. It was then my breath hitched and I caught her lips in a fast, searing kiss. It reaffirmed our reality, our love. Us. No more second-guessing my decisions.

Then I pulled away, locking my fingers at the nape of her neck. I inhaled in one big gulp. Fought for control. "Talk. We don't have much time."

"I know." JT caught my gaze once again. "I did *not* kill Krasski."

"I know you didn't." I did truly believe that. "But why—"

"Why did I not tell you about him?" JT finished for me and sighed. I raised my eyebrows expectantly. "Well, yeah."

JT's arms dropped, and she hugged herself as she backed away. The loss of her physical presence was palpable. Bright orange was so not her color.

She stared first at the ceiling, then at the door, then finally back to me. "It's a long story. I let my emotions get the better of me, and well, I don't want to get into it here."

"Babe." I took a step toward her. "I know what happened with Taffy at that church when you were a kid. Well, I know Taffy's version, anyway."

JT visibly paled, and I quickly moved beside her in case she decided to pitch headlong to the floor. I pulled her toward the table, turned her around, and urged her to slide onto the hard surface. She did so without argument. I stood between her knees, one hand on the side of her neck, the other resting on her shoulder. I had no idea what to do with my usually rugged, savvy, street smart cop.

"Hey," I said softly, tugging her chin up. "It's okay."

"I'm sorry. I should've told you. I should've explained. Way back when, when I realized you had absolutely no idea about any of that mess, I just—I just couldn't bear to see your inevitable disappointment."

"I think if you see disappointment in anyone, it's just a reflection of your perception." I gave her a gentle shake. "I, for one, would've done the same damn thing." I paused a beat. "And you know it."

JT let out a ragged breath. "I do know," she said wearily. "My head knows that, but apparently the Catholic guilt the nuns beat into us didn't."

I raised my eyebrows. "You're sure you really didn't off Krasski and shove my pickle down his throat, right?"

That finally garnered a ghost of a grin.

I said, "I have to ask. Why on earth did you have pickle chunks and pickle stains all over your shirt?" I leaned toward her and sniffed. "I could smell it."

"Oh God," JT barked a harsh laugh. "That's Robert's smoking gun. He's so damn sure he has me dead to rights. Asshole. Anyway, I found a different pickle slinger, and he was busy doing a Gallagher with his pickles instead of with watermelons. With a big ass wood sledgehammer. I have to admit the pickles splattered quite impressively and I was standing a bit too close. I got sucked in watching his shtick and lost track of time."

"So you managed to get me my 'big, hard specimen'?"

"I did. Looked like a good one too, if you're into that kind of thing." Her mouth puckered in memory.

"What happened to it?"

"I lost it when I had to do hand-to-hand combat to get through those Ren Fest security people. They meant business."

Time was ticking. As much as I just wanted to stand there holding JT, I needed to get us back on track. "Have you heard anything about a lawyer?"

Any humor in JT's voice disappeared, her tone hardened. "No. I've got two problems. One, it's the freaking weekend, and two, Clint Roberts. I swear that man—"

The door burst open, and in strode "that man" himself. "What the *hell* is going on in here?!" His face was beet red and his eyes were wild.

JT slid off the table and drew herself to full height. "Roberts, you really should properly meet my girl—"

"You. Are. A. Prisoner." Roberts advanced on JT with every word. "What part of that don't you understand?"

For a minute he looked like he might haul off and try to belt JT. I took a half step in front of her, not really sure what I was going to do if he made a move, but damn well ready to do something. In all reality, putting myself between two trained law enforcement officers wasn't probably the smartest thing I'd ever done.

He ground out, "You are not hanging out at the local country club. Jesus. When I find out who allowed this, their ass is mine." He turned his attention to me and shoved a finger none-too-gently into my shoulder. If it bruised, maybe I could sue. The veins in Robert's forehead pulsated like little worms. "And you, you don't even think about attacking me again, or you'll wind up sitting in a cell next to her."

Holy shit. I glared at Roberts. Poor Detective or Deputy or whatever-his-title-was Rasmussen. Then my big mouth got the better of me and ran away with itself. "What's wrong with you? JT hasn't done a thing. There's a killer out there, you damned idio—"

Roberts grabbed JT by the arm and backed me against the wall, dragging JT along for the ride. He shoved his face into my space, no more than two inches from my own. "The only killer here is Bordeaux. She's going down. You mark my words." His lips actually trembled. Anger leached off of him in waves. He was the one who needed anger management classes.

The fury he was failing to suppress and the fact that he was whipping JT around like a rag doll, and moreover, that she was letting him, startled my already-on-edge Protector. My vision narrowed, my muscles tensed, and my body literally started to vibrate.

From somewhere far away, JT shouted. "Shay! Shay. It's okay. I'm all right." I blinked. Somehow she had managed to detach herself from the clamp of Robert's hand and now stood in front of me, fear filling her eyes. I blinked again. Tracked for Roberts. Spotted him, bent over and gasping for breath. What just happened?

She shook my shoulders. "Shay." I tore my gaze off the defective detective and focused on JT.

"Listen to me," she said, urgency making her voice crack. "Tell Tyrell to track down Geller and Handy Randy. One of them—"

"That's it. Bordeaux," Roberts had recovered enough to lay his ugly paws on my girl again. "Come on, you bitch." He hauled JT out the door, and I was surprised that she acquiesced. She stumbled as she tried to keep her feet under her.

Her snarl filtered into the room. "This isn't the academy, dickhead."

I took a step, and then another, intending to go after them when I heard JT yell, "I love you, Shay. Tell Tyrell—" Her words were cut off amidst the sound of a painful grunt.

I stopped and sucked in two deep, calming breaths. Then I again headed for the door and stuck my head out. JT and Roberts were nowhere to be seen. I was alone in the bowels of hell.

TEN

Twenty minutes later, I retrieved my license, reunited with Coop, and gunned the engine toward home. First I tried calling Tyrell but caught his voicemail. That wasn't a surprise. I left a message for him to check into the two names JT had given me.

To Coop, I recounted what went down in a voice that slowly stopped shaking, and now we were mulling over Shawn Geller and Handy Randy.

Coop said, "We know about Geller. But who's Randy and why is he handy? Does JT think they might have offed Krasski, or is there something else about them she wants Tyrell to know?"

"I have absolutely no idea."

We lapsed into silence.

Traffic was picking up on highway 169 as the Sunday cabin crowd trickled back to reality. The twentyish-mile long stretch of 169 between Shakopee and Maple Grove was one of the few expanses of freeway where the speed limit hadn't yet been raised to at least sixty. It was a speed trap for those who weren't paying attention, and I was sorry to count myself as one of those inattentive drivers. I'd been on the receiving end of those flashing lights more than once, so I tried to keep a careful eye on my speedometer.

A sign indicated my exit was a half-mile away. I prepared to put the signal light on and slow. "Why do you think Roberts is out to railroad JT?"

"Don't know. How do they know each other?"

"That crack about the academy. Maybe they were there at the same time."

"Could be."

"Who was it that mentioned someone had gone to the Minneapolis police academy with JT?" I pressed one hand on my forehead, trying to squeeze out the memory. Then I had it. "Dimples. He called me Peaches, along with Taffy. I think I have split personalities." I frowned. "Anyway, yeah. Peaches. Peaches Reker."

Coop pulled out his cell. "Peaches? Really?"

I shrugged.

"So," Coop said as he hunched over his phone. "Peaches Reker. Do you know when JT graduated from the academy?"

I did some quick math in my head. "She's been a cop at least the last eight or ten years."

Coop's thumbs were a flurry over the tiny keyboard.

"How can you do that?"

"Do what?"

"Type so fast."

"Practice."

"You are really gonna hack the MPD? On your phone?"

Coop ignored me. Then, "Well, not exactly the MPD, just their server. Don't see a computer in here, so I guess the phone will have to do."

"Sarcasm really doesn't flatter you."

More ignoring. "There."

A car paced us on the left, blocking me from passing a slow-moving Challenger that was directly in front of my fender. Those cars were supposed to go fast. It would fly if I were behind the wheel. I huffed in frustration. "There, what?"

"I'm in. Now to find Peaches. You don't think she really went by Peaches, do you?"

"Good question. Wonder if Cream is her middle name."

"Aren't you the sly one. Peaches and Cream. Sick." Coop messed around with the device for another couple minutes. "Okay. I've got two Rekers graduating at the same time that JT did. A Heidi and a Christina."

"How'd you do that?"

"Do what?"

"Use your phone to hack a law enforcement agency."

Coop laughed. "Ah, Grasshopper, that is for me to know, and for you to wallow in ignorance forever. Safer for you that way. Back to our Rekers. Twins?"

"Gee, thanks for your concern for my safety. And I have no idea. Could be twins. Twins do stuff together a lot I think. Could be that they both chose the copper route. Or maybe they're not related at all. Anyway, where do they live?"

"Patience, Grasshopper."

"Where is this Grasshopper crap coming from? Are you watching reruns of *Kung Fu*?"

"Now where ever would you get that idea?" Coop grinned.

"I'm going to start calling you Eddy."

He ignored my comment. "I've got the addresses. Both are in Minneapolis. Christina's is in the Stevens area, and Heidi's is near Lake Calhoun."

I cut off on Dunwoody and followed it to Hennepin. "Okay, where to for Christina?"

"Uh, drive like you're going to Loring Park."

I followed Coop's directions as he read them off his map. We wound up and down one-way streets, finally ending up at a two-story brick apartment building. The postage stamp lawn in the front of the apartment was brown. I pulled to the curb and killed the engine.

"So how are we going to do this?" Coop asked.

"Let's just go on in and tell her the truth." I considered that. "Okay, maybe the abbreviated version of the truth would be better."

"After we figure out if Christina is indeed Peaches."

"Good point."

We bailed from the truck and hiked into the building. In the tiny vestibule, formerly white one-inch tiles covered the floor. Cream-colored plaster on the walls had started to crack with age. Oak woodwork surrounded the entrance and the two secure doors leading to the interior. Six-foot-long panes of glass were mounted in each door. They sure didn't make 'em that way anymore.

The faint aroma of fried hamburger and onions lingered in the lobby. Names that had been printed out on a curling sheet of paper were taped above a call box. I ran my finger along the list. Two-thirds of the way down, I found C. REKER—#23.

I pushed the pound sign and then the digits on the pay phone–like button pad. The vestibule echoed as a screechy sound blared out from a two-inch speaker below the keys. One, two, three, four rings. No answer.

"Maybe she's working," Coop said.

After another round of annoying rings, I disconnected. "Damn. I guess we go try Heidi."

We piled back into the truck and headed for the second address.

Heidi Reker's place was in a nicely kept, four-story brick apartment building. The lobby was spotless and smelled of cleaning stuff and carpet glue. A list of apartment dwellers was posted behind glass on the wall next to a call box. I buzzed the only Reker on that list. An annoying boinging sound as the thing attempted to connect echoed around the enclosed space. There was no response. Damn. I really didn't want this to be an 0-for-2 blowout.

Disappointed, we headed out the foyer to the truck. I pressed the key fob to unlock the doors, and the headlights flashed on. They momentarily illuminated a shadowy figure that had just rounded the sidewalk at the end of the block. The person jogged toward us, the silhouette of a dog trotting at their side. When the jogger came into the glow cast by a nearby streetlamp, the shape coalesced into that of a woman dressed in a light-colored sweatshirt and tight running pants.

I was about to step off the curb and get in the truck when the gal turned off the sidewalk and headed for the door to the complex we'd just exited.

Coop saw her too. He called, "Heidi? Heidi Reker?" Fat chance it'd be her.

The woman turned around. Her dog remained glued to her side. Now that they were closer, I could see the pooch was a German shepherd.

"Yeah," she said warily, "I'm Reker. Who're you?" Her face was fine-boned, and her dark hair was tied back. Loose strands stuck to her damp skin and intelligent, curious eyes assessed us.

The dog sat on his haunches as soon as Ms. Reker stopped moving. He, or I guess it could be a she, waited quietly at her side. The dog appeared keenly alert, ready to take action if needed. Heidi rested a calming hand on the pooch's head.

Well, I'll be switched. Something was actually going to go smoother than expected. I said, "I'm Shay O'Hanlon, and"—I poked my thumb at Coop—"that's Nick Cooper, but he gets ornery if you call him Nick, so he goes by Coop."

"What can I do for you?"

Oh man, where did we begin? I said, "Do you know JT Bordeaux?"

"JT Bordeaux? Yeah. Why?"

As soon as I uttered JT's name, I could feel the woman's walls slam up. It was probably best to simply lay the truth on her. "I'm JT's girlfriend. She's in serious trouble, and we need help."

Heidi blinked. Her demeanor softened, although she remained cautious. "I heard JT had hooked up with someone. So you're the lucky girl, huh?" She looked me up and down once, then returned her eyes to my face. "What kind of scrape did JT get herself into this time?"

I said, "It's a long story. We need to ask you about—" I glanced at Coop, who gave me a blank look. Sometimes his brand of assistance didn't match what I thought I needed. "About a sensitive situation that JT's managed to get tangled up in. Can we come inside? I think it'd be better if we didn't conduct this discussion out here."

Heidi apparently decided we weren't a threat. She said, "What do you think, Radar, should we let these two come in?"

Radar gave a low woof, eyes glued to us.

"Is he friendly?" I asked.

"If you're a friend, he's friendly. If not, he'll kick your ass. And he's got sharp teeth."

I held out my hand. The dog sniffed my offering, his wet, quivering nose nudging my fingers. Then he gently touched the tip of his tongue to my skin. I tentatively passed muster.

Coop followed my lead. Radar pretty much bypassed the sniffing part and dove right into "oh please pet me" mode. Dogs could somehow tell Coop had a kind, gentle soul. He could probably be the next Dog Whisperer when Cesar Millan decided to retire.

Thus vetted, we followed Heidi and Radar through the front door and up well-worn stairs to the second floor. Hers was the second door on the left. She unlocked it and let us inside. We followed her through a short hall and made a right turn into a combined kitchen/dining/living room.

Immediately, one thing became very clear: Heidi Reker was a Smurfs freak. Posters starring the white-hatted, blue-bodied gnomeish beings lined her walls. Shelves were filled with Smurf figurines and plush Smurf toys. Even Gargamel was represented, both on a framed poster and as a stuffed toy. A throw populated with Smurfs was tossed over the back of her couch.

Coop's eyes grew wide as he took it all in.

Heidi watched us look around. "I confess I'm a blue-blooded Smurfaholic. Have a seat and let me get out of these sweaty clothes. Radar, you stay and keep these nice folks company." With that directive given, Heidi disappeared down the hallway. Radar strolled across the room and plodded directly to Coop, who lowered himself to the couch and gave the mutt some attention.

I remained standing and crossed my arms, watching them with amusement. "He knows who the pushover is."

"Yeah, yeah. You're just jealous because he can see my warm, tender heart."

There wasn't much to come back to that with. Coop was absolutely right.

A freestanding shelving unit divided the kitchen from the living room. One single shelf was devoid of anything Smurf-related. Instead, framed photos were lined up with military precision. One of the pictures was a group shot of maybe twenty people, all wearing the blue and black uniform of a Minneapolis police academy recruit. JT was standing next to Heidi, who actually looked the same as she did now. Her arm was draped over Heidi's shoulder in a friendly fashion, and the entire squad beamed for the camera.

One recruit in particular wasn't smiling, and in fact didn't look pleased at all. The glare on his face sent a shiver down my spine. I realized I'd seen that same face and same scowl earlier today. It was Clint Roberts. I wondered what had happened to him to make him such a hard ass jerk.

Heidi reentered the living room and pulled me out of my rumination on the mysteries of Roberts's psyche. She'd changed into a pair of sweats and what else but a Smurfs T-shirt. I barely restrained myself from rolling my eyes. Heidi was probably thrilled to pieces when they released that new Smurfs movie awhile back.

She asked, "Can I get either of you something to drink?"

Both Coop and I politely declined, and I moved to sit on the couch next to Coop.

Heidi settled on the edge of a recliner. Radar bailed on Coop, padded over, and settled down at Heidi's side. She reached over the arm of the chair and absently rubbed the top of the dog's head. "So what is this about?"

I wasn't sure exactly where to start. If Heidi were in the same position that Tyrell had been, she would have absolutely no idea that JT was in custody on suspicion of murder, or homicide, or whatever the authorities called it. I really didn't want to repeat any of this stupid tale again. In fact, I just wanted to snuggle into bed with JT and gleefully stick my cold feet on her warm legs. I wanted to wake up to a new day with none of this hovering over our heads.

Unfortunately life wasn't that cooperative. I heaved a resigned sigh, then recounted for Heidi the events of the craziest Saturday I may have ever had. She listened with rapt attention. When I related the details about JT's arrest and told her the name of the arresting officer, she literally hissed air in between her teeth.

"That bastard. I can't believe he still has it out for JT after all this time." Heidi stared blankly into space, apparently ruminating over the bad history JT shared with Clint Roberts. After a couple of seconds, she zeroed back into the present. "What happened after Roberts took her away?"

Coop and I recounted the zigzagging path we'd followed throughout the day. When I got to the part about JT's grandfather confusing me with someone named Peaches, a woman JT had apparently attended the academy with, she laughed. "I can't believe he remembers that after all this time."

Ah ha. We really did find Peaches.

I couldn't help but ask, "Was your nickname Peaches, or was it just a nickname he used?"

"Nickname. I've had it since I was a kid. Everyone in my family, even to this day, calls me Peaches, and my twin sister, Christina, Cream." She rolled her eyes. "Peaches and Cream. Sad, isn't it? No amount of threatening anyone made a damn bit of difference. At least Peaches is way better than being called Cream. My poor sister."

Poor sister indeed. I was sort of right about Peaches and Cream, and I'd been joking.

"So why does Detective Roberts have it out for JT?" I asked. "What did she ever do to him?"

"Oh God. That was such a mess." Heidi sighed.

This wasn't going to be good.

"It all started when we were at the academy. Roberts was bull-headed right from the get-go. He was an opinionated misogynist who felt—probably still feels—that anyone without a dick has no place in law enforcement. All of the women in our class butted heads with him. He's just lucky no one decided to use him for a target during firearms drills."

Coop asked, "So did he have the same animosity toward all of the recruits that he has toward JT?"

"As I said, he didn't like any of the women, but JT in particular tripped something in his itty-bitty brain. JT scored at the top of the class, neck and neck with the bas—with Roberts—every step of the way. He couldn't fathom a mere girl challenging him at anything. When someone came along who was actually better than he was at more than one thing and who didn't have a penis, well, he popped his cork.

"The instructors yanked him out of class more than once over his behavior. I hoped—we all hoped—he'd get booted, but somehow he managed to hang in there, no matter what crap he laid on the rest of us." With eyes squinted almost shut in memory, Heidi continued. "Rumors were always flying among us as to why Roberts didn't get the heave-ho. They ran the gamut. From him being related to one of the brass, or that maybe he managed to bribe his way in—man, he could find out secrets and make life a living hell for whoever he targeted."

Heidi paused, measuring her words. "In fact, his behavior was exactly that of a schoolyard bully. Frankly, I'm surprised he's still a cop. I was sure that by now he would've done something to someone that would have gotten him fired, or worse."

No doubt about it, the man was straight-up bad news.

"Back to JT," I said gently, trying to pull Heidi out of her memories. "That was awhile back. Wouldn't he have let things go by now? Well, obviously he hasn't. But why?"

"As class went on, animosity between JT and Roberts grew every day. When we graduated, she'd aced him out of the top spot. It was a come-from-behind thing. Believe me, he wasn't happy playing second fiddle to anyone. You know, come to think of it, I believe he began to truly hate JT after she wiped the course with his ass when we were in St. Cloud learning how to PIT, which was right toward the end of the academy."

"Pit?" I'd heard JT talk about a lot of police stuff, but I didn't recall hearing about any pit. It sounded like what was left after eating certain fruits and veggies.

Coop shocked the hell out of me by explaining. "Pursuit Intervention Technique, I think. P-I-T."

I glanced at him, impressed and more than a little puzzled as to why he'd know that. He caught my look and tapped his noggin with a knuckle. "I have more useless trivia up here than you'd ever expect."

Heidi gave him a nod. "I guess you do. It's a technique that, under the right conditions, we can use to stop a fleeing vehicle. JT, as usual, mastered the how-to in no time flat. She somehow managed to find herself partnered up with Roberts for the hands-on driving portion on the second day. Let me tell you, it wasn't by choice. She avoided that man like a plague of killer wasps. By the end of day two, their relationship shifted from barely tolerant to outright hatred. I don't know what was said in that car while they ran the course, but something had to have been.

"Afterward, I asked her what happened. Numerous times. But she just shut her trap. After awhile I just quit trying."

Poor JT. To be stuck in a tiny space with someone she couldn't stand would've seriously sucked.

"So," I asked, "what happened after you guys graduated?"

"We hit the road with field training officers. Eventually some of the guys moved into other areas within the Minneapolis police department. JT went into sex crimes. I did a stint with mounted patrol then wound up in backgrounds and SWAT hostage negotiations. A few of the guys left for other agencies. Roberts wanted a promotion, but no one was willing to give him one in the MPD. Probably because he was riddled with use-of-force complaints. He bailed to the burbs, and from what I heard, cleaned up his act enough to get promoted to detective."

I said, "So then at least he was out of JT's hair."

"He was until the blowout with Russ Krasski." Heidi sighed. "After that, he dogged her again. Talking shit. The cities are big, but this burg is a pretty damn small place when it comes to that kind of thing."

Coop asked, "Did JT ever talk about that night? About what happened with Krasski?"

Heidi considered that. "After I heard what happened, I called her. We met at a coffee shop in Uptown. That Alice in Wonderland one."

I bit down a wry grin. "The Rabbit Hole."

"Yeah. That's the place. I don't often get over there, but the coffee's good."

That was nice to hear. I considered telling her I owned the joint, but it wasn't pertinent to this conversation. There was a fair chance I'd worked the day that JT and Heidi met, and I would've been completely oblivious. It was an unsettling feeling.

Heidi said, "JT was wrecked. Who wouldn't have been? She singlehandedly screwed up a case they'd been working on for a really long time. The only saving grace—well, I guess you could call it more than one saving grace—was that all of Krasski's cronies who were there at the time were taken down. But JT was furious with herself for losing it."

Coop asked, "Did she tell you what Krasski said to her that set her off?"

Heidi was quiet a long moment. "She would never tell me specifically what he said, only that it was so—what was the word JT used? Reprehensible, that was it—so reprehensible and disgusting that she just snapped." Heidi pinned her eyes on mine and stared directly into my heart. "JT was a good cop then. She's a good cop now. Yeah, she might've lost her mind, but that monster got what was coming to him. It's just too bad the beat-down didn't happen in prison at the hands of some child-molester-hating murderer."

Poor JT. She bore all of this without ever even giving me a hint that she was carrying around this kind of pain. That just sucked. It hurt more than I expected, actually. But I understood as best I could without actually hearing the details from the woman herself.

Lord knew I had my own share of uncontrolled anger. There were times I had to work really hard to keep myself in check. I intimately knew blinding, red-that-actually-tinted-your-vision rage that could boil up in an instant under the right conditions. But that was me. I absolutely had no idea this kind of thing had ever happened to JT. She worked so very hard to remain cool, calm, and collected, even in the place most people figuratively and literally bared and shared it all— the bedroom. Now for the first time, I guess I really comprehended why. She and I had more in common than I thought, but it was totally disconcerting to have it revealed to me in quite this way.

We thanked Heidi for her time. Once we piled back in the pickup, I started the engine but left the truck idling at the curb. The impact of what we'd just learned about someone I loved, and loved even more intensely the more I heard, rattled me. It wasn't that I felt JT had failed in any way, but that she'd had to go through this by herself.

Well, she damn well wasn't alone anymore. She finally had someone on her side, someone who'd been there, who totally understood and got where she was coming from. She and I could only hope we didn't turn this—I wasn't even sure what to call it—this rage of conviction, for want of a better phrase, on each other or we'd be toast. The one thing that still got me was that she'd shielded such a huge, painful part of herself from me, and from the rest of the world, simply so she could continue to function.

It all boiled down to secrets. JT obviously had hers, and I suppose I did too. I rarely looked too deeply inside myself, didn't take much time to consider my own deepest feelings. It was too scary in that place. It was much easier to let the Tenacious Protector take care of the things that I couldn't deal with.

I imagined it was easier for JT to remain solidly in control, concentrating on whatever needed her attention so she wouldn't have to consider the demons that had pitched their own tents inside her. If she delved too much, the monsters would be unleashed with a vengeance, and the control she so carefully cultivated would melt like a grape Popsicle on a late-July day.

I leaned back in the seat and pressed my head against the headrest. I didn't need to get myself all bogged down. JT needed me, and I was going to be there for her. Warmth spread through my chest the way the first sip of something hot on a frigid winter's evening flowed through your veins after you'd frozen your ass off outside. Maybe this is what love really was all about. But hell, it was confusing.

Coop said quietly, "You okay?"

It was a good thing my friend was a patient man. I had no idea how long I'd sat immobile in the driver's seat contemplating secrets, tempers, and Minnesota weather metaphors. I didn't often do a whole lot of self-analysis, and when I did, it tended to freak me out. In this instance, my inner assessment solidified what I was—what *we* were, actually—working toward. It was time to get serious about tracking down a murderer, even if he had offed someone who should've been deep-sixed a long time ago, and bring JT's butt back home where it belonged. That was priority number one.

I shot Coop a steady glance, newfound resolve steeling my words. "It's time to kick some serious ass."

ELEVEN

IT WAS JUST PAST eight thirty when we rumbled up the alley and I parked in front of Eddy's garage behind the Rabbit Hole. Dawg and Bogey were busy chasing each other around the yard. After slobbery hellos I left the two to their game of tag. I thought again how the life of a dog was a hell of a lot easier than the lives of humans these days. Pee. Play. Nap. Eat. Play. Poop. Get some human love. Nap. Pee. Pee again. Eat. Repeat.

I trooped into the kitchen, leaving Coop outside to feed his nicotine addiction and suffer a little more canine slobber.

The kitchen simmered with the mouthwatering fragrance of Eddy's homemade enchiladas. My stomach reminded me it had been awhile since it had been properly filled and wasn't particularly happy about it. What an unending, crazy-ass day. I was ready to chow down on just about anything that was edible, and maybe some things that weren't. The good news was that Eddy's cooking was always more than edible.

The woman herself, clad in black footie pajamas emblazoned with the rock band Kiss's logo, stood at the stove stirring something.

Without turning around, she said, "About time you showed up. I've got a late supper going. Chicken cheese enchiladas. They'll be done in fifteen minutes. I'm cooking up parsnips for Coop, and a salad." She turned away from the softly bubbling root vegetables to face me. "Where is that boy? Kate said he left with you. What kind of shenanigans did you kids get yourselves into while I was stuck with the Knitters? Although," she said almost as an afterthought, "I made twenty-six bucks on the deal."

Ah yes, the Mad Knitters doing what they did best.

"As to your first question, Coop's outside."

"Puffing on those damn cancer sticks." She didn't wait for my affirmation. "We need to light a fire under that boy. Thought he had 'em beat last time. Maybe he should take up cigars."

Yuck. I had hopes that Coop's last effort to kick the coffin nail habit would've stuck, but at least he had a good attitude about trying again. And again. And again.

I mentally reviewed the day's events. It made me tired to think about it all. From my morning visit to the Hole, snagging Coop and Rocky from the phone book biz to help with my police station snooping exercise, the near-disastrous water dance with Dimples and Eddy, locating Taffy at the sperm bank and meeting her menagerie, to the heart wrenching trip to see JT and finally tracking down Peaches, or rather, Heidi. It was quite a list to run down when I reviewed it.

I said, "You aren't going to believe the visit we had to Taffy's place. Eddy, you should've been there."

"'Course I'm gonna believe. You might not be a child of these old loins, but you're as close to a daughter to me as anyone could be. I dang well know when you're laying it on thicker than clumpy molasses."

That was true. The woman had this freaky sixth sense when it came to me copping a lie or spilling the honest dope. I couldn't count the times the wooden spoon went *whack!* across my backside when she finally pried the truth from my mouth. It had taken some good *thwacks*, but I learned to either keep my mouth shut or tell the woman the truth. Which, in the long run, was probably a good thing.

Eddy grabbed a fork and stabbed a parsnip. "These are done. You fetch Coop and I'll get Rocky."

She drained the parsnips and dumped them in a frying pan with a slab of butter. Then she zoomed off in her footie jammies, the sight of which still cracked me up every time I saw her wearing them. She'd become a *Simmons Family Jewels* fan, and the sleepwear had been a natural hit.

I swung the screen door open. "Coop," I called into the night. "Eddy cooked. She made you parsnips." The vegetable was one of his favorites. I thought they were rather unappetizing, myself.

I held the door open as Dawg and Bogey strolled in, snuffled me in greeting, and then wandered out of the kitchen and into the living room. Coop followed them inside and closed the door, sighing appreciatively as he sniffed the air.

I said, "Bet you wish you ate meat right now, don't you?"

"I can use my schnoz to appreciate that which I'm not going to stuff in my pie hole." Coop sniffed again. He moved toward the stove. "Sweet. Looks like I'm just in time to keep these beauties from burning." He grabbed a spatula and started flipping.

"Nick Coop!" Rocky burst into the kitchen, with Eddy trailing along in his wake. "Shay O'Hanlon," he added when he caught sight of me. "You will never guess what!" He bounced on the balls of his feet.

It was easy to get caught up in Rocky's enthusiasm. He did a little dance, his entire body getting into the motion. Then he took a big breath and said, "As Shay O'Hanlon likes to say, my flower, my flower, oh boy, oh BOY! My flower is *coming*!"

"What?" Coop turned toward Rocky, spatula frozen in mid-flip. A lone parsnip slid off the utensil and dropped into the sizzling frying pan.

"What?" I echoed, my voice sounding decidedly feeble. Did he really just say Tulip was coming? Holy shit. Rocky and Tulip were both adults as far as the law was concerned, but they were a bit shy of a fully operational deck. Not that either one of them were dumb, not by any stretch. They just lacked a few—okay—more than a few facets of common sense, while they were beyond brilliant in other aspects.

"Oh yes!" Rocky clapped his hands in sheer delight. "Tulip is coming here! To the Twin Cities! To Minneapolis! To the Rabbit Hole! To see me! Oh boy. I am so excited!" He hopped from one neon-orange Converse clad foot to the other. The shoes had been a gift from Eddy, and the sight of him walking around glowing usually made me grin. This time, however, the sight failed to do its job. Panic of a new kind was too firmly imbedded inside me.

Eddy had stopped behind Rocky. Her eyes were round and her mouth gaped in a shocked O.

I swallowed hard and cleared my throat. "Is she coming alone?" I was afraid to ask and was afraid of the answer. I couldn't recall ever hearing anything about a caretaker who might give Tulip a hand. I momentarily wondered if they might produce kids as strangely brilliant and as weirdly unique they were. Then I banished that thought. It was a little like thinking about sex and a close relative.

Rocky clapped his hands again, excitement radiating off him in palpable waves. "She is coming with Miss Marple, the wonderful woman who is exactly fifty-seven years, three months, and twenty-two days old. Miss Marple loves Tulip. She likes me too. And this is the very, very, very best part of all." He gulped in a huge breath, and then said through a face-splitting grin, "We are going to be joined in ultimate holy matrimony and bliss."

For a heartbeat, utter silence descended on the kitchen. Then the sound of the spatula hitting the edge of the frying pan and clattering to a rest on the countertop broke the spell.

Both Coop and I looked from Rocky to Eddy. She looked as flabbergasted as we were. In fact, I was afraid for a moment she might pitch headlong to the kitchen floor. She covered her eyes with her hands, inhaled, and calmly said, "Let's eat."

———

Ten minutes later we were seated around the kitchen table, stuffing our faces with enchiladas, parsnips, and salad. One part of my brain recognized the food was as awesome as it always was whenever Eddy slapped her cooking hat on, but a much larger part of me paid no attention to the taste. Instead, Rocky's bomb ripped repeatedly, loud and clear, through my brain.

Usually when Rocky ate, he shoveled one thing at a time into his mouth. He'd hardly look up and rarely uttered a word before the task of feeding himself was complete. I'd learned early on that something in his makeup compelled him to chew his food a certain number of times before he swallowed it, and if he lost count, he'd have to start over. Tonight, however, his jaws flew as he masticated his grub. For the first time since I'd known him, Rocky finished eating before anyone else. And none of us were exactly leisurely diners.

Rocky swallowed his last bite and downed the rest of his grape-flavored Kool-Aid. He set the empty glass down with a thump.

"Shay O'Hanlon, we want to be joined in ultimate holy matrimony and bliss in the Rabbit Hole."

I nearly spewed out the milk I had just sucked into my mouth. "I—uh—don't…"

Eddy shot me a withering look.

"Ah, yes, of course you can, Rocky." I quickly shoved in another mouthful of salad.

Rocky bobbed in his chair like a jack-in-the-box and turned his attention to Coop. "Nick Coop, you are going to be my best man."

Coop raised his fist and did a knuckle bump with Rocky. "You got it, my man. Do you want a bachelor party?"

I yelped, "Coop!" I couldn't believe he just said that. Our Rocky—at a strip show?

Coop gave me an innocent look. "What?"

Oblivious to our interchange, Rocky shifted gears again. "Eddy, I want you to be our sermonizer in ultimate holy matrimony and bliss."

Eddy paled under her brown skin. She said, "Your…your—oh dear. I'm not a person of the cloth, Rocky."

"You can be," Rocky told her. "You just have to go on the Internet, and you too can become a person of the cloth even if you do not like the cloth. I looked."

I stared at Eddy with wild eyes. She was quite wild-eyed herself.

Rocky was oblivious to our facial antics. "Kate and Anna are going to be Tulip's bridesmaids."

Before any of us could formulate any kind of appropriate response, Rocky was off on another statistical frenzy. "In 2008, two million one hundred fifty-seven thousand people who were in love got to be joined in ultimate holy matrimony and bliss." He swooped his head dramatically toward Coop. "Eight hundred forty-four thousand people got *un*joined in ultimate holy matrimony and bliss." With that Rocky jumped up from the table. "I have to go. It is time to Facebook with Tulip."

I opened my mouth, but Coop beat me. "Rocky, when's she coming?"

Rocky paused at the threshold between the kitchen and the living room. He called over his shoulder, "Day after tomorrow. We will get joined in ultimate holy matrimony and bliss Wednesday. I do not know what time my Tulip wants to be joined in ultimate holy matrimony and bliss though." Then he disappeared into the living room.

"Wednesday?" I whispered.

"Oh." Eddy fanned her face with her hand. "I need to think about this."

It was a rare moment when Eddy was struck speechless. If I weren't so stunned, I'd have taken great pleasure in that.

For a full minute the only sounds were forks scraping against Corelle. Then I said, "Can he really get married?"

"Why not?" Coop pushed his chair away from the table and gathered his and Rocky's dishes. "Could be cute." He brought them over to the sink.

"Nicholas," Eddy said sharply, "did you ever talk to that boy about S-E-X?"

I couldn't help but taunt him. "Yeah, Coop, didja?"

Coop industriously scrubbed at his plate.

"Well, Nicholas?"

"I meant to. Really. I will. Soon. Oh God."

Eddy brought her plate and silverware to the sink and handed them to Coop. "Here you go. Maybe a little manual labor will improve your memory."

I cleared the table and added my load of memory improvers to his pile, still reeling. First JT, now Rocky. What could happen next? I didn't dare contemplate the possibilities.

Eddy rummaged around a cupboard, pulling out mugs and plunking them on the counter with a bang. Her voice was hollow behind the cabinet door. "If there ever was a time for liquid backbone, this is it."

She was more shaken over Rocky's news than I realized. She skipped her special concoction ingredients and went right for the whiskey. She set the three glasses, each with about two shots of straight alcohol, on the table.

I picked up the tumbler and watched the amber liquid swirl around the bottom quarter of the cup. I took a tentative sip. The liquor burned its way down my throat and settled hotly in my stomach. I was pretty sure I was going to end up with an ulcer before this was all over. Maybe I needed to learn to meditate to deal with my stress. But who had time to meditate when their girlfriend was accused of murder and locked up by a madman masquerading as a cop?

We needed to keep our eyes on the prize, which was finding Krasski's killer. Without losing track of Rocky and his upcoming—I could hardly form the word in my mind—nuptials.

To Tulip. Oh man.

Coop finished his manual labor and rejoined us at the table. He settled into the chair with a groan. "I'm too old for this."

"Young man, you don't even know what old means." Eddy fixed the stink-eye on him. Then she said, "Okay. Tell me all about your day. Don't leave a single thing out."

I filled her in on finally seeing JT and what had happened. Then, between Coop and I, we gave her the rundown on Taffy and the zoo, and Heidi, AKA Peaches. When we were done, Eddy didn't say anything for a long minute. Finally, she said, "A live goat—in the house?"

After all that, she got stuck on the goat.

"Yeah," I said. I was starting to loosen up as the booze flowed through my system. "And a chicken. The goat and the chicken were friends. They played with each other."

"Okay. That Peaches—"

"Heidi," I said. "Her name's Heidi. She used to go by Peaches."

"Anyway, she knew our JT. Do you feel better now, Shay, after hearing what she had to say?"

"Yeah. As a matter of fact, I do." I peered into the depths of my nearly empty cup. "Now we just need to get our act in gear and figure out who the hell pickled Krasski."

I was about to down the last of my liquid backbone when my cell rang. The readout on the caller ID displayed Tyrell's number.

"Hey Ty, what's up?" I hoped maybe he'd say everything had been a huge mistake and that I could go now and scoop JT up from the evil clutches of Detective Clint Roberts.

"Got a couple things for you. First, the bad news—word on the vine is Roberts is sure he has his woman and isn't looking for any other suspects. Which, as you and I both know, is bullshit. Second, the potentially worse news—just heard from the friend of a friend of a not-so-good friend that preliminary ballistics came back. The bullet found at the crime scene matches a handgun that was found down the stink hole—"

"The 'stink hole'?"

"Yup. Exactly what you think it is. I feel for the poor grunt who sifted through all that shit, no pun intended. Anyway, you gotta keep this under wraps, okay?"

"Yeah, yeah. I won't say anything to anyone who counts." So much for positive thinking. "What about fingerprints?"

"One tiny ray of sunshine. They couldn't pull a single print off it. You know if JT was carrying when you went to the festival yesterday?"

Was she? I thought about it. It was a rare occasion she didn't stash a weapon somewhere on her person while off duty. I hadn't mauled her before we left home, or I would've known for sure. "Probably. Why?"

"The gun they fished from the crapper was the same kind I know JT uses as one of her off-duty weapons. A Smith & Wesson Bodyguard. Do you know the one I'm talking about?"

My heart beat heavy in my chest. I didn't pay any attention to what guns JT used. I knew she had a locked crate for her weapons, but that was it. "Oh shit."

"Yeah, oh shit. We have to hope the gun they found isn't registered to her."

"Wouldn't they have taken swabs of her hands to see if they had gunpowder on them or something?" That's what the CSI guys always did on Eddy's shows.

"Yeah. I'm sure they did. Haven't heard anything on that yet, though. Trying to get information through the Clint Roberts filter is worse than having a tooth yanked with string and a slamming door."

"I could take a look in her gun locker and see what's there."

Tyrell sighed. "If you get a chance, let me know. And, hey. I talked to someone who's checking into the two names she gave you. Nothing yet. I'll call when I can if I hear anything else. Chin up, okay?"

I disconnected. That tiny, wee sliver of doubt regarding JT's guilt flared as bright as a flash-bang grenade. Then my overextended but still sort of functioning brain tamped the flare out almost immediately. I itched to get home and take a gander in JT's strongbox. If this Bodyguard gun were there, it would prove her innocence, right?

When I was little, the ragtag bunch of neighborhood kids I ran with often played the pickle in the middle game. The object was to keep the ball, or whatever it was we decided to toss back and forth, away from the person in the middle of the pack. The pickle in the middle.

In this case, the truth was my elusive ball, and it went sailing over my head, first one way, then the other. Every time I reached out to grab that truth, it just barely slipped through my fingers. The game frustrated me to no end as a kid, and that's how I felt now. Every time I came to a conclusion about what JT may or may not have done, something happened that made me question my own perceptions. But come on. This was JT we were talking about. The one who cared about justice, about people. Who, for some reason, loved me. It didn't matter if JT had a gun on her person at the fair. She didn't kill Krasski.

Still, that insistent knocking in my heart and conscience meant that I knew I'd be making a beeline for that gun locker as soon as I got home.

Coop's and Eddy's piercing stares knocked me out of my ruminations. I told them what Tyrell had shared. When I finished, Eddy rolled her eyes. "That girl did *not* shoot anyone. We simply need to find who did. What were the two names JT said Tyrell should look into again?"

"Geller. Shawn Geller. And Handy Randy. Shawn Geller was the human trafficker recently released from prison, if I remember right. Handy Randy? I don't have a clue."

"Well, what are we waiting for? Let's go find Geller, wring his neck, and see if he shoved a pickle in his old boss's mouth. Coop, fire up that contraption of yours. Do your thing and find out where

Geller's staying. Shay, you go do whatever you need to do to print those names off your phone. I can't see a damn thing on that little bitty screen." Eddy was a great drill sergeant on a moment's notice.

For once I was ahead of the eight ball. "I can do better than that. Coop, I stuck the stuff you printed out at JT's in your bag." I'd forgotten I'd done that when we'd hauled ass out of the house and headed to the lockup to see JT. "Can you dig them out while I pop over and see if things are holding together in the Hole?"

Sundays we closed at nine. I glanced at my watch. It read 9:20 p.m. I walked though Eddy's living room and through a short hall into the café. The front door was locked, and the neon OPEN sign was off. Anna was busy scrubbing the remnants of multitudes of coffee creations off the espresso machine.

"Hey, kid," I said.

She yelped and almost toppled head over keister. "Whoa—" Anna slapped a hand to her throat. "You could be a little noisier, you know. I doubt the health inspector would appreciate a dead barista messing up this not-yet pristine floor."

"Sorry, Anna. Don't worry, we'd make sure you were safely tucked away in the dumpster."

"Oh you—" She attempted to snap me with her wet towel. I barely avoided a stinging *thwap* to the hip as I escaped into the kitchen.

The kitchen wasn't huge, but it worked. One wall was taken up by wire racks loaded with supplies for the café. A long stainless-steel counter with a three-well sink occupied most of the opposite side. Dripping dishes rested on the drying rack. At the far end of the room was a 6x8 closet we'd recently turned into a dinky office.

Since I wasn't living in the apartment above the café any longer, I hadn't wanted to take all of the store paperwork I'd accumulated to JT's. So now a lot of it was stowed in the four-drawer filing cabinet we'd crammed into the space, along with a midget-sized desk that one of Eddy's Mad Knitters had donated to our cause.

I leaned against the doorjamb, crossed my arms, and watched Kate, whose head was bent over her work. She was busy counting cash, the bills making a rhythmic *whooshing* sound as they slid through her nimble fingers. She sensed my presence and glanced up mid-count.

"Hang on." She finished and then tapped the money against the surface of the desk, set the pile aside, and wrote a number on the deposit slip. "What's up?"

"Can you take the dogs overnight?"

"Sure I can." Kate's eyes drilled me. "What the hell is going on now? Is JT out of the klink?"

I heaved a sigh and caught her up. When I was finished, she leaned back in her chair. "Jeez. How do you guys always manage to get into such crazy-ass shit? I swear trouble follows you around like a…like…when I think of an appropriate comparison, I'll let you know."

"Sounds good," I said wryly. "Anyway, if you can take the mutts, that'll be one less worry."

"Yeah, no problem. You want me to open for you tomorrow, too?"

Five in the morning was going to come mighty early, especially depending on what we got ourselves into next. "That would be totally awesome."

"Not a worry. I have my slave girl to help if needed."

Poor Anna. Good thing she thought the ground Kate walked on was sacred—except when Kate pissed her off, which luckily didn't happen very often.

"Thanks, as usual." I waved and spun around, then paused in mid-step. I backed up and stuck my head through the door. "Hey, you hear about Rocky?"

"What about Rocky?"

"Tulip's coming to town."

"Really? When?"

"Tuesday."

"As in this Tuesday?"

"Yup. Guess what else?"

Kate looked up sharply at my tone. "What?"

"You and Anna are going to be Tulip's bridesmaids."

"What?"

"You sound like a parrot. Rocky and Tulip are going to get hitched. Wait. They are going to"—what the hell had Rocky said?—"be joined in ultimate holy matrimony and bliss. Rocky wants Eddy to officiate, Coop to be best man, and you and Anna to do bridesmaid duties."

Kate's mouth opened and closed a couple of times. I could see the wheels in her brain start and stop and start again as she tried to process my bomb. "Bridesmaids? How can Eddy—"

I smirked. "The Internet is a miraculous thing. For a couple hundred bucks, I guess one can be endowed with all the necessary licenses or whatever to legally marry people." Bad Shay. I was getting a kick out of watching poor Kate flounder. "Wait," I said. "It gets better."

"Oh no. What?"

"Rocky wants to get married here."

"That's not a problem."

"Wednesday."

"Wednesday what date?"

"He wants to get hitched here, at the Hole, on Wednesday."

Kate's eyes just about popped from her head. "It's Sunday, nearly Monday. Two days from now? That Wednesday?"

"Yup."

"Oh man. We can't do it on this short notice."

"I know. I'm hoping we can con him into changing his mind. See if we can get him to delay it a couple days. At least long enough to give notice to the customers. By then this JT mess better be straightened out."

"I'll talk to him as soon as I have the deposit done. Is he upstairs?"

"I think so. Thanks."

"Hey, it's both our asses I'll be saving. Don't thank me yet."

I left Kate mumbling to herself and hustled back through the French doors that connected Eddy's place with the Hole.

Coop was still putting his laptop through its paces. Eddy was next to him poring over the printouts. Shawn Geller's information was on the top of the stack. She squinted as she looked over the face staring back at her. "I need my reading glasses. Shay, they're in the living room on the TV tray next to the recliner."

I traipsed off and in a moment returned and handed over Eddy's cheaters.

"Thank you, child. This Geller kinda looks like he's about to pee himself. Let's see." She scanned the page. "He's supposed to be staying at the Shamrock Motel in St. Paul."

"Already on it," Coop said without looking up, his fingers going a mile a minute. I was always surprised he didn't get knuckle whiplash at the rate he typed. Way better than my hunt, peck, backspace method.

"Okay," Coop said. "The motel is close to Dale and University. I can't find anything in the system about it though." He frowned at the screen. "The phone number is listed here, but there's no website."

"Well, child, have you considered the fact that there's still plenty of people out there who don't do computers?" Eddy disliked technology, but she would put her game face on and give it a whirl when the need arose. Luckily for her, the need arose very infrequently. And the cell phone battle raged on; one of these days I'd convince her they weren't spawn of the devil.

"That's true," Coop said, "but you have to admit, Eddy, once in awhile, even you've shied away from a business that doesn't have a website you can check out."

She was quiet a long moment. "You're right. It's a sad thing, but you are right."

Coop scrawled something on a piece of paper he had next to the laptop. "I've got the directions. I don't think it's the greatest of areas—Frogtown."

Frogtown was a St. Paul neighborhood that had long since seen better days. Had seen better decades, actually. It was a poor area, and at times, a rough one. It was definitely nowhere I was particularly keen on adventuring into on the hunt for a potential murderer.

Eddy said, "You let me get changed out of my fine jammies, find my Whacker, and we'll head on over there and see if Mr. Geller is receiving visitors."

"Now?" I said. "Don't you think it's a little late? It's almost ten o'clock." In my estimation, the advantage of daylight would be much better to confront a potential murderer with an affinity for pickles. Then again, JT was behind bars, right now, this very minute. Come daylight, she was still going to be there.

Eddy echoed my subconscious. "Now's the time to strike. Besides, it's Sunday night. Bad guys tend to lay low on Sunday night."

Coop said, "How do you know that?"

"Because that's always how it is. I am a woman of great knowledge." With that, she shuffled away to her bedroom.

I looked at Coop. His eyes were red-rimmed, and I'd have wondered if he were doing drugs if I didn't know him better. He was one tired Green Bean. I felt completely strung out myself and I hadn't done a single drug either. Well, if you didn't count the whiskey.

TWELVE

"I'M READY," EDDY ANNOUNCED as she scooted down the stairs a few minutes later, dressed in black from head to ankle. Bright green high-tops were tied firmly on her feet. She wielded her Whacker—a mini Twins baseball bat—tight in her right hand. After the scrapes we'd run into the last year, her Whacker mantra had shifted from "can't break up coffee house brawls without it," to "can't be part of no break-in without it."

Snap on the safety belts, kids. Here we go again.

Five minutes later, we sailed down I-94 toward St. Paul. The glow of the in-dash clock read 10:22 p.m. Traffic was light, almost nonexistent. Most people were tucked in their houses, maybe snug in bed, getting ready for the workweek to begin anew. I wished that was where JT and I were right now.

I kept a watchful eye on the speedometer. It wouldn't bode well to get pulled over while we were on the way to confront a potential killer. The steering wheel felt slippery under my palms. I wiped one damp hand, then the other, on my pants. What on earth were we thinking?

We were a motley crew of nobodies who thought they were going to figure out something the cops were probably onto long ago. This was lunacy.

No.

I shoved that thought from my head. The cops—or at least the ones who counted here—figured they had the right person locked up. The bottom line was that we had to prove they were wrong. To do that we needed to find the pickle-stuffing murderer.

Coop called out directions, and before long we'd exited on Dale and crossed University. We made a couple rights, a left, and after a number of blocks, I pulled into the rutted parking lot of a run-down, worn-out motel. The sign atop the building designated this dump as the Shamrock Motel. The name, at least, would've gone well with my dad's bar, the Leprechaun. The sign was less than half lit, the red neon illuminating only the letters S, H, O, and T.

Coop caught sight of the sign. "I hope that's not an omen."

I said, "Me too."

Eddy stuck her face between the seats. "What are you two jawing about?"

I pointed to the flickering sign.

She spelled out, "S-H-O-T." Then it sunk in. "Oh. Oh my goodness. Good thing I brought the Whacker."

I wasn't so sure how well that mini baseball bat would stop a bullet.

The single-level motel, which appeared many decades old if the crumbling walls and flaking paint were any indication, was built in an L shape, with the office/lobby at the top of the L. The front door of each unit faced the dark parking lot.

I pulled into a spot next to the office. Dim light filtered out through dirty windows.

We scrambled from the car. Eddy took two steps toward the entrance when Coop put his long arm to good use and dragged her back.

"Let go, child. What are you doing?"

Coop hissed, "Stop. Wait. What are we going to tell whoever's in there?"

Good point. Why did we always seem to be just a step behind ourselves when it came to this kind of thing? We should've been discussing how we were going to con the desk clerk into telling us what room Geller was staying in the whole way over here. We could be a bunch of idiots sometimes.

Eddy said, "We'll just go in and ask if Shawn Geller is registered here. Then we go knock on his door."

"But," Coop said, "what if whoever's on duty won't tell us?"

Eddy twitched her Whacker.

"No," I said, "we're not going to give him a crack."

"You two kids. Couple of wusses. Come *on.*" Eddy hightailed it toward the front door. Coop and I exchanged a look of terror and hustled to catch up just as she opened the door and cleared the threshold.

I caught the door just before it slammed shut and we snuck through the portal in Eddy's wake. The aroma of cigar smoke almost knocked me on my ass. The rug underfoot was filthy and had been either pea green or industrial gray at some point in its life. Now it was just skanky.

The desk was maybe six feet long, constructed of battered, dark-stained, graffiti-laden wood. Cubbyholes mounted on the wall behind the scarred workspace held old-fashioned keys for the motel doors. There were twenty numbered slots, and at least two-thirds, if not more, of the spaces had a key within.

Eddy elbowed me. "I don't see a guest register we can sneak a peek at."

Coop asked, "Where is the night clerk?"

I stepped closer to the desk. A tarnished brass call bell sat next to a cheap plastic nameplate mounted on a jaggedly cut 2x4. It read S. Neilson, Proprietor.

What the hell. I banged on the bell, the *ding* echoing throughout the space. At least a hundred seconds passed. I hit the bell again.

Coop raised his eyebrows at me, and Eddy's frown turned into an icy glare.

Another half-minute passed, and I was about to smack the thing one last time when a loud crash sounded from behind a closed door situated to the right of the key cubbies.

The angry tones of a deep voice seeped through the wood. Then said door slammed open, bashing into the side of a counter next to it. A tall, silver-haired, barrel-chested man limped into the lobby. He wore a garish orange and black Hawaiian shirt covered with white flowers and faded jeans. The stub of a smoldering cigar nestled in one corner of his mouth. The nonstop stream of foul language that erupted from the other half would've put a blush on the most sea-weary sailor.

He reminded me of a cartoon character, but for the life of me I couldn't say which one.

The man said, "What the hell do you want? I think I broke my goddamned kneecap." He planted two beefy fists on the top of the counter and glared at us, smoke curling from the end of his cigar.

Eddy, ever the brave soul, stepped up to the desk. She fanned the now-smoky air. "We're wondering if you might have a Shawn Geller registered here."

For a moment, the entire room was silent, like it was holding its breath for the beast to speak. Then the beast spoke. "What the fuck. You mean to tell me you pulled me away from my *Debbie Does Des Moines* DVD to ask if someone was staying here? You're goddamn lucky my pause button works. Get the fuck outta here."

I was ready to make tracks. Coop had already edged toward the door. Eddy, however, stood her ground. One did have to admire that about her. I would do just that, as long as we all lived to contemplate such things.

Eddy said, "I'm sorry to have interrupted your—um—television viewing, but we need to track down Mr. Geller. His mother is dying. The family sent us to see if we could find her only child."

Holy shit, good one Eddy. Where she came up with that load of malarkey I had no idea. But it was impressive nonetheless.

Proprietor Neilson's strangely familiar face had started out beet red, his forehead beaded with perspiration when he burst into the lobby. As Eddy spoke, the redness faded into a less death-impending pink. The sweat remained, soaking his hair.

"His mother's sick, huh?"

Ah ha! I wanted to raise my hand and wave. Neilson had just confirmed that he at least knew who Geller was.

"Yes," Eddy told him. "We need to speak to Mr. Geller right away. It's truly a matter of life and death."

Neilson's Einstein brows inched together like two night crawlers trying to mate as he sized us up. "Okay. But it's gonna cost ya."

I was afraid to ask what he wanted in exchange. Eddy, however, had no such compunction. "Just how much you want, big boy?"

I blinked. She was a third the size of this man, a good number of years older, and she was flirting with him.

Neilson crinkled his nose, and his upper lip twitched. "Lady, you couldn't handle me. I'll give you his room number, but like I said, it's gonna cost." He rubbed his thumb and forefinger together in the international signal for cash.

Oh God.

Eddy rummaged through the pockets of her black jeans. One by one she came up empty. Finally she turned to Coop and me. "What do you have? I forgot to bring bribery dough. Or my wallet."

Great. Just freaking great. We were about to be murdered, and Eddy's corpse would get buried wherever they stuck unidentified bodies. At least Coop and I had our driver's licenses on us and our next of kin would be notified. That got me to thinking about JT and me. If we managed to get out of this alive and JT got sprung from the slammer, we'd better talk to a lawyer about powers of attorney, living wills, and all that.

"Shay!" Coop *thwacked* my arm, knocking me out of my lawyer zone.

"What?" I rubbed my upper arm.

Eddy glared at me and said, "How much money do you have, girl?"

"I don't know." As I spoke I noticed a pile of bills lying on the counter top. And S. Neilson wanted more. Bastard. I rummaged in my pockets and pulled out two singles, a ten, and two twenties.

I looked into Neilson's greedy, beady eyes. "How much do you want?"

He smirked. "All of it."

"Oh, come on. That's all the money I have until I work again."

"Not my problem, sweet cheeks." He held his grubby paw out, and I slapped the money into it. "You need to make some extra dough," he said, "you just come see Uncle Steve. I'll hook you up with some nice paying customers."

Understanding dawned and I was instantly nauseous. "That's disgusting."

"Just sayin'." Neilson leered at me as he grabbed the greenbacks. "Geller's in thirteen. Guess it's not a lucky number for him, is it?" He guffawed at his own joke, and it finally occurred to me who he reminded me of. Barney. Barney Rubble, Fred's best friend in *The Flintstones*. But I didn't think I'd call Neilson anything close to a member of the modern stone-age family. He was stuck at cave man.

"It's been a pleasure. Don't let the door smack you in the ass," Neilson cheerily called to our rapidly retreating backsides.

We gathered in front of my truck. My heart was thumping madly in my chest. I glanced down the length of the building, but it was too dark to make out the room numbers.

"Okay," I said. "Here's what we're going to do." *Yes, Shay? What exactly are we going to do?* I racked my brain. It had frozen up, like the inside of a too-small air conditioner on a hotter than the devil's own home day.

After a couple of seconds, Eddy said, "Well?"

The clock ticked on. I tried. I really did.

Coop said, "Shay?"

Ack. What the hell. "We find room thirteen and knock on the door."

"Sounds good to me." Eddy was off again. Coop and I hurried to catch up.

The farther away we got from what little light the dirty office windows cast outside, the darker it got. Two unlit lampposts stood at cockeyed angles in the middle of the mostly gravel lot, like maybe someone's bumper had gotten a little too close. Repeatedly.

I counted the shadowy hulks of parked cars as we trooped along the sidewalk. Five vehicles, make that six with ours, occupied the lot. Most of the rides looked old.

A large window was situated to one side of the door to each room. All the windows we passed were covered by heavy drapes. In a few of the rooms, light bled around the gaps where the cloth didn't fully cover the glass. The muffled sounds of television sets at varying volumes trickled out of gaps in warped doors. Some of the sounds that filtered through the cracks were of the X-rated kind. Was this a short-stay motel—a wham-bam-thank-you-ma'am kind of place—on top of being just plain trashy? Did Minnesota motels even charge by the hour?

Eddy stopped in front of the door marked 13. The window was blacked out, but a thin line of light snuck through at the top. She raised her fist. I caught it just as it was descending toward the pitted wood surface.

She yanked her hand from mine and whispered, "What now, for goodness sake?"

"Plan," I whispered hoarsely. "We need a damn plan. We can't just go pound on his door. What was I thinking?" Someone, please tell me why we never thought anything through. Carefully. "We can't just trounce in there and ask him if he offed Krasski. He'll kill us."

Coop murmured, "Maybe we should tackle him when he opens the door. Ask questions later." It was hard getting used to such a change from my peaceful protester pal.

Eddy waved her Whacker. "Let me at him—"

In a blink, two things happened almost simultaneously. The first was that the end of the Whacker met the surface of the door with a loud bang. The second was that the door was abruptly yanked open.

THIRTEEN

BRIGHT LIGHT FROM INSIDE the room temporarily blinded me. I blinked hard. A man stood in silhouette, filling the doorway. A wife beater covered his heavyset, hairy chest, and baggy blue-and-white-striped boxers covered his lower half. Thin chicken legs poked out below the boxers, and no-longer-white socks drooped around his ankles. Wisps of what hair he had left on the top of his head floated every which way above his pasty pate. His eyes flashed.

He roared, "Whaddya want?"

Eddy's arm was still outstretched, the Whacker wobbling in her fist.

His eyes dropped to the mini bat. "What the—" He grabbed for it, and before I knew what happened, he and Eddy were playing tug of war.

Eddy kicked at him.

He sidestepped, then gave the Whacker a great yank.

The force pulled Eddy off her feet and launched her in the air. She smashed into the man's flab with a soft splat. That was enough, combined with his own backward momentum, for him to lose his footing. He crashed to the ground, flat on his back. The back of his head hit the carpet-covered cement floor with a resounding thud. Eddy landed square on top of him, knocking the breath from his lungs in an audible woosh.

For a brief moment, Coop and I stood transfixed. Eddy squeaked. She flailed atop the downed man, her Whacker accidentally bonking him hard on the forehead.

Coop and I each grabbed one of Eddy's arms and hauled her to her feet. Somehow, she'd managed to hang onto the Whacker through the entire incident. In the background, I heard someone repeating over and over, "Oh shit, oh shit, oh shit."

"Shut up, Nicholas," Eddy hissed and jerked her arms out of our grasp. "Help me get him all the way inside. You don't think I killed him, do you?"

My heart hammered in my ears. I couldn't breathe. Then, all of a sudden, my brain kicked back in. The scene became crystal clear.

"Come on, Coop." I grunted as I plucked up one of the man's limp arms. Coop snatched the other, and we dragged him all the way into the room, his heels bouncing across the doorjamb.

Eddy stepped inside and shut the door. "Didn't see no neighbors sticking their heads outside, so hopefully nobody saw me and the goon going at it." Eddy stepped closer and bent over the downed man. "Is he dead? I really didn't mean to kill him."

Coop said, "You have a mirror? If you hold it under his nose and it fogs up, he's breathing."

"Do I have a mirror? Nicholas, do you see my handbag with me?"

"Well, no, but—"

The guy moaned.

Both Coop and Eddy scrambled backward.

We needed to ask him questions. Somehow I didn't think he'd play nice and cough up the answers without a little persuasion. I glanced around. It was evident he'd been living in here for a while. A pile of dirty clothes filled one corner, personal effects were scattered across a rickety table, and beer cans and pizza boxes were tossed in another corner.

The motel room smelled like a bar. Spilled booze, body odor, and cigarette smoke mixed with the lingering tang of old pizza. Reminded me of the inside of my father's bar, but without that comforting homey feeling.

Rumpled bedding was strewn across the top of the mattress. More out of instinct than intent, I formulated a plan. We were going to get some answers from El Stinko if I had to take him apart piece by piece to do it. Time was of the essence.

"Help me. Hurry." I yanked the top sheet off the bed and attempted to tear it.

Both Coop and Eddy scrambled over the prone figure, who was starting to twitch.

Between Eddy's pocketknife and our tugging, we managed to rip the sheet into narrow strips.

"Roll him over," I barked.

Coop grabbed one of the man's arms and pulled. "Crap. He weighs a ton."

Eddy knelt down and started pushing while Coop yanked. If I wasn't on the edge of complete hysteria, I would've laughed and taken a picture of this ridiculousness for posterity. However, a photo like that would've helped us score prison sentences of our own. Why did bad guys take pictures and videos of their crimes, anyway? Dumbasses. Nothing like helping the cops make their case against you.

I shook off my rambling thoughts and rapidly gathered up the strips of cloth.

Eddy stood and dramatically dusted her hands off. "My work here is done. Tie this man up."

I handed Coop a piece of the sheet. He took it and muttered, "I can't believe we're doing this."

"Could be worse. He could be flatlined." I wrapped a strip around his wrists and tied it tight as Coop bound his ankles. "Look at it this way. We've either got a murderer tied up, or we've just made a really big mistake."

"If that's the case," Eddy said, "Better blindfold him so he can't recognize us. It was pretty dark in the doorway. I doubt he got much of a look at us before I knocked his sorry keister out."

In record time we had the man hog-tied and blindfolded. Coop and I wrestled him into a sitting position. Then we propped him up against the edge of the bed. His moaning was getting louder. We were going to have to literally stuff a sock in it if he didn't quiet down.

Eddy pulled up the only chair in the room, a spindly-legged, creaky affair, and settled next to our now-secure suspect. "Too bad I don't have smelling salts." She poked one of his thin, pale legs with her foot. "Wake up."

He grumbled something, then fell back to moaning.

I stood and headed for the bathroom. As soon as I walked in, I was completely ooged out. The little room was filthy. The sink was coated with toothpaste spit and whisker shavings. The toilet seat was up, and it was obvious the ding-dong out there either had a crooked ding-a-ling or didn't know how to aim. Stashed on the tile floor between the sink and the tub was a long-necked bottle of Jack Daniels. That should do the trick. I grabbed it and scooted back out to the prisoner.

170

"This might help." I unscrewed the cap and waved the bottle under his schnoz.

The pungent aroma hit his nostrils. They twitched. He inhaled and then snorted. Raised his head. I let him take one more sniff of the alcohol, then recapped it.

Eddy elbowed me. "Give it here."

I handed it over.

"Whaaa 'appened?" His speech was slurred. From the sound of it, he'd already been hitting the bottle hard.

Then a thought occurred me. What if he'd sustained a concussion from the fall? Concussions were a big problem in sports nowadays. If a player had been knocked out, they often appeared drunk when they came to. If this dude wasn't dead, which he obviously wasn't, but had his bell rung a little too hard, we could be in serious trouble. Good thing Eddy told us to blindfold him.

"Shawn Geller?" I asked. My hands trembled either in terror or from the adrenaline hit.

"Whaaa …"

Oh boy.

Eddy uncapped the booze and gave him another snootful.

"Who the hell are you?" This time he managed to cough up an entire sentence.

I repeated, "Are you Shawn Geller?" Best to know for absolutely sure if the person we were about to torture was actually the right bad boy.

"Yeah. Who the fuck *are* you? Old biddy from hell." At least his memory was working to some degree.

"No," I said. "*She's* the little old biddy from hell. *I'm* your worst nightmare."

Coop stood with his arms crossed, looking at me as if I'd lost my mind.

"Hey," I whispered to Coop. "It sounded good."

He just shook his head.

I refocused and nudged the dude's calf with my toes. "Focus. Are you Shawn Geller or not?"

"Yes, for Chrissake. What the fuck you want?"

There was something to this power game thing. I felt a rush go through me at the realization that, at least to start with, our man was cooperating. Maybe this was why some cops fell for the seduction of power that a badge can provide. "Where were you yesterday about five?"

"I was right here, in this stinking hole."

"Can you prove it?"

"Can I prove it? Who the hell *are* you people? You're not the fucking cops."

"No." I bent in close to his ear. "You'll only wish we were. Did you kill Russell Krasski?" That sounded pretty good, if I did say so myself.

"What? Kill Krasski? What are you talking about? He's not dead. You're a crazy fucking broad."

Eddy said, "Were you at the Renaissance Festival yesterday evening?"

"No, I said." Exasperation tinted his words. "I was right here."

Coop said, "Prove it."

Geller was silent long enough that I wondered if he needed another sniff of the hard stuff.

Eddy, however, had plans of her own. She raised her Whacker and gave Geller a smart rap on the forehead.

"OW!"

"You," Eddy said, "were asked a question. Can you prove you were here or not?"

"I ordered in pizza about seven. Jesus."

Eddy whacked him again.

"OWW! What the fuck was that for?"

"Stop taking the Lord's name in vain, young man."

I said, "If you ordered pizza about seven, that would still give you enough time to do Krasski and get back here. You could've even called the order in from your car."

I pictured JT in that conference room just before Detective Roberts manhandled her away, yelling at me to tell Tyrell about Geller and Handy Randy. If she thought one of them might have killed Krasski, there had to be a reason. We just needed to find out what that reason was.

"Hey," I poked Geller in the shoulder. He jerked back in reaction to the unexpected prod. "What was your relationship with Krasski?"

"What is this? I didn't have a fucking relationship with him. Are you calling me a fag?"

Eddy popped him in the noggin again.

"OW!"

She said, "Don't be calling anyone 'fag.' That's hurtful. Got it?" She whapped him another one.

"Ouch! Yeah. Yeah. Crap. Stop with the forehead thing already. I got a bad enough headache."

I almost felt sorry for him.

Eddy told him, "You're the one who tried to steal my Whacker."

"Steal your what? You tried to hit me with that little fucking bat."

"I did not. You startled me when you opened the door so fast—"

"Stop!" I tried hard to keep my voice low. "Let's get back on track. Geller, did you have a problem with Russell Krasski?"

"Krasski? He got off while the rest of us went down for his shit. But no. I don't hold that against him. Why would I? Just cause I spent years in the can while he was out? Free to do whatever the hell he wanted?"

He was obviously lucid enough to effect sarcasm. There it was: motive.

Then Geller asked, "Is he really dead?" The pure delight in his voice twisted my insides.

I said, "Yes."

He was either a good liar or was actually telling the truth. But the bad guys always lied. How were you supposed to tell? Maybe police work wasn't for me after all.

Geller said, "If that bitch cop hadn't lost her mind and beat the shit out of him, I mighta walked. Instead, after she fucked everything up, they came after all the rest of us. We were just doing a job—"

At the mention of JT, my brain momentarily seized. The red haze flared. The desire to sock Geller in the nose made my hands tremble. Before I had a chance to allow the Protector free rein, Eddy took care of it for me.

She struck like a snake, hard and fast. Really gave Geller a crack. He yelped.

She said in a deadly voice, one I hated to have directed at me, "You leave 'that cop' out of this. Selling one human being to another isn't a job." *Wham.* "Doing what you did to those innocent kids." *Bam.* "You are the lowest of low. You should be locked up forever. Or maybe dead would be better." *Whack.*

A huge part of me was gleefully cheering Eddy on. However, I grabbed Eddy's hand before she could bash him again.

"Listen. Please." Geller's tone had changed from aggression to full-fledged whine. "Please. Don't hit me anymore. I know what we did was wrong. I said I was sorry. I did my goddamned time. What more do you want?"

Crack! "I told you not to take the Lord's name in vain."

Geller cringed, leaning as far back as he could, which wasn't too far at all. His head bumped the mattress.

Pathetic, Geller was. Killer of Russell Krasski? No. My gut told me he didn't cram a pickle down Krasski's throat or shoot him in the head. Damn. It would have been so much easier if it had been him. But maybe there was one more thing we could wring out of the perv. I asked him, "Who's Handy Randy?"

Geller slowly rocked his head back and forth, as if hoping the action would realign the sprockets so he could follow the change in conversation. "Handy Randy? Big Mike."

"Big Mike?" I asked.

"Mike Handler. Why?" Geller's voice was filled with a cross between suspicion and curiosity.

I looked at Coop. His arms were crossed, his expression grim. He nodded. At least now we had someone else to check out.

I straightened up with a groan. "Come on. Let's get the hell out of this pit."

"Wait. What about me? You can't fucking leave me tied up like this. I can't see a guh—uh—damned thing." Geller said, his voice a number of octaves higher and tinged with panic.

Coop said, "The hell we can't. You just relax and work on those knots. You'll probably get them undone soon." He looked around the filthy room. "Unless the rats get to you first. But don't worry, you won't see it coming."

Holy shit. Coop had a gentle soul. But when someone got to him—*really* got to him—he was becoming much better about expressing it.

We filed outside, and I gently pulled the door to room 13 shut. S. Neilson was right: thirteen was certainly not Geller's lucky number.

I had to be in a lucid dream. We'd just tied up someone and Eddy'd used his head for batting practice. Amazingly, I didn't feel one bit bad about it. A certain degree of sadness crept under my skin. I was a good person. So why didn't I care that we'd just left another human being bound and blindfolded? Geller was no better than Krasski. Considering what he'd done, he deserved whatever came his way.

The darkness seemed even more absolute as we rapidly retraced our steps to the truck. The office was completely blacked out. "Uncle Steve" was probably enjoying his DVD. I shuddered at the thought.

We hopped into the pickup in record time. I pulled out of the parking lot and pointed the nose of the truck toward home.

Coop finally broke the silence. "Do you think he'll call the cops on us?"

"So what if he does," Eddy said from the back seat. "He was blindfolded. The little shit."

I signaled and took the ramp onto I-94 west. "Uncle Steve in the office could turn us in."

"What about people in the other rooms?" Coop asked. "They had to have heard something."

"No," Eddy said. "We paid the creepy office guy off. I'm sure worse have come in before us. I don't think the Shamrock Motel houses much in the way of what one might call genteel folk. Probably there's always squawking and carrying on. Bet no one even pays attention anymore."

The rest of the ride home was quiet, each of us lost in our own thoughts. Now that the excitement was over, I felt bone weary. It was like someone stuck a big straw in the top of my head and sucked the get up and go right out of me. My legs were jelly. The old spine kind of felt that way too.

I dropped Eddy off, and we agreed to meet back up in the morning.

Coop offered to come home with me and spend the night in the spare bedroom. In my little apartment above the Rabbit Hole, I'd never had a place to stash sleepover guests unless they didn't mind bunking with me or sacking out on my sad excuse for a couch. Having an extra bedroom was one benefit of living with JT. Well, there were a lot of benefits, actually.

Besides, it'd be easier to jump right back in the hunt in the morning if Coop were right there with me instead of at his apartment. Yeah, that was it. My desire for company had absolutely nothing to do with the fact I was totally freaked out.

Rationalization was sometimes a very important coping mechanism.

By the time I pulled into the garage and clomped inside, leaving Coop having a smoke on the porch, it was almost midnight. Without the dogs rattling around or JT's presence filling the space, the silence of the house was nearly unbearable. I was pathetically glad Coop was staying.

While Coop hit the bathroom, I trudged upstairs to a room and a bed that were way too big for one. I shed my clothes in a pile on the floor and dropped onto the mattress. Luckily, instead of spending countless hours praying for slumber and chasing racing thoughts around and around my mind, sleep claimed me almost before my eyes were closed.

FOURTEEN

I WAS RUNNING THROUGH the brain of a madman. Somewhere along the line, the brain had morphed into one of those funhouses that were built in the back end of a rusty semitrailer found on carnival midways. Lights from nowhere and everywhere flashed, hurting my eyes. Curved mirrors distorted my reflection. Swinging green-and-white-striped punching bags got in the way of my quest to find the exit. A bridge with spinning tubes instead of planks impeded my progress. Try as I might, I couldn't get past its midpoint. The cylinders spun underfoot every time I tried to take a step forward. JT was at the far end of the bridge, her arm outstretched, desperately reaching for me. I leaned as far as I could, tried to grab her hand. I slipped, fell forward, watched transfixed as the rolling pipes rushed up.

I jerked awake with a gasp and groped blindly for JT's solid, reassuring presence. When my hand found nothing but tangled, cold sheets, memory returned with the impact of one of those rolling pipes from my nightmare. I managed to prop myself up on my elbows, sucking air, heart pounding. I tried a couple deep breaths, hoping to slow my racing heart.

Spatial awareness kicked in. The bedroom was still dark. Not a drop of light leaked around the edges of the curtains. I glanced at the alarm clock on my nightstand. 6:23 a.m. Whoa. Welcome to Monday morning.

I dropped back to the mattress, pulled the blanket tight around my chin and replayed the previous two days on my mind's movie screen in about twenty seconds.

That little show took care of any thought of additional zzz's I may have hoped for. With a resigned sigh, I unwound myself from the bedding and trudged into the bathroom. I flicked the light on, squinting at the harsh glare. The image that looked back at me in the mirror was decidedly scary. Dark smudges made my eyes look sunken and the pinched look on my face reminded me of a particularly dour teacher I had in junior high. My mostly black hair was longer than I'd worn it in awhile, and it looked a little like an upside-down rag mop.

I hit the shower and dressed. Afterward, I slowly opened the door so it wouldn't squeak and stuck my nose out in the hallway for a look-see. The door to the spare bedroom was still closed. I quietly headed downstairs.

As I stood at the kitchen counter and chewed on a piece of toast smeared with peanut butter, strawberry jam, and Nutella, I thought about JT's gun. She kept everything locked in a small gun safe in the closet in her office. The pull of taking a peek at her weapons stash was irresistible.

While I'd seen her take one weapon or another out of the safe numerous times, I'd never considered going into the thing. Guns didn't particularly freak me out, but I certainly wasn't an aficionado, either.

What was it Tyrell had called the gun? A Smith & Wesson something or other.

I stuffed the last bite in my mouth and washed it down with a swallow of milk. I rinsed the glass in a show of my newfound neatness and headed for JT's office.

I paused at the doorway to flip on the light. JT's office, like mine upstairs, was a converted bedroom. She had the requisite desk; three well-used, uglier than sin, olive filing cabinets; a love seat; and a wide, cushy recliner stowed in the room. I'd fallen asleep in that recliner on a number of occasions as she'd worked on cop stuff late into the night. The walls were light blue, a color I thought fit her cool-till-you-got-to-know-her demeanor. Awards and certificates for various cop-related activities hung above both the couch and chair.

The desk was neat as a pin, following my girl's personality. She was a neatnik, which I was sure was going to be the cause of many a head butt when I first moved in. Instead, my messy influence helped her to chill while her careful attention to detail helped me to organize my own stuff into something more workable. It was a win-win. Who knew?

JT's gun locker was in the corner of the closet. I steeled my resolve. This was for JT's own good. My feet made no noise on the carpet as I strolled over to the closet door. I was a heel for sticking my nose into my lover's stuff. However, her freedom outweighed the dreaded snoop factor.

The closet folded open with a clunk. I pushed the hanging police duds out of the way and crouched down to the gun locker hidden in the shadows at the back of the space. The heavy hunk of metal was dull black and knee high, with a digital number pad instead of an old-fashioned dial. I tapped my fingers impatiently on my knee, trying to guess what code she would've used as a combination.

It was highly unlikely she'd have employed the date we called our anniversary, which, I realized, was coming up quickly. I filed that tidbit in the back of my mind for future action and concentrated on the present. Her birthday? I keyed it in, both with the four-digit year and then tried the two-digit, just in case. The buttons beeped as I pushed them, but neither set of digits did a thing except make a red LED glow.

As I poked the buttons in another possible combination, I hoped to hell the safe wasn't rigged to trigger an alarm somewhere when wrong codes kept being entered.

No luck—the LED remained red.

I tried JT's house number, her mom's birthday, and then the date of her graduation from the police academy. Zip.

My knees were starting to ache, so I stiffly stood up and limped around the office so the blood would resume flowing through my legs. As I passed JT's desk, I saw she'd left the 8.5x11 planner and address book she usually carried with her laying next to the keyboard. Had she been un-JT-like and maybe jotted the code somewhere within it? I doubted it, but since I wasn't getting anywhere as it was, I had nothing to lose in looking.

The worn red leather cover of the address book felt soft against my fingers. The planner was refillable. Maybe that's what I could score JT for an anniversary present. On second thought, maybe that wasn't quite an appropriate first-anniversary gift.

In typical JT fashion, the inside of the front cover listed out her complete contact information just in case she lost it. However, JT was too careful with her stuff to let that happen. I figured way back in school, when the teacher would hand out fill-in-the-blank worksheets, she'd make sure to complete each and every open slot. She was a through and through t-crosser and an i-dotter.

JT's neat printing covered page after page, last name, comma, first name. She knew way more people than I realized. Birthdates and anniversaries were written in for friends and relatives. I carried the book over to the closet and tried various numbers I ran across. No go. I flipped through the book again. In the middle of her M's there was a first name listed, but no last name, which was odd. Every other entry included both.

This one simply read Maria. A circled star asterisked the name. I flipped through the pages again and there were no other similar entries.

I knew a couple of Marias from years back, but, to my knowledge, neither JT nor I currently associated with anyone by that name.

Frustration was playing with my temper. I stuck my bottom lip out and blew a breath that lifted the hair at my forehead. I pushed myself to my feet and backed up until I felt the edge of JT's chair hit my legs. Then I plopped unceremoniously into the seat, address book still in hand. The edge of the planner hit my leg, and some of the sheets of paper that had been tucked in the back spilled out.

I gathered the sheets and tapped them on my thigh to straighten them. An envelope slipped out and fell between my legs to the floor. JT's name was on the front, addressed to the precinct she worked out of. I picked up the envelope and took a closer look. The return address, printed in block letters, listed a Maria Delgado at an address in Ramsey, which was about thirty miles north of Minneapolis. I held the envelope closer. The post office date stamp was less than a week ago. Interesting.

With devil-may-care-nonchalance, better known as nosiness, I slid the letter out of the envelope. It was a short typewritten note on a white piece of paper. I unfolded the sheet, read the first two lines, and just about dropped it.

Hola JT,

I miss you.

Holy shit. My eyes scanned the rest of the letter as my brain churned to make sense of this.

Hola JT,

I miss you.

I want to see you again soon. I had so much fun last night at The Depot. I can't wait to do it again. And again. I'm sorry I got you so wet. Well, no, not really. You have to remember your swimsuit next time.

Te quiero, Maria

Te quiero? That was something about love: Love, Maria.

Love, Maria?

I blinked. Blinked again, hard. Squinted as I reread the note.

I stuffed it back in the envelope and peered again at the date stamp. Last Tuesday.

Air whistled from my lungs in one big gust. I slouched against the backrest, my mind churning like a hurricane-buffeted ocean.

Think, Shay.

Monday night. JT had called to say she was going to be stuck on an overnight detail. When did I see her the next day? I'd worked the Hole early that morning. JT had wandered in sometime in the early afternoon. That was that. I'd never had call to question her odd hours, her occasional nights away from home.

Oh my God.

A boulder settled in the bottom of my stomach. Then the Protector stirred, winding its way insidiously up through my chest, squeezing the air from my lungs.

Maybe it was a good thing JT was safely behind bars. If she was cheating on me, I'd kill her. And whoever she was doing the horizontal mambo with.

A still-rational piece of my psyche ordered, *Chill out, Shay. You're jumping the gun. Bad idea.*

I firmly told that voice to shut the hell up. I was running now on about three-quarters anger that was rapidly developing into full-fledged fury. After all my worrying, after all the work Coop, Eddy, and I had done to try and find the person who'd killed Krasski in order to free JT, I find this? Well hell, maybe JT did do Krasski after all. The bastard deserved to be dead, preferably not by JT's hand, but that was no longer the point. If she was dancing the tango with this Maria floozy, she could rot in that cell for a good long time.

I wrapped my self-righteous outrage around me like a down jacket on an ice-cold winter day.

My original task was forgotten. The need to find out who this mysterious Maria was—and getting the truth out of her—burned under my skin, the flames ready to explode from within. If I had to wring the woman's neck to get a full and complete confession, all the better.

I slapped the address book on the desk and stalked out of the room, the envelope in my fist.

Usually when I was in the midst of the Tenacious Protector's grip, the situation involved somebody else. Someone I loved or cared deeply about was being threatened. This time, the threat directly involved me and JT and our future. If we had a future. The power of the Protector steamed through me in a rush, and I gasped. I rarely let anyone—especially a woman—get this close to me, for damn good reasons. I was a fool.

I blindly grabbed a zip-up sweat jacket off the back of a dining room chair and let myself out. Coop would be fine till I came back. In fact, he'd probably still be sleeping.

Unless I didn't return at all because I'd been arrested for murder. Maybe JT and I could share that jail cell after all.

An involuntary choking sound burst from my mouth as I backed out of the garage.

I'd driven down the alley, made a couple turns, and was on Franklin headed toward Hennepin and the freeway when I realized I had absolutely no idea where I was going. I pulled to the curb in front of a shop called Patina that was next to my favorite ice cream joint of all time, Sebastian Joe's. If I'd been in a better mood, it would've been hard to resist the siren call of ice cream, even at this early hour. What time was it anyway? I glanced at the in-dash clock. Still a bit before eight. Served the bitch right that I make an early stop at her place. Unless she was already off to work, doing whatever it was that home-wreckers did to make money.

To hell with it. I'd take my chances and see if the bimbo was home. I wedged my iPhone out of my pocket and tapped the address in. A moment later, a map with alternate routes popped up on the screen. A-fricking-mazing. In thirty-seven minutes and thirty-two miles, with a little luck, I'd have my answers. Whether I liked them or not.

The trip north past the wilds of Brooklyn Center, Brooklyn Park, and up into Coon Rapids and Anoka went relatively quickly. Luckily all the traffic was headed for the city, so I had little to deal with in the way of jam-ups and slow-downs. I passed a huge HOM furniture building when I merged onto Highway 10 westbound.

Fifteen minutes later I passed a sign on the side of the road telling me I'd now entered the city of Ramsey. I turned off on a ridiculously named road called Sunfish Lake Boulevard and wound my way past streets that sounded as if they belonged in a geology class, not a map. I was light-years removed from the city. All the space, huge houses, gigantic yards, and even cornfields were giving me the heebie-jeebies. I could never live out here, in the middle of nowhere, practically away from life itself.

I slowed and stopped at the curb in front of a mini castle. The number on the siding matched the number on the envelope. All the houses on the block were McMansions. Did people really live in these things? How on earth could they afford it?

I smoothed the now wrinkled piece of incriminating evidence on my leg as I surveyed the area. There wasn't a tinker's chance in hell I'd be able to put it back in JT's address book without her knowing something very wrong had happened to it. Oh well.

It was now or never. This was it. I repeated Eddy's mantra: action was always better than contemplation. It was never truer than at this moment. I got out of the truck and hoofed it up to the front door before common sense and fear of the truth stopped me cold.

A sturdy, dark-wood front door loomed intimidatingly over a raised stoop. I lifted a hand to pound on the door when I spied a door-bell off to one side, imbedded in the mouth of a three-inch stone dragon mounted on the edge of the door casing. I did a double take. If I hadn't been in the frame of mind that included murderous intent, I would've taken a moment to admire it.

My finger made quick work of the unique doorbell. The re-sounding clang chimed deeply in numerous tones, and faded away. I was about to attack the bell again when the door swung open.

"Can I help you?"

Holy crap on a cracker.

A woman, whose friendly smile lit up an open, intelligent face, stood before me. She held a squirming, towheaded toddler propped on her hip. A glob of something whose origin I had no desire to find out was slowly dripping down the front of the woman's Hello Kitty nightshirt. Her bottom half was clad in matching sleep pants, and her feet were bare. If JT was planning on trading me—trading us—in for *this,* I simply had no comeback. If this poor woman was Maria, I was going to pass out cold right here on the doorstep.

I closed my mouth so hard my teeth clacked.

Home-Wrecker frowned at me in concern. "Are you okay?" she asked. Behind her I heard the unmistakable chatter of more than one child.

"I, uh..."

She shifted from concern to wariness. "Are you all right?"

Speak, Shay. Jeez.

I swallowed. Swallowed again. "Is—are you Maria?"

Home-Wrecker's eyes shifted from wary to guarded in an instant. "No, I'm not Maria."

Oh Jesus. What was I doing? "Does"—I looked down at the envelope still clutched between my fingers—"Maria Delgado live here?"

A black-haired girl of maybe ten or twelve, who'd apparently been standing behind Maybe-Not-A-Home-Wrecker, peered shyly at me around the obviously confused woman's shoulder.

What was the saying? In for a penny, in for a pound. Of course, now it'd be "in for a dollar, in for a Euro," or something like that. I tried valiantly to vocalize one more time. "Do you know JT Bordeaux?"

At the mention of JT's name, the girl gasped out "JT!" and slid past the woman and darted out the door. I half-spun as she passed by and watched her run across the grass toward my truck. "What—"

"Maria!" the woman yelled. She brushed roughly by me to stand on the edge of the concrete walkway, still holding the toddler. "JT's not here, honey," she called.

Well, knock me over with a cream puff. Preferably one right to the kisser. I was an idiot.

JT's Maria was a little girl.

FIFTEEN

TEN MINUTES LATER, I was seated in Michelle Osterhus's toy-strewn, chaotic, cheerful living room. Three kids, all knee-high, played in the corner with oversized Lincoln Logs, periodically clobbering each other with the pieces.

Michelle sent Maria to her room with a treat and had given me a glass of milk and a handful of Oreos, an instant remedy in every mother's repertoire. She finished feeding Gomer, which was the really, *really* unfortunate name of the kid who'd been on her hip when she answered the door.

She set him on the floor and gave his diaper-covered butt an affectionate pat. He scuttled, crablike, over to play with the other three kids.

I'd already downed three Oreos and now sipped at the cold milk, slowly feeling my rational brain kick back in as I watched this scene of domesticity.

Michelle rubbed at the smear on the front of her pajama top with a damp cloth. "Mashed banana and oatmeal," she explained as she scrubbed. After a moment she gave up and threw the rag on a side table with a resigned sigh. "You want kids," she said, "you might as well learn to live in harmony with a mess. So tell me, why are you looking for Maria?"

I sunk deeper in the chair. I was embarrassed and, yes, ashamed. Yeah. I was terribly ashamed of myself for jumping to conclusions. This wasn't going to be an easy conversation.

"I'm—well, actually—" I looked at her, my mouth open again without any sound coming out. Words stuck like glue in the back of my throat. I cleared it and tried again. "I … I'm with JT."

A facial chorus played out before my eyes. Blankness melted into puzzlement, which morphed into understanding. Michelle said, "Are you Shay?"

Holy shit. "How do you know my name?"

"Hasn't JT mentioned either Maria or me to you?"

"This is all I know." I handed her the crumpled envelope.

Michelle took it and turned it over in her hands. She slid out the note and read it, then carefully folded it and tucked away. "I can see why you might have questions." Finally Michelle looked up and met my eyes. "I helped Maria write this." Any trace of humor had faded and was replaced with concerned empathy. "This is going to call for more Oreos."

Uh oh.

Michelle disappeared into the kitchen and reappeared with the entire container of Oreos and more milk for the both of us. As the kids played (blessedly quietly) with their Lincoln Logs, Michelle told me a story.

She asked, "Are you familiar with Russell Krasski?" Sharp eyes watched my face, gauging my reaction.

Cripes. Did everyone but me know the man? "As of Saturday, yes."

"So you know about his and JT's background—about what happened?"

"I do now. It's been quite a learning curve I've navigated in the last couple days."

Michelle looked sympathetically at me as she took an Oreo. "Help yourself. That's quite a bit to take in on short notice. You ready for more?"

I followed her advice and helped myself. "Bring it on." I nibbled at the top of the cookie and wished life was as simple as licking the white crème insides out and dunking the rest of the cookie in my glass of milk.

"Okay." Michelle chewed thoughtfully. "I'm not sure where to start. The night that the cops arrested Russell Krasski, Krasski and his cohorts were in the midst of moving the kids somewhere. They'd gotten a delivery of kidnapped children from a supplier"— she waved half a cookie at me—"can you believe they call those abominations suppliers? Anyway, these kids were in the house where the bust went down." Michelle swallowed, took a shot of milk, and grabbed another cookie. "All the attention was on poor JT and the failure of the Minneapolis Police Department in the takedown of that ring. The real story, the reason for the arrests, was the kids."

It was obvious Michelle loved children. The affection in her voice affirmed that truth.

She continued, "That night, after JT went to town on Krasski, before she was put on leave, she managed to get the kids who'd been in the house into protective custody. We—my husband and I—have three of our own," she nodded to the crew playing in the corner. "We foster kids as well. Gomer, as well as Maria, are staying with us until someone adopts Gomer and one of Maria's family members can come and escort her back to Mexico."

I helped myself to another Oreo. "It's been almost two years since this happened. You've had Maria that long?"

"No. The system is slow and sometimes doesn't move forward at all. Maria came to stay with us after a string of foster homes didn't work out for her for one reason or another. She's a bit of a handful. But she's going to be okay.

"Anyway, from the start, Maria got under JT's skin. JT kept an eye on her through every home Maria's been to. After the last go-round, JT recommended us. Maria's been here ever since."

"Since when?"

"The last year or so. JT's not been able to get up here too often, but she emails with Maria and still manages to visit maybe once a month. Sometimes she'll take Maria on an outing, on some exciting overnight adventures."

Things were becoming clearer. "Like the one last week Monday?"

"Exactly. Maria was so excited to go to The Depot in Minneapolis. She loves trains, planes, semis—anything big that moves."

That, as they say, explained that. I was a complete and total ass. There goes Shay again, jumping the gun, diving in without thinking, without knowing the entire story.

Michelle continued, "In fact, I believe JT's worked on each child's case, helping locate relatives. Maria is the last one of the bunch. Finding her family has been next to impossible, but JT pulled off another miracle, and we're this close"—Michelle held up two fingers a hair apart—"to sending Maria home."

Hesitation shadowed her voice.

"But?" I prompted.

"JT managed to get a hold of an uncle—Hector Delgado, who actually drove up here from Mexico. He arrived last Thursday. The social worker who's assigned to Maria's case brought him up to see her

Thursday night." Michelle smiled in memory. "You should've seen Maria's face light up when she saw Hector. I didn't think we were going to be able to pry her away from him. She wanted to go home with him right then and there. Hector had to start the paperwork process Friday and came back here for a few hours after a meeting at Child Protective Services. He's a really nice guy, if a little hard to understand. But we've been boning up on our Spanish since Maria's been with us."

"So Maria will be going home soon, then."

"Once the paperwork is all filed and whatever else has to happen, yes. But," Michelle looked around, then leaned toward me and whispered, "Hector—he was supposed to come and take Maria out Saturday night. But he never showed up. Then he was going to come to church with us Sunday and spend the day here. And…"

"He never showed up for that either," I finished.

"Nope." Michelle gazed at the kids, two of whom were playing around the third, who'd fallen asleep with a log clutched tight in his chubby fist. "I could see he adores that girl. I don't get why he didn't come back. Poor Maria's heartbroken."

I could just imagine. Maria must've been ecstatic to see a member of her family, and then for him not to come when he said he would had to have been unbelievably hard.

A number of reasons why Hector didn't show popped into my mind. Illegal entry into the States made the top of my short list. If Immigration and Customs Enforcement nabbed Hector and was holding him, it might be a good long time before they released him. And then it would most likely be on Mexican soil. Without Maria.

The Protector unfurled its tail again and stretched, extending claws and kneading my innards. That poor little girl. To have already gone through so much only to be left high and dry again?

No.

I asked, "Did you try to call Hector?"

"I did. He left two numbers, one for the Starlite Motel in Blaine, or was it Spring Lake Park? Or Vadnais Heights maybe? Room two two four, I think he said. I can't remember for sure. He also left one for a cell phone. I tried both numbers, left messages. He still hasn't returned my calls."

"If you can give me the contact numbers he gave you, I have a friend who's pretty good at tracking down that kind of stuff."

"That would be great." Michelle hurried off to jot down the information. I took the opportunity to sneak another Oreo.

She returned after a couple of minutes with two phone numbers scrawled on a blue Post-It. "Here you go. I hope you have better luck than I did. My husband's gone all weekend attending a sci-fi convention in Chicago, so I haven't been able to get out with the troops in tow or I'd have checked on him myself."

"I totally understand." I stood up, and so did Michelle. "Thank you so much for telling me this. It shines a whole new light on a side of JT that I never knew existed."

With a promise to keep Michelle updated, I left. Shame haunted each step I took back to the truck.

———

The ride home was a blur. The events of the last two days had rattled my brain so hard I was pretty damn sure I had an emotional concussion. My head spun as if I just stepped off my fourth ride in a row on the Corkscrew at Valleyfair—I knew my feet were on the ground, but everything was still twirling.

What I thought I knew about JT was being rearranged and put into new compartments so rapidly I could barely keep up. No, frankly, I wasn't keeping up at all.

Now that I knew something about the abuse she witnessed in the past—and I prayed witnessing was the extent of it—and how that experience colored her actions and decisions, it made me love her all the more. She'd always been a champion of the less fortunate, the downtrodden, of those in need. It was almost a cliché, but it was real. But this...this entire thing went well beyond that. As I learned more about what really made JT tick, my appreciation of the person she was grew exponentially. As did my missing-her quotient.

Without conscious thought, I'd pulled up and parked at the curb next to the Rabbit Hole. I pulled myself out of my own head and focused on the present. At a few minutes after ten, the morning mob had thinned and the lunch crowd had yet to arrive.

I wondered if Coop had any luck finding any more on Mike Handler.

Holy shit.

Coop.

I forgot Coop at my house! Hopefully he was still snoozing. Some friend I was. A new wave of guilt flared and crept up my spine, overshadowing my earlier mortification. I tamped the guilt back down with the thought that there was a good chance, if I got a move on, I'd make it home and Coop would be oblivious to the fact I'd even left. *In fact*, I told myself, *you might as well get a caffeine infusion since you're here.*

I dove for the bait and shut off the truck.

The chimes jangled softly as I opened the front door of the Hole. A couple customers were seated at the tables with mugs at their elbows. One guy was reading a tattered, lime-green paperback whose cover featured a drooling dog. The other sat poring over the newspaper.

Coop was seated in one of the easy chairs, which he'd moved to the edge of the stone hearth in front of the fire. His crossed feet were propped up in front of the spark screen, yellow-red flames popping merrily behind it. A laptop was balanced on his thighs. A coffee mug sat within easy reach, and white headphone cords wound up to his ears. He didn't look up at my entrance, and his fingers didn't pause their tapping on the keys.

Great. He'd most likely walked from JT's. Not that it was all that far, but jeez. At least it wasn't freezing outside yet.

Metallic clanging echoed from the kitchen, where someone was working on the morning dishes.

Eddy was behind the counter, wearing her favorite, hand-made blue apron with the Rabbit Hole logo embroidered on the front.

As soon as her eyes settled on me, Eddy's forehead crinkled in a particularly unhappy fashion. I closed in on the counter, but before I could utter a word she growled, "Where have you been, child?"

By this time, Coop spotted me. He heaved himself from his chair and tramped over to the counter. "Where'd you go?"

I looked from Eddy's mask of angry concern to Coop's face, which reflected more curiosity than anything else. He always gave me a bye for stuff he probably shouldn't.

"Coop, I'm so sorry. I didn't mean to just bail without leaving a note or something—"

He waved my apology off. "Tell the tale."

I wasn't sure where to even begin to sort out the previous couple of hours. Or if I even wanted to. I sucked in a breath and slowly expelled it. "I talked to Tyrell yesterday. He said the gun used to shoot Krasski was found, and—"

195

"Where?" Eddy asked.

"You don't want to know. Trust me. Anyway—"

"I'll bet it was in a pickle barrel. What do you think, Nicholas?"

"Could be. Or maybe it was—"

"Hey," I held up a hand. "I'm trying to tell a story here." I shot both of them a look, and they rewarded me with wide-eyed silence. For about a half second.

Eddy said, "Well, child, spit it out. Where was the gun?"

She wouldn't stop until she had an answer. I said, "In the Porta Potty."

"In—by that horrible stinky urinal they have in there?"

"No. *In,* as in down the pooper."

Eddy half-squealed, half-gagged. Coop just groaned.

"Anyway, as I was trying to tell you, Tyrell said he heard the weapon was similar to one JT carries."

Coop said, "Yikes. That doesn't sound good."

"I know. So I thought if I took a look to see if JT's gun was there, maybe it could help. Well, to make a short story long, I couldn't get in the gun safe. It was locked and I don't know the combo. So I started poking around JT's desk, hoping she had it written somewhere."

"Ooh, girl," Eddy cut her eyes at me. "Snoopin' never did a body good."

"I wasn't trying to snoop. But that's some nice advice coming from one of the biggest snoops around."

If Eddy's skin wasn't so dark, I thought I might've actually seen her blush. She waved a hand at me. "Go on with you."

"So I accidently found this letter in JT's address book." I hurried my words before guilt had me tripping over them. "It was from someone named Maria. It looked kind of like a . . . well, like a love letter."

"Ah," Coop said. "I think I see where this is going. Continue." He crossed his arms and leaned a hip against the counter.

"There was a return address, in Ramsey."

"The county?" Eddy asked.

Coop said, "There's a town called Ramsey too. North of here, far, far away. I think maybe in another galaxy."

I said, "So I sort of lost my mind. Momentarily."

Eddy narrowed her eyes. "You went to—?"

"Ramsey. I wasn't exactly thinking clearly. I drove up there. Found the address."

I proceeded to tell them the abbreviated version of my trauma. When I finished, I was amazed that no customers had come in and interrupted my recitation.

"That poor JT," Eddy said. "And that little girl."

"I know. It's awful. I can't imagine…" I put a hand over my eyes and then rubbed my temples. "So Coop, did you find anything out about Handy Randy?"

"I haven't had much of a chance to look, but I did get an address." He shrugged. "Whether it's valid or not, who knows."

The sound of canine nails clicked against the wood floor, and Dawg came wandering around the counter into the café. He looked groggy. One ear was lying inside out on the top of his head.

"Wow. Someone had a rough night." I crouched down. "Hey, bud." I flipped the errant ear back and hugged his warm, solid body tight. What was it about dogs that was so comforting, so grounding?

Eddy said, "Told Kate to leave them dogs here last night. They were sleeping like angels when she and Anna finished up. I didn't want to wake them."

Holy cow, she'd come a long way from dog hater to dog mushball. I was impressed.

Dawg favored me with a slurp on the jaw. After a couple more rubs, he trundled over to greet Coop. A couple seconds later, Bogey plodded in and I repeated the process.

I stood and watched the mutts meander toward the rug in front of the fire. When the logs were crackling and the flames were dancing, that rug was their favorite spot. It occurred to me that Rocky hadn't been popping in and out, as was his usual MO when the café quieted down.

"Where's lover boy?" I asked.

Eddy shot me a look. "There is absolutely no need to refer to him in such terms." She muttered under her breath, "Lover boy. Hmph."

Coop said, "When I got here earlier, he was in the backyard loading up his wagon with phone books. I helped him, and off he went. He's made quite a dent."

Eddy said, "He's been working on that pile of books day and night. I swear, that boy gets something stuck in his brain and nothing deters him."

It was true. Following that logic, we'd better be getting ready for a wedding. Oh jeez. I just could not think about that right now. It took more brain cells than I had to go around. "So where were we?"

"Handy Randy may or may not be at some address, and you have a missing uncle," Eddy said. "I'd love to go investigating with you kids, but"—she jerked a thumb over her shoulder—"Kate's decided today would be a good day for cleaning. I told her I'd handle the crowd."

"Well," I said, "let's go see what we can find. Time's a wastin'."

"Let me pack up, and we're outta here," Coop said.

"Hey," Eddy called after us. "Drop by Maria's uncle's motel first. In case he had a heart attack and keeled over or something. Bet he doesn't have one of those 'Help me, I've fallen and I can't get up!' thingies they show on the television."

As we snarfed leftover grub from Eddy's refrigerator, Coop Googled the Starlite Motel. It was actually in Columbia Heights. Michelle, Maria's foster mom, had part of the city's name right, anyway.

We cleaned up and soon I was following Coop's directions, headed north on I-94.

He said, "You know, I could check with Luz, see if she's heard of this Hector Delgado."

"Can't hurt."

"Okay. Just in case I'm not off the phone, go east on 694 when you get to it, and then south on Central. It's probably less than a mile, I think on the right-hand side."

Luz picked up right away, and Coop summarized our predicament for her. I zoned out as he spoke, letting the act of driving and the monotony of the highway mesmerize me.

"Well," Coop said, jarring me back to the moment after he disconnected, "Luz hasn't heard of Hector, but she said she'd talk to her remaining contacts."

"Okay." I turned right off of Central Avenue, crossed a frontage road, and pulled into the parking lot of the Starlite Motel. "We're looking for room two two four. That's the number Michelle thought Hector was in."

Coop looked around. "This place belongs in Vegas. I don't really want a repeat performance of the Shamrock Dumptel. Let's just try the room and if he's not there, we'll check again later."

"Absolutely." I wasn't in any rush to cough up more bribery dough to shady proprietors.

The motel itself was a U-shaped, two-story from the late Fifties or early Sixties. The sign out front was an upside-down triangle with an arrow pointing into the parking lot. A big white star sat on top of the arrow. At night, I was pretty sure the whole thing would light up obnoxiously.

An old van and four other cars were parked on recently laid blacktop. I pulled into one of the diagonally painted spots at the outside corner of the motel and killed the engine. This joint was a step up from the Shamrock, but it was still light years away from the Hilton.

"Here goes nothing." I climbed from the truck and scanned the building. A staircase at the end of the motel accessed the second level. An open-air walkway ran the length of the building and extended over the sidewalk below.

The sidewalk and regularly spaced pillars holding up the second-story overhang were all that separated the parking lot from the motel.

A number 127 was mounted on a raised plaque secured to a door almost directly in front of the truck's grill. If logic followed, Hector's room 224 should be just above us, a few doors down the way. I headed for the stairs, Coop close on my flank.

Without pausing on the landing at the top of the steps, we rounded the corner of the stucco structure. The first room was 227. I glanced over the railing into the lot. My pickup was tucked in the spot right below us.

Cars on the main drag whizzed noisily by, and if the motel rooms weren't soundproofed well, the racket would bleed right through the walls. I had a hunch a lot of bleeding went on here.

The next room we passed was 226, then 225. Part of the 5 had fallen off the plaque. The low rumble of a television seeped through the door to room 224.

Coop whispered, "Someone's home."

"Yeah." I rapped on the door, waited a few seconds, and tapped again. "Hector Delgado?" I called, hoping he'd be able to hear us as well as we could hear the TV. The chatter was suddenly silenced. Maybe if Hector heard something about his niece, he'd open up. "Mr. Delgado, we're here about Maria."

For long moments there was nothing. Then a muffled, accented voice said, "She is okay?"

"Yes, she is," I said. "Can you open the door?"

The door opened just a crack. I said, "Mr. Delgado—Hector, I'm Shay O'Hanlon, and this is Nick Cooper. I just visited Maria."

Hector hesitantly opened the door the rest of the way. A thick, muscular man, probably somewhere in his thirties, stood before us. Black hair was cut to a quarter inch. A wide, neatly trimmed moustache ran across his upper lip, down each cheek, and stopped right above his jawbone. He was dressed in a navy-blue T-shirt, gray sweats, and black tennis shoes.

The one thing that stood out, aside from the gigantic moustache, was that Hector's right eye was just about swollen shut. A bruise the size of a grapefruit covered half his face. Ouch.

Coop and I stepped inside, and Hector shut the door. The curtains were drawn, and the only light came from a lamp on a table. The television flickered the noon news on channel 4, but the sound had been muted. Pizza had been recently consumed—as evidenced by a grease-stained cardboard box propped on the floor next to the wall. Pizza was evidently the sustenance of choice for motel dwellers.

Hector limped over to the table and sat heavily on the only chair in the room. A bag of ice lay on the tabletop leaking water, which was soaking into a mounded pile of newspapers. A glossy green and white magazine topped the stack.

I noticed the knuckles on Hector's right hand were swelled up and raw, the skin scraped off in places. Looked like a brawl to me.

"Maria is all right?" Hector repeated hoarsely.

"She's fine," Coop said.

I stepped into the circle of light. "I saw her today. She's wondering where you've been. Michelle's really worried. She tried to get a hold of you…"

Hector closed his non-blackened eye. "I know. I did not want Maria to see me—" He waved his hand at himself.

"In your—condition, I understand." I wouldn't want her to see me looking like that either. I glanced down at the table. The magazine on top of the newspapers looked familiar. I peered closer. It was actually an event brochure, folded open to the center. I'd seen that brochure before. It displayed half of a stylized, hand-drawn map. What were the chances? "Hector," I said slowly, "Were you at the Renaissance Festival Saturday evening?"

My head snapped up and I met Hector's suddenly squinty eye. His absence and wounded state suddenly made complete sense. My eyes widened as the horrifying realization and its repercussions sunk in. I stood there frozen, mesmerized, watching Hector's face vacillate from confusion to suspicious comprehension of my own comprehension.

He was the one who stuffed a pickle in Krasski's mouth. He was the one who pulled the trigger and blew off the back of Krasski's head. And now Hector knew that I'd figured out his dirty little secret.

Holy hell. We were in the same room as a killer.

SIXTEEN

My heart dropped past my stomach and slammed into my heels. I spun around and bounced into Coop, nearly knocking him on his keister.

"Run!" I gasped, grabbing onto his belt to steady then drag him toward the door.

I yanked it open, lurched onto the walkway, and careened into the railing. I used it to propel myself down the walkway. Coop scrambled right behind me, legs churning.

"Wha—" He was interrupted by Hector's howl of desperation.

I glanced over my shoulder. Terror overtook panic. Hector leaned out of the room, a gigantic silver gun in his mitt.

We'd never make it to the end of the walkway and around the corner of the building before he blasted one of us.

Two more strides. The truck came into view through the iron grates of the railing, right below us. "Coop, jump!" I hollered as I leaped over the railing, praying the hood of the pickup was as close as it seemed.

As I flew through the air, everything slowed. I clearly saw the truck hood right below my feet, unmarred and shiny. Coop launched off the walkway and flew over my shoulder past me. I heard him impact the roof just as my feet hit the hood.

A tiny part of my brain registered the fact that my poor truck was never going to be quite the same.

For a split second, the metal hood dipped until it slammed into the engine block. The resulting impact jarred the oxygen right out of me. My momentum threw me into the windshield, which somehow, thankfully, didn't shatter.

I managed to roll off and land on my feet next to the driver's door. Coop leaped to the ground from where he'd bounced to a stop in the pickup bed.

We nearly bashed heads as we frantically dove inside. I scrambled for the key in my pocket, yanked it out, and promptly dropped it. It hit my knee and disappeared somewhere in the vicinity of the gas pedal. I swore and awkwardly fumbled around the floorboard.

"SHAY!" Coop bellowed. "Hurry!"

I popped my head up. Hector had made it down the stairs. I was afraid he was going to take a run at us. The gun in his hand flashed in the sunlight.

"I'm trying!" I ducked under the dash again and swore some more, cursing my klutziness. Wouldn't it just be something to be taken out because I couldn't find the goddamned key in time? Finally my fingers wrapped around it. I straightened and jammed that sucker home. A horrified yowling filled the cab, and I was afraid the terrible sound came from me.

The engine roared to life. I shifted into Reverse and floored it. The back tires squealed as they spun, finally gaining traction. We zoomed backward. I slammed on the brakes and twisted the wheel. Rubber screamed on asphalt.

As we started to roll forward, Hector veered away from my pickup and ran flat out toward a rusty maroon and silver van.

I shifted into Drive and hammered the gas, squealing out of the lot and turned left onto the frontage road. In the rearview mirror, I saw the van peel out of the parking lot amid the high-pitched squealing of tires.

"Jesus!" Coop yelled as he twisted around to look out of the back window. "He's right on our ass."

Flameburger was coming up on our left. I was going too fast to make a hard right onto Central. Ahead, the frontage road ended in the parking lot shared by Dammit Jayne Liquors and Walgreen's.

"Holy fuck!" I searched frantically for another out as we whipped past Flameburger.

Then decisions were literally ripped out of my hands as the van violently rammed the back end of my truck. The steering wheel spun but wouldn't respond. I stomped on the brake pedal with both feet. The truck shuddered as the tires tried to grip the rough roadway. We launched into a full-on skid. Directly in front of us, a bright red 6x4-foot CLOTHING AND SHOES ONLY donation drop-off bin loomed in front of the Dammit Jayne Liquors sign.

"COO—" I screamed as we careened head-on into the metal container. There was a loud popping sound as metal screeched and crunched. Something blasted me in the face, momentarily stunning me senseless.

Then there was silence.

I struggled through disorientation. "COOP!"

He made a strangled gasp. "Gah. You okay?"

"Think so. Come on!"

He wrenched his door open and fell out onto the ground in his haste to exit.

I found the handle on the driver's door and shoved. My body felt like it was floating. *Focus, Shay.* My feet hit the ground with a *thump* that rattled my teeth. No more floating.

The driver's side of the van was wedged up against the bed of the pickup. The tailgate blocked the van's driver's door. Hector was attempting to crawl across the seat toward the passenger side. In my stunned stupor, I wondered why he didn't try going out the big rolling side door instead.

Before I could take in any more, Coop was at my side. "Come ON!" He grabbed my arm and yanked. I stumbled. My feet weren't working as fast as my brain wanted them to.

I found my footing and raced after Coop, who was making a bee-line for the front door of the liquor store. I cast a desperate glance back. Hector had made it out of the van and was streaking toward us, a rampaging bronco on crack.

"RUN!" I doubled down, trying to squeeze more speed out of my already pistoning legs.

We were so close I could smell the barley-infused stench oozing through the entrance. Then Coop flung the glass-plate door open so hard it banged against the brick façade of the building. We zipped inside and skidded to an abrupt halt just before we bulldozed a display of Effen Vodka bottles stacked to the ceiling, shaped like a huge jug of the stuff.

Two workers stood transfixed behind the checkout counter.

My mind processed the scene in snapshots, like an off-kilter camera.

Both Coop and I spun as the door slammed open again. Hector burst over the threshold in a frenzy. His hands were empty, no gun in sight. He must have lost it in the crash. But with adrenaline rage fueling him, I didn't think the gun's absence counted for much.

I grabbed the only weapon within reach—a bottle off of the display behind me.

Hector paused long enough to take in the scene, then surged forward.

I wound up that Effen bottle and swung as hard as I could. It impacted Hector's noggin with a hollow crack. The reverb ran up my hands into my arms. It took everything I had not to drop my impromptu bat.

The man's forward momentum slowed but didn't stop. I managed to somehow step aside as he lost his footing, and we watched him do a slow motion barrel roll in midair. His body glanced off Coop's and crashed into the display of vodka bottles. The carefully stacked arrangement began to topple, one bottle at a time. The collapse picked up speed as supporting bottles fell. Some bounced off Hector while others skittered and spun or shattered when they hit the cement. In a few short moments, Hector's feet were the only thing left visible from under the Effen avalanche.

Someone was shouting in my ear. "Let it go, Shay. Come on, let it go."

It was as if a rubber band snapped me in the back of the head. Instantaneously, my thoughts realigned and reality returned. I came back to the here-and-now with a jerk.

Coop's voice seeped into my consciousness as he continued to try to talk me out of the bottle of vodka I wielded in front of me. My hands were locked around its neck.

I blinked hard, then again. Coop was on one side of me. The two workers, alarm radiating from their faces, flanked the other. I lowered my bludgeoner.

One of the employees—a short, brown-haired, round-faced gal whose nametag, honest to God, read BAD CAROL—breathed, "Oh, my goodness. Are you okay? Is this a robbery?" Her eyes were as wide as the bottom of the Effen bottle.

A thin, dark-haired woman, whose nametag read DAMMIT JAYNE, silently perused the state of her store and rolled her eyes. She tried to appear stern, but the corners of her mouth curved upward. If I wasn't mistaken, she was getting quite a charge out of the commotion. Then she gently extracted the weapon from my hand, and surveyed my face with a critical eye. "Nope, Carol. It's not a robbery. This one looks banged up, but she'll be fine, I think. Grab the first-aid kit." She nudged Hector's boot with her shoe. "It's dingleberry here under this mess who's going to be really sorry."

The stinging smell of the alcohol pooling at our feet began to seep into my senses.

All of a sudden the adrenaline I'd been riding dissipated, replaced with exhaustion so heavy I wasn't sure I'd remain upright. I sagged against Coop, thankful he was still beside me. Half my face was wet, and my chin felt like the skin had been rubbed right off. It hurt to breathe.

Jayne walked over and set the bottle on the countertop with a gentle *thump*. That was the last straw for the poor container. It shattered into a gazillion little pieces. Booze and shards of glass spilled across the countertop and onto the cement.

Effen Vodka—innocuous stuff till it hit you in the head.

SEVENTEEN

Bad Carol doctored both Coop and me as best she could until the cops—and then an ambulance—showed up at the liquor store. Hector sat on the floor with his head in his hands, not trying to run or fight, mumbling to himself. Dammit Jayne kept a wary eye on Hector, ready to crack him another one if the need arose. When the police showed, they unpacked Hector from his Effen pile and loaded him into a squad.

Tow trucks appeared and sorted out the mess of twisted metal that had been my pickup and Hector's van. I didn't hold out much hope either was going to be repairable.

Coop and I got what I was sure was going to be a not-so-free ride in an ambulance to the emergency room. I tried to con the driver into putting the lights and sirens on, but she was having none of it, and the paramedic attending to my face wasn't happy with my squirming around.

The ER intake folks processed us right away, and I was amazed to be shuffled into one of the tiny, curtain-walled "rooms" almost immediately. We must have lucked out and hit the Monday afternoon lull.

Coop was tucked into a space somewhere nearby. The curtained walls blocked visuals but didn't impair hearing, and I could hear his voice. A baby screamed bloody murder, and with any luck I wouldn't do the same thing. I sure hoped that whatever brought the tyke in was something that could be fixed fast; that noise was murder on my skull. Poor thing.

I sat on the edge of the hospital bed/gurney and dangled my legs impatiently. My head pounded in time to the beat of my heart, and everything hurt. I so wished I could wake up and start the entire weekend all over again.

Earlier at the liquor store, two detectives—replicas of Starsky and Hutch—told Coop and me they'd meet us at the hospital to take statements. As the minutes ticked by without the appearance of either a doctor or Starsky or Hutch, it occurred to me that maybe I should try to get a hold of both Tyrell and Eddy.

To my surprise, Tyrell picked up on the third ring. He listened in silence as I related the trials and tribulations of the last couple of hours, and he only asked clarifying questions. When I was finished, he offered to come and pick us up when we were cleared to leave, but I told him I'd call Eddy for that duty if he'd do whatever he could to get the ball rolling with JT's release.

Tyrell and I had barely disconnected when a nurse poked her head in to make sure I hadn't collapsed. I assured her I was still mostly alert and somewhat coherent. She hustled off to her next patient, and I dialed Eddy. That conversation wasn't one I looked forward to having, especially when she heard about the cracked-up truck and crazed man chasing us with a gun. She finally calmed down, and, as I expected, offered to come get our sorry butts. She hung up, and I let out a deep sigh. I didn't envy the unfortunate souls who would be on the road at the same time as her when she stormed over here.

Finally a harried ER doctor showed up. He was short and a bit stout, with a friendly round face and a perpetual smile. After introducing himself as Dr. Singh, he started in on removing the bandage from my face, tsk'ing a few times as he concentrated on his work. I was afraid he was going to take some skin off along with the blood-matted gauze. However, he accomplished the removal of the goopy dressing with gentle hands and lots of warm water. He critically assessed the gash after he gently cleaned it. I wasn't sure I wanted to hear the fact that another quarter inch and I could've kissed my eye good-bye. Nice.

And another fun fact: stitches were in my very near future.

Dr. Singh evaluated the airbag burn that started on my chin and continued down the side of my neck. Airbags were amazing things, but holy cow, did they pack a wallop. The whole area stung every time I turned or bent my head, making me grumpier than the cut on my face did. All things considered, though, I was damn lucky.

When I was in the middle of the chaos, I'd been simply doing and not thinking. Adrenaline and a desire to stay in the land of the living overrode any fear I may have had, so I just reacted. Now that I looked back on what had happened—and what could have happened—I was freaked out big time. My hands were actually trembling. Kind of how I felt after a Tenacious Protector moment. Rubbery and jittery.

My shoulder hurt like a bitch where the seatbelt had locked up and dug in, and the ribs on my left side ached. The doc performed a number of pain application techniques that he claimed were simple physical assessments, mumbling under his breath as he did. Luckily, he didn't find anything more serious than multiple strains and bruises.

In the midst of the torture, one of the detectives showed up. He waited patiently at my side until the doc finished poking and prodding. While he was Hutch in my book, he told me his last name was Caribou. I wondered if he frequented Caribou Coffee. With his five o'clock shadow and tired eyes, he sure looked like he could use a jolt. He took my statement while Doc Singh stitched me back together.

The doctor raised his eyebrow but continued his slow, steady sewing when I told the detective about the dead man with a pickle in his mouth in the privy. Once I finished the entire sordid tale, I tried to impress on the good detective the importance of speaking with Tyrell about the history behind this mess. The way agencies didn't play nicely in the same sandbox scared the crap out of me. JT could be in the clink for a long time before everything got straightened out, and that was the last thing either one of us needed. What I really wanted was her solid strength right here next to me.

The doc finished up, and while I waited forever to be discharged, I called Tyrell back. I gave him the contact info for the detective I'd talked to, and he promised to do what he could.

Coop and I were finally kicked loose nearly an hour later, and Eddy escorted us out of the building. After she reassured herself that we were generally in one piece, she gleefully listened as we rehashed our visit to the Starlight Motel and Dammit Jayne Liquors. Her only regret, aside from her mortification that she had been the one to suggest we check up on a killer, was that she'd missed out on all of the action.

Eddy actually drove like a sane woman on the way home, perhaps in deference to our all-too-recent experiment in demolition. That was a good thing because I wasn't sure my heart could take much more. She dropped Coop off at his apartment and came inside with me when we arrived at JT's place. She wanted to help get me out of my

212

bloody clothes and clean me up, but I told her I wasn't incapacitated, just sore.

After reassuring Eddy I was going to be fine, she fussed over me a little more and finally took off for home.

The quiet of the house settled around me, making my antsy again. My muscles were already stiffening up, and I wondered how much worse it would be in the morning. I hobbled upstairs to my office and lowered myself gingerly into a chair. I sat still while the events and calamities of the last few hours replayed in my brain. What was I supposed to do now? I hated waiting around and feeling like everything was completely out of my control. I wanted JT home, safe and sound. I wanted this nightmare over and done.

My gaze settled on the wax rose from the Renaissance Festival. I recalled the look on JT's face as she'd given it to me. Sure, I'd seen love and affection. But there was something more in her eyes, a look of unadulterated devotion. How did I wind up with someone who felt that way about me?

My world shifted these days when I *really* thought about what JT meant to me. When I learned what she'd been through, the horrors I hadn't even been aware of, I was shaken just that much more. Despite all that had happened, she survived, whole and strong, much like that resilient Renaissance rose. Its stem had been battered and broken, but the heart and the beauty of the flower remained complete and true. And so it was with JT.

Action is better than contemplation. *Thank you for that mantra, Eddy.* I stood with a pained groan and carefully wrapped the rose in Kleenex and stuck it in my jacket pocket. JT kept a spare set of car keys on a hook by the back door, and I grabbed them and let myself out. It was time to bring my woman home, one way or another.

The closer I got to my destination, the stronger my resolve became. JT was coming home tonight, period. If I had to bust her butt out of the joint, I was going to do it. Of course, I hadn't thought too deeply about how I might actually accomplish that little feat, but hey, give me an A for effort. If I got pitched in the hoosegow for my actions, it damn well better be directly into JT's cell.

Tyrell called as I pulled into the jail's parking lot. He said he talked to Detective Caribou, and things were actually rolling along nicely. Right off the bat, Hector confessed to popping a cap in Russell Krasski and wanted a deal. Apparently Maria's uncle had some unsavory contacts, and it was via that route he'd somehow managed to locate the slimeball.

Hector's intent had been to avenge his niece. Tyrell said the guy had originally meant to mess up Krasski enough that he would never again be able to do what he had done to another child. The "lesson," as Hector called it, involved a sharp knife and Krasski's family jewels. Hector had managed to get Krasski into the handicapped Porta Potty at knifepoint, and they'd somehow wound up fighting. Krasski had been packing a gun, and in the end, instead of turning him into a eunuch, Hector got a hold of the weapon and shot Krasski instead.

In a blind rage, Hector stuffed Krasski's pickle down the dead man's throat and left him propped on the seat in the privy. Then he'd run like hell. Apparently the fatal gunshot had indeed occurred at almost the same time the Tortuga Twins ended their show. The crowd had gone ballistic, and that was why the explosive sound hadn't drawn any attention.

Detective Caribou told Tyrell he contacted Scott County immediately after his interview with Hector and tried to speak to Detective

Roberts. Roberts wasn't taking calls, but Caribou eventually managed to reach Roberts's supervising officer, a captain who happened to be an old acquaintance of his.

Sometimes it seemed that everyone knew each other in the law enforcement realm. It was a smaller world within an already small world.

Roberts's captain hadn't heard that another cop was being held for the Ren Fest murder and was none-too-pleased that Roberts had not shared that information with him. He was furious that Roberts was working a secret agenda that really had little to do with catching a killer and instead continued a beef he had with JT. As I said all along, Roberts had skipped his due diligence and hadn't looked at all the angles before throwing the metaphorical book at JT.

I was also delighted to learn from Tyrell that Roberts was already on thin ice with his department over a few bad decisions. He also had an unusually high number of use-of-force complaints.

I hoped they'd can Roberts's judgmental, vindictive ass. I was more than willing to lodge an unlawful arrest charge or some such other fancy term against him if it would help speed that outcome along.

Tyrell told me the upshot was that JT would be processed out and should be released soon. I thanked him and tucked my phone away. Good thing I'd listened to my instincts and headed to the jail.

The place was quiet as I explained my situation to a surprisingly affable deputy—no more than a kid, really—who manned the front desk. He picked up a clipboard from a hook on the wall and studied it. Then he nodded. "JT Bordeaux?"

"Yes."

"She should be out shortly. You can wait over there." He pointed to the bench along the wall where Coop had waited for me yesterday. God, was that really only yesterday?

I lowered my aching body to the seat and waited as minutes ticked by like sands through an overly narrow hourglass. I shifted uncomfortably on the cold metal. Padding on the narrow expanse would be a big improvement, even for those whose bodies weren't banged up. My butt was falling asleep, and the position made my ribs ache. Maybe standing was a better idea.

With an impatient breath, I looked at my watch for probably the forty-fifth time. It was well after midnight. *Come on already, JT. Where are you, babe?* I was about to get up and check with the deputy again when a door opened, and JT emerged into the lobby at long last. She looked rumpled and more than a little crabby, but otherwise unharmed. But as soon as she caught sight of me, her entire demeanor brightened.

I eased myself to my feet, watching her move across the floor with graceful, determined strides. She was dressed in the same clothes she'd been wearing Saturday, although they were now looking decidedly worse for wear. Her glittering brown eyes bore into mine, and then flicked across my face as she catalogued my beleaguered appearance. I shivered at their intensity and opened my arms. JT walked right into them.

Her breath tickled my ear. "Oh my god, Shay—what the hell happened to you?" I returned her embrace with cautious enthusiasm, trying not to gasp as she squeezed me. She felt solid and warm.

"Come on," I said, "let's get you out of here and I'll tell all." I swung her toward the front door. Once we stepped out into the starlit night, I stopped and pulled her to me again. She was real. This nightmare was finally over.

JT's hands came up and cupped my cheeks, her thumb gently tracing the gash and its accompanying seven stitches. She carefully tilted my head back and looked under my chin at the missing layer of skin. I wasn't sure how much she could make out in the dimness, but her resulting soft gasp told me she managed to see more than enough. I dipped my chin back down and peered into her beautiful, troubled eyes. "I'm okay."

"Jesus, Shay, you look like a tank ran you over. Are you hurt anywhere else?"

"I'm sore. A few ribs are bruised."

She bent her head and ever so softly, her lips met mine for a brief moment. Then her eyes searched my face.

I could see she wanted answers, and she wanted them now. I kissed her nose and said, "Let's go home."

"Absolutely the best offer I've heard in the last forty-eight hours. But—"

"No buts." I grabbed her hand and led her to her Durango.

"Where's your truck?" she asked and shot me a confused look as I beeped the doors unlocked.

Hadn't they told her anything when they let her go? "Long story," I said. "Goes with the face. I'll explain on the way home."

I settled gingerly into the seat and clicked my seatbelt into place. The shoulder belt rubbed painfully, and I eased it behind me. I caught JT watching me, a concerned frown marring her face. I clicked off the radio in the middle of Simon and Garfunkel's "Bridge Over Troubled Water." The words made me smile.

She said, "That song's pretty appropriate."

"Yeah, it is. Look, before we get into this, I have something for you."

One shapely eyebrow arched.

I handed her the Kleenex-encased rose. She unwrapped it and turned the colorful flower over in her hands.

I said, "I thought the entire flower was going to be squashed after those two cops landed on me. When I got home and realized that was still intact, it felt…" I trailed off, not sure how to put my emotions into words. "Lately the things I knew that held me up were crumbling down around my ears. But the most important part of the flower survived, and that's how I feel about us, JT. We might be battered and banged up, but our relationship—the heart of us—is okay."

"Shay." JT's voice cracked. "Thank you. I've been worried about you, about everything."

I grabbed her hand and our fingers twined together familiarly, comforting. "I know you have. I've got questions, and I know you do too, so let's get this done."

The ride home went by in a blink as I gave JT a totally bare bones rundown of what had happened in my world since Saturday afternoon. I didn't want to get too deep into anything now, because if I did, we would never get to bed.

JT had always been a great listener, and she proved it again by stopping me only to ask clarifying questions and to gasp in appropriate places. When I got to the part about finding the letter from Maria, she visibly cringed and looked appropriately chagrined, but she let me continue my brief summary.

By the time I pulled into the garage, I'd pretty much wound down. I said as much as I was going to say for the night, and my brain was becoming mighty slow on the uptake.

JT looked at the conspicuously empty half of the garage and said, "So where *is* your truck?"

"No idea. They towed it somewhere."

"We'll get that figured out. Don't worry." She slammed the door shut and met me in front of the SUV. I hit the button to close the garage door and we entered the quiet house. After a questioning look from JT, I informed her that the mutts were at a sleepover. She nodded, the movement mechanical. I could see exhaustion etched below her eyes and tenseness in the set of her jaw. As I led the way up the stairs toward the bedroom, JT said hoarsely, "I have a favor to ask."

I stopped and turned around.

"I know I need to explain some things—"

I gave her a look that silenced her. "More than *some*," I amended softly.

JT dropped her head for a second, then looked up at me. "Yes, you're right. But I'm wondering if you could wait until tomorrow for my confessions." She rubbed her face. "I'm so tired I don't know if I could tell you anything that would make much sense at this point."

I was relieved, since I was running on fumes myself, and thankful a bottle of pain pills sat on the bathroom counter calling my name. I touched my fingertip to her nose. "You got it, Cupcake."

"Cupcake? Have you been reading Janet Evanovich again?"

"Nope. But we watched the movie a couple weeks ago, remember?"

JT rolled her eyes and herded me into the bedroom. We didn't speak as she shed her clothes in a pile and pulled a form-fitting, white tank top over her head. I was nowhere near as speedy, and she gently helped me finish. She found my Vicodin in the bathroom and scored me two pills along with a glass of water. Then she wrapped herself around me and simply held me for a long time. Eventually we shifted to the bed and snuggled under the covers, so tangled in each other it was hard to know where I ended and she began. I tried to ignore my aches and pains, absorbing the love that flowed off of her like a tidal wave.

She lifted a finger and traced my facial wounds. "You look a little like something out of one of the *Friday the 13th* movies." Her tone was teasing, but her eyes were serious.

"I'll take that as a compliment, jailbird."

"That's the last time I want to be on that side of the bars. You have no idea how glad I am to be home."

"I think I do." I kissed her nose. "I like you much better on this side of the bars too."

JT smiled lazily and gently tucked the uninjured side of my head beneath her chin. Reaching over me, she turned out the light. "Night, Shay."

I mumbled, "Night, love." It wasn't long before I felt JT's breathing even out and her body relax. I lay pressed against her chest, listening to the steady beating of her heart.

As exhausted as I was, sleep was slow in coming. Thoughts flowed in and out of my brain like a river that couldn't follow its own path.

JT was an amazing person, a good cop. She was a bright light in an oftentimes dark and insane world. She was a fighter of the good fight, even when her demons threatened to consume her. My Protector, calm now, rumbled contentedly in the back of my head. I knew without a doubt I loved her with every ounce of my being, and that I'd do whatever was in my power to protect and defend this incredibly brave, incredibly frustrating human being. Not that she needed a whole lot of help in that capacity, but…

It still irked me to think about how much pain and sorrow she'd hidden from me, things I had no idea about until everything exploded Saturday night. Tomorrow, I was sure she'd give me another whole new perspective and understanding of this debacle.

I sighed and tightened my grip on JT, finally allowing the tides of sleep to pull me under.

EIGHTEEN

THE NEXT DAY'S MID-AFTERNOON sun shone brilliantly through leaves that blazed glorious fall colors. I sat with JT on a wooden bench at the surprisingly quiet Lake of the Isles off-leash dog park. At this time of day, only a few other people were there to watch their canine companions frolic through the wooded copse.

In the sun-dappled distance, Maria tussled and tumbled with Dawg and Bogey. Her thrilled, high-pitched giggles floated through the air, reminding me of this past summer when JT and I had taken a day off and visited the Como Park Zoo. Kids had squealed in delight as they rode Cafésjian's Carousel, a 1914 merry-go-round located at the edge of the zoo. It almost made me feel maternal. Almost.

After we'd finally gotten up that morning, JT had called Michelle Osterhus and explained what had happened. She'd agreed to bring Maria and meet us here.

Michelle stood close by Maria, keeping a sharp eye on the dogs and her charge. I'd purchased two Angry Birds squeaky toys, and they were getting a slobbery workout. The pooches were already wrapped around Maria's really little finger, and even from this distance I could see they were both being gentle when they returned the toys to her.

I heaved a sigh and gently smoothed stray strands of hair that had escaped JT's ponytail. I studied her profile as her eyes followed the antics of our dogs. When she'd finally woken up and gotten dressed, she pulled on one of my Rabbit Hole T-shirts and topped it with a navy cable-knit sweater. A faded pair of blue jeans covered her long legs. She'd never looked more appealing to me than in that moment, absolutely vulnerable yet strong as steel.

I reached up and ran my knuckles along JT's jaw. She pressed against my hand, then said, "I think it's time I gave you some explanations."

JT kept her eyes on Maria and the dogs.

"I guess I'm—I'd really like to know. About a lot of things." I gently squeezed her thigh, which had gone tense as a bowstring.

Her head dropped. "Shay, I hardly know where to start."

"At the beginning, I guess."

At first it was hard to hear JT because she spoke so quietly. "I was so angry. So ashamed. I'm not even sure if shame's the right word. Appalled at myself, maybe. I completely destroyed a case we'd been working on for so goddamned long. All because I lost my mind over a few words from a moronic jackass."

"I learned some things from a few friends of yours that might explain your reactions."

JT shot me a look of dread-laced curiosity. "Exactly who've you been talking to? You kind of glossed over those specifics last night."

"Dimples, for one."

"Dimp—you talked to my grandfather?"

"Eddy and I did. You'll have to ask her about her dip in the pool."

"Oh no." JT's eyes grew wide as half dollars.

"Oh yes. But it was worth it. He led us to Taffy."

"Taffy. You looked up Taffy Abernathy?"

"Yup. Did you know she works in a sperm bank? And lives in a house that's actually more barn-like than house-like?"

"Really?"

I smiled. "Yup."

"I haven't talked to her in way too long. She's unique, always has been. Always rode her own horse to the parade. Her whole family's a little like that." She blinked. "Maybe a lot like that."

"Then we went to visit Peaches."

Both eyebrows rose. "You *have* been busy."

"And then Michelle told me about the work you've done for the kids who were involved with Krasski, and she really illuminated things. You're amazing, you know that?"

JT's mouth tightened. "Amazing is one thing I'm not. I wanted—I had to do something. After what happened, it was the least I could do for those kids. I owed it to them." The muscles in her jaw bunched as she clenched her teeth.

And, I thought, *you felt like you owed it to yourself too.* Maybe it was best to let her admit that, though. I said, "It was a great thing you did. That you've been doing. I just don't understand why you never told me about any of it." That was the crux of it, really. Her double life had to stop. I could only hope she'd let me in this time.

"Oh, Shay," she said with a sigh. "I'm so sorry." She finally met my gaze. Her eyes and expression radiated pain and a fury that was barely kept in check. I ached to take away the hurt that was reflected there.

JT tucked her fingers through mine. I gave them an encouraging squeeze.

She sighed and stretched her neck from side to side. "When we first got together and I realized you didn't know anything about what had happened, it was a total shock. After it'd been on the news, in the papers..." She trailed off and gave me a disbelieving look.

"Hey, I can't help it, I don't pay attention to the depressing stuff. I suppose I must have heard customers at the Hole talking about it, but I obviously never linked it to you."

"It was a relief. An absolute relief. You have no idea what it was like—still feels like, sometimes—to think I was being judged by practically everyone. With you, I didn't feel that I was a total and complete loser. Honestly, I didn't want to see the disappointment on your face if I told you what I'd done."

"JT. Honey. I know you. I know your heart. I know how much you believe in doing the right thing." That felt good to say. However, there was a piece of this puzzle that still nagged at me. "What exactly did Krasski say to you that set you off that night?"

JT swallowed and then locked her eyes on the dogs and Maria again. "Well, I haven't repeated it to anyone before now." She gently cupped my head and whispered to me some of the most vile words I'd ever heard having to do with children and things they should never, ever experience.

I stiffened, and violently expelled the breath I'd been holding. "That fucking bastard." I felt physically sick and could easily see how JT had snapped. There is no doubt in my mind I would have done the same thing. I wanted to jump up and go kick the shit out of somebody or something myself.

JT clamped a hand on my knee and dug her fingers into my skin to bring me back. "Hey, easy does it, Shay. I know, believe me, I know." When she was sure I was back in control, she continued.

"Anyway, after awhile when no one at the Rabbit Hole said anything to me about the whole Krasski fiasco, well, it was just easier to say nothing." She gave a harsh laugh. "I was so sure Eddy or Kate would've known. I always wondered if maybe they were too polite to say anything. You, on the other hand, hardly ever watched TV or paid the slightest bit of attention to the news, so I wasn't too worried there." JT rubbed her jaw and glanced at me. "You remember when I first started coming to the Hole?"

"Yeah." Did I ever. I remembered how Kate had been dying to score a date with JT, and I'd admitted to a crush as well. However, our interior guidance systems ran in two different directions. Kate had been shot down by JT more than once, while I kept my attraction to myself.

JT said, "Before all that, when I told you I'd gotten a transfer and that's why I wouldn't be coming in any more, well, it was actually because of the Krasski thing. I was transferred, but I didn't stop coming in because of that. I just couldn't face seeing disdain on your faces."

I tugged JT's hand into my lap and wrapped my other hand around her knuckles. "You have to know I wouldn't have thought any less of you. Neither would Kate or Eddy. Or Coop."

"I do know that now. I think I did then too, on some level. But the emotions I was working with at the time freaked me out too damn much to really believe it."

I could relate. When the Protector was in control, I just reacted. It wasn't until I'd calmed down that I could think clearly, and even then it was sometimes a challenge to see things as they really were and not colored by the events that had rattled me to the core in the first place.

The bright sound of Maria's giggle floated to us on the lazy breeze. She and Michelle were now both on the ground with Dawg and

225

Bogey, who, by their wiggling body language, were loving every moment of attention they were getting.

I could totally understand JT's reluctance to revisit her hell, especially as time went by. That I got, loud and clear. But then there was the little issue of Maria, sweet Maria, who she'd been in contact with at least once every few weeks. For the entire span of time we'd been together. That really stung. Even after hearing JT's side of things, that part still pissed me off. However, I was just going to have to buck up and deal with it.

It was time. I said, "Tell me Maria's story."

"Yes." JT squeezed my fingers and studied her lap with intense interest. "Maria."

Trying to keep my voice even, I said, "It's one thing to not tell me about the Krasski mess, horrible as it may have been. But it's entirely another to ... to keep up the charade, to hide the facts of what you were doing to help that little girl. How could you think I wouldn't understand that?"

JT's head hung even lower. It might have been funny if it weren't so sad.

I untangled my hand from hers, shifted to face her on the bench, gritting my teeth as pain shot through my bruised ribs. "Hey." I reached out and tucked her hair behind her ear again. "Babe, look at me." I caught JT's chin and tugged. Reluctantly she met my eyes.

Unshed tears glittered in those brown depths. She drew in a breath. "I have no excuse. I'm so sorry, Shay."

I pulled her into a fierce hug, trying to be careful of my side. She held onto me and buried her face in the crook of my neck, thankfully on the non-airbag-burned side.

"You," I whispered into her ear, "have nothing to be ashamed of. You're amazing. So you lost your freaking temper? That bastard deserved it. Maria, well, we'll work on that. Sometime soon I want to hear the entire story about how you've helped those kids."

She nodded against my shoulder.

My hand tangled in her hair and tugged until her face came up, scant inches from mine. "But if you ever hide something like this from me again, so help me, JT Bordeaux, I'll fillet you myself and feed you to one of Taffy's goats."

A weak smile fluttered across JT's face. I let go of her hair and gingerly met her lips in a reaffirming kiss that spoke not of passion but of forgiveness and hope.

————

After about two hours, we bid Michelle and a very excited Maria goodbye and headed for the Rabbit Hole. JT reassured the little girl that her uncle was okay, but he couldn't take her home. JT told her that she'd get a hold of another family member as soon as she could to come and whisk her back to Mexico, and if she had to, she'd bring the little girl there herself. Now there was the JT I knew and loved.

On the way to the Hole, Tyrell called. After informing him that the object of our concern was sitting next to me, I handed the phone over to JT. She mostly listened to whatever he was saying to her, with a few "uh huhs" thrown in. She signed off with a promise that we'd get together with Tyrell and his wife sometime soon.

I glanced sideways at JT, waiting for her to fill me in. As I waited for her to order her thoughts, I took a detour from our regularly scheduled route back to the café and pulled to the curb in front of the Leaning Tower of Pizza. It was almost feeding time, and a couple of pizzas with the works sounded excellent. In addition, it would be a nice surprise for Eddy and the rest of the crew.

JT smiled when she realized where we were. "I like your thinking. So. Ty told me he'd found out a bit more about Hector. He's the oldest living male in Maria's family, and I guess it's been a pretty rough road for all of them. Couple of brothers were killed in drug-related dealings. Her dad died some time ago. Maria's the baby of the family." She put her hand over her mouth for a moment and gazed through the windshield, eyes locked on something in the distance.

"When Hector found out what had happened to Maria, he vowed to seek revenge." She choked out a bitter laugh. "That's exactly how I felt, Shay."

"I know." I sucked my bottom lip in and put my hand on the back of her neck, gently stroking the silky strands of hair that flowed over her collar and down her back. Hector had done what he felt he needed to do. I realized that when Coop and I showed up, Hector must have felt terrified, completely trapped with no way out, much like a wild animal cornered, with no escape route. If it had been me in his situation, I can't say I would have done things much differently.

Hector came after Coop and me because he was backed into a corner and didn't know what else to do. He didn't really mean either one of us harm. I knew in my heart that if Coop had all the same facts I did, he'd feel exactly the same way. "JT," I said, and swallowed carefully, "is there any way we can get Hector home?"

JT shot me a surprised glance. "What do you mean?"

"I ..." What *did* I mean, exactly? I frowned. "What happened to Maria can't be changed. We both know that. But Krasski's now in a place where he can't hurt anyone ever again. Hector did that. For everyone. I know killing another human being isn't right. Oh hell, JT, maybe sometimes it is. Krasski wasn't anything I'd call human, and he deserved to be broiling in hell long before now. I just hate to see Hector locked up for the rest of his life for eradicating a menace." I shrugged, feeling discouraged and helpless. Both emotions pissed me off.

JT looked at me thoughtfully without speaking.

"What?" I finally asked. "You of all people have to under—"

She held her hands up. "Hey, easy. I do get it." Her dark, piercing eyes were indeed full of compassion, and under that, a layer of rebellion. "No promises, but let me see what I can do."

I left JT mumbling to herself and walked into the Leaning Tower of Pizza where the tang of pizza and the rich smell of pasta and alfredo sauce made my stomach rumble. I placed an order for a large Leaning Tower and an Italian Stallion to go, and on second thought, added a Holy Trinity of Cheese for Coop, in honor of his vegetable munching ways.

———

Forty minutes later, JT and I were seated at Eddy's kitchen table with Eddy, Coop, Kate, and Anna. Eddy's friend Agnes was busy holding down the café. She wasn't particularly competent, and I had to admit the thought of her working the counter gave me the jitters. It was a good thing we'd be done here soon.

With Coop's and Eddy's help, JT and I put the entire story together for a flabbergasted and appalled Anna and Kate.

Throughout the tale, Eddy periodically exclaimed and slapped the tabletop, making both the silverware and me jump. "You are a little spitfire, girl," Eddy said to JT.

JT looked more relaxed than I'd seen her since I brought her home the night before. Her eyes were no longer angry obsidian or smoky with shame. They were warm and full of affection for the people seated around the table. When her gaze fell on me, the love that emanated from her cut into my very soul.

I thought, too, that it was a good thing JT had a chance to talk to everyone about Krasski and Maria. She was able to see firsthand that the only reaction each and every one of them had was of understanding and respect. I still didn't get why my perfectionist of a cop had been unable to see that. *Well*, I thought smugly to myself as I scooped up another piece of Italian Stallion, *that attitude was long overdue for a change.*

I'd taken a big bite and was chewing away when Dawg wandered in, snuffling for a handout. He wiggled over to me, and I put my non-pizza-filled hand on his warm head.

"Where's Bogey?" Eddy asked.

Anna said, "When I left the Hole, he was sprawled in front of the fire. By the way, Shay, Eddy's going to cover the rest of my shift so I can go home and study."

I waved a hand at her. "No problem, bookworm. Agnes can hang out and help her. By the time Eddy gets behind the counter, Agnes'll probably be so wired from espresso shots she'll be up for the next three days." Agnes had a good heart, but vodka and more recently espresso were her two downfalls.

Dawg poked me in the belly with his nose, and I snuck him a pizza crust. I was about to snitch another one from Eddy's plate when Bogey came trotting in, which wasn't remarkable except for the fact he had a big red ball on the end of his snoot. He sneezed and wagged his head, trying to dislodge the thing.

"What is that?" Eddy asked.

"Bogey, come here." Coop put the piece of pizza he'd been stuffing into his mouth on his plate, licked his fingers, and patted his thigh. Bogey ambled over to him. Coop grabbed the ball and pulled it off, much to Bogey's relief. The dog snerfed and shook himself. Coop turned the object over as he examined it. "It looks like a ball you attach to something. An antenna, maybe?"

Before we could delve deeper into the mystery of the red ball, Rocky bounced in, his arms full of bulging bags. "Thank you for inviting me for pizza, Shay O'Hanlon. I was busy Facebooking with my lovely Tulip last night. Deciding wedding things." He handed each of us a bag.

I opened mine. In it was a red and yellow striped cloth and a pair of huge, red, oversized shoes that Ronald McDonald might wear. I tugged the cloth out of the bag and held it up. It was a jumpsuit. A very large jumpsuit.

"What—" I began, and then I saw that each of us had funny-looking shoes along with striped jumpsuits in various colors. JT and I exchanged mutual looks of horror.

Rocky clapped his hands. "It is for Tulip. Her dad was a clown. So I decided we are going to have a clown wedding. On Saturday in the Rabbit Hole so we can let all of the customers know and they can be there too."

I croaked, "A clown wedding?" Oh my god, I'd completely forgotten about Tulip and the I do's.

"Yes, isn't it wonderful?" Rocky giggled with glee. "The Ringling Brothers and Barnum and Bailey Clown College has been in existence since 1968. Almost one thousand three hundred clowns have graduated since then." He hopped up and down a couple of times. "I will be a clown for my lovely Tulip. And so will you."

Where was my Effen Vodka when I needed it?

April McGuire, Back Porch Studio

ABOUT THE AUTHOR

Jessie Chandler is a board member-at-large of the midwest chapter of Mystery Writers of America and a member of Sisters in Crime. In her spare time, Chandler sells unique, artsy T-shirts and other assorted trinkets to unsuspecting conference and festival goers. She is a former police officer and resides in Minneapolis. Visit her online at JessieChandler.com.